Payoff Pitch

ED McCLOSKEY

To my lovely wife Rosi, whose love encouragement, faith and patience makes this book and especially my life joyful.

"Outside of a dog, a book is a man's best friend. Inside of a dog it's too dark to read."

~Groucho Marx

CHAPTER 1

"C'mon, McKenna, get your butt outta bed, breakfast is ready and we gotta lot to do today," came the mellifluous screech from my pretty wife, Hannah.

"Wow, what a joyous way to get roused outta bed, especially on a lazy Saturday morning." I lurched my bleary-eyed way down to breakfast to join my lovely wife. I probably looked like an unmade bed. I know I felt like one. The wall clock said it was 6:45 a.m.

"Your timing is perfect. The French toast is nearly ready," Hannah said.

"I love it when a plan comes together," I said, as I slumped at the breakfast counter. We were joined by our idiosyncratic Black Lab, Riley T. Dog, who had just come back from his morning ablutions with Ivan, our House Manager and friend.

"I do. Now listen up. We're leaving here at eleven to catch the subway, she said in a gentle but still strident tone. You're gonna have to lose the Dagwood hair, my sweet."

"Uh oh, whatcha got us into now?" I asked with arched eyebrows which I hoped etched sufficient curiosity onto my face, my true feelings.

"You'll see soon enough."

Frowning I declared, "C'mon, if you want me to go somewhere—anywhere—after rousting me outta bed on a Saturday, I gotta know the where, okay?"

"You're no fun. If you must know, we're going to the stadium to see the Yankees."

"All right then, that I can do. What's behind the dawn wake up?"

1

"I just thought you might like to join me after reading the papers."

"I'm missin' something... unless..."

"Unless what, Mr. Obtuse?"

"See ya up there," I said with my best ogle.

After an extended foray into the world of erotic behavior, I reflected on how Hannah had bribed me in the past to get me to take part in stuff.

I recalled a persuasive romp last year to get me to help a friend save a car company from ruin. It all worked out well. Company saved, friends helped, handsome profit realized, lots of jobs created, all good things. I especially savored the romp. I bet Hannah hopes this, whatever it is, goes half as well, as do I.

Zero hour arrived. We dashed out the door. Hannah decided now was a good time to pin me down and get answers to the unanswered questions she asked a while ago. She also thought it would be an effective way to dodge my query. It wasn't because she feared telling me, feared negative response, feared no response, what she actually feared was imposing on me again.

Even though the National Motors project was off and running successfully we paid a heavy price in personal grief. Since then, I had done nothing productive in a year. She didn't want to watch me become moldy and stagnant, I suppose. She wasn't about to let that happen.

"Okay, Mr. McKenna, you promised to tell me how your grandfather, Red, got his name. You said it wasn't due to his hair color, so what's the story?"

"I'll tell you later, Mrs. McKenna. I promise." Pointing at my watch I said, "Now we need to hustle to catch the D train if we're gonna get to the Bronx in time for the first pitch."

Off we ran down the crowded street, reminiscent of kids who'd swiped apples from the neighborhood bodega. I ran interference like the tight end I was in college.

"Damn right you will," she said with a stern expression as she followed close behind her personal bulldozer. Down the packed subway entrance, through the stiles, ending on the D train to the Bronx we rode—albeit standing—holding onto a single strap as we jostled along.

I always felt I knew what the inside of a well-used sweat sock smelled like whenever I took the subway. Once again my olfactory memory was refreshed.

We were no sooner seated in our upper deck, right field seats, when a laser-like fly-ball screamed into the second tier seats, over the FOX BUSINESS sign in right field. After a tangle of hands and arms a young fan held the ball up in triumph only to have it snatched from him by some greedy mook. A fight broke out when the boy's father decked the guy to get the ball back for his son. Only in New York!

"Wow, what a shot," I yelled enthusiastically. The homer opened the Yankee scoring in the bottom of the first inning. First baseman, Mark Teixeira's home run drove in the two runners ahead of him for a 3-0 Yankee lead.

I turned to assess Hannah's reaction. I knew she wouldn't have the same appreciation for Yankee success as I did.

As a Red Sox fan—despite hailing from Rochester, New York— she professed an intense dislike for my favorite team, the Yankees. I believed I could read her mind, despite her efforts to conceal her thoughts with a smile.

"Damn Yankees, right?" I said with a twenty-eight piece grin of pearly white Chiclets. We're all supposed to have thirty-two teeth but hockey and football took out four of mine.

"What, now you're a mind reader?" I smiled, fully knowing I nailed it.

Despite my Detroit birth, for some inexplicable reason I never rooted for the Tigers. I didn't hate or dislike them, I just loved the Yanks, always had. I figured it was since the Yankees were my father's favorite. I never knew him, since he was killed in service to his country just a few weeks before I was born. He still has a profound influence over me.

"So I suppose you're happy, huh?"

The stupid grin on my mug told her I was.

"What's not to be happy about? Beautiful day, beautiful ball park, beautiful girl, the Yankees ahead... and watching you squirm. Just beautiful, all of it," I said.

"So you like to see me squirm, huh?"

"Not really, I just thought gloating would be too much."

"I'll tell you what's too much, smug Yankee fans being smug Yankee fans," she said with as much attitude as she could muster, blue eyes flashing and a grim expression of disapproval.

"Twenty-seven world championships will do it to people, ya know."

Basking in the sun, surrounded by nearly 50,000 roaring fans enjoying some of the best players in the world ply their trade was a distinct pleasure. Still I was eager to learn what Hannah had up her sleeve.

After the game, won by the Yankees 9-4 we rode the subway to South Central Park and climbed into a booth with a view of the oil painting of The Mick in the foyer. Mickey Mantle's was a favorite restaurant of mine. Hannah was setting me up for a tough pitch. After we ordered drinks and dinner I looked at my love's baby blues and asked, "How come you didn't root for the Orioles growing up?"

"I did until they dumped their AAA team in Rochester for Norfolk. I just couldn't bring myself to become a *Damn Yankee* fan. My mother's from Boston so I switched allegiance to the Red Sox."

"Well, nobody can ever accuse us of being homers, can they?" We both laughed then I asked, "So what is it you want from me? You never said."

"Can't a wife just take her husband to see his favorite team?"

"Of course, but I've seen this play before, if you recall," I said with feigned indignation.

"Okay, I'll fess up. Remember the call I got from my college friend, Libby Reynolds, a couple of days ago? You know the one in Elmira?"

"Vaguely."

"Her husband, Ted, wants to bring a minor league team back to their home town. They lost their major league affiliation years ago. I just thought you'd like to see a game and..."

"See if I'd be interested in looking into the world of pro baseball. I'm right, huh?"

"You are, damn it," she admitted with an irresistible smile much like Elizabeth Taylor's. Hannah had often been compared to the infamous Liz.

"A very expensive and convoluted way of finding out. I know what those tickets cost these days. You coulda just asked, you know. Did ya have to sell the house to pay for 'em?"

Hannah squirmed then said, "No, just a mortgage. This way you get to see your favorite team, be wined and dined at the Mick's and now I figure you owe me," she said.

"My, my, you are a devious one, aren't you?"

"I know, but effective right?"

I shook my head at the dazzling woman across the table and said, "Right, so what do you think we can do? I don't know anything about running a baseball team, do you?"

"Of course not, but we've proven to be clever and resourceful people. I'm sure we'll figure it out. Plus you need to get off your lazy butt and get involved with something before you turn into a moldy science project," she said.

"Road trip?"

"Precisely," she said looking peacock proud, or more appropriately peahen proud.

At the crack of slumber, we packed up Riley, and enough stuff for a week's stay in the Finger Lake Region of New York State—specifically Elmira. To say I was ambivalent about this idea was on the money. I didn't know these people. I didn't know anything about running a baseball team. But I did know Hannah and I trust her. So here we are on the road. *Nice view,* I thought.

"This area never gets the credit it deserves in the fall," I said gazing at the luxuriant foliage blanketing the rolling foothills of the Appalachian range. "I guess New England has a better PR firm. What've you got to say about it, missy?"

Hannah, a very successful owner of a PR firm herself, took umbrage for a moment but concealed it. However, she didn't fail to be impressed by the surrounding hillsides too. They were resplendent in as many shades as a big box of Crayolas.

"I'm glad to see your razor sharp wit is still honed, dear... misplaced though it is."

"So tell me about your friend. What's going on there?" I said.

"Well, Libby and her husband Ted are natives of Elmira. There was a professional baseball team there some time ago, called the Pioneers. They belonged to the Double-A Eastern League, then a Brooklyn Dodgers affiliate. When the Dodgers moved west they moved their minor league teams to be nearer L.A. Eventually, the Orioles stepped in to fill the void left by the Dodgers' departure." Jutting out her jaw for emphasis and tipping her head back a tad she said, "I did some research after Libby called."

I was paying close attention. "Those first years saw the building of the nucleus for the first Oriole glory days, right?" I said.

"You seem to know your sports history."

"About some stuff," I said.

"To answer, yes. Lots of future stars came through Elmira on their way to Rochester then ultimately to Baltimore. It lasted until Major League Baseball demanded all teams upgrade their minor league facilities to a certain standard. Elmira couldn't afford to do it to MLB's satisfaction at the Double-A level."

"Okay," I said.

"The Red Sox put a Single-A team there for a few years. Twenty years ago, I guess. Then MLB mandated still more upgrades. Once again, Elmira couldn't afford to comply. Ultimately, they lost their affiliation. Now they have a team playing in an amateur collegiate league."

"Why do your friends want to bring back pro ball? More important, why do they think they can?"

"It's why we're going up there. By the way, we're staying up at Justin and Kimberley's cottage on Keuka, where we stayed last year for the race at Watkins Glen."

Hannah was referring to her former college golf teammate and her husband, the president of National Motors. We had worked with them two years ago to help introduce their wildly successful family of hydrogen fueled cars.

"I love their place. Riley will have the best time in the water. I will too, even though I fear this is more of a long shot than the automobile business." I paused to pet Riley and said, "Think mission impossible."

CHAPTER 2

Hank Lewis, seated behind his ornately carved mahogany desk, slowly spun his Super Bowl sized onyx ring, with the full carat diamond in the center around a large finger from what could only be characterized as a paw. It glistened prism-like in the sunlight as he deliberated his next move. Glancing at his gold Rolex his fidgety behavior exhibited annoyance. Rance Butler was late again.

Finally, Butler strode into the opulent office. He paused a moment in admiration of the joint. Glancing at Henry, he shook his head and said, "Sorry I'm late."

Hank recognized the reaction—pure envy—most people had when they entered. Hank figured Butler would be no different. He wasn't wrong.

"Yeah, yeah, whatcha got for me, Rance?"

Butler tried to stretch his wiry, five foot eleven inch frame to meet the six foot four Lewis. Of course, he failed.

"You were right. Reynolds seems to be interested in the Big Flats property. At least he's been inquiring about it."

Hank looked out his window unmindful of the view, leering like a large reptile about to have at his prey and said, "Finally, I've got you, you rat-bastard."

Turning to Butler he said, "All these years of eating his crap is over. I'll finally break the back of the son of a bitch," said Hank. Hank turned his back on Butler and gazed out his window and barely audible said, "Ted Reynolds, you're dead meat. And that goes for your simpering wife too."

"Wow, you really mean it, huh?" asked Butler.

"You bet your sweet ass I mean it. I'll discover his plan and then I'm gonna steal it. Let's see how he likes the meal I'll serve him. You don't know how many times I've gone head to head with Reynolds on a project bid, only to lose."

Hank pounded his right fist into his open left hand repeatedly, finally pounding his desk so hard the knick-knacks on it jumped.

"Somehow he always seems to beat me. I've even lost to him once when I put in a higher bid."

"You're kiddin'," said Rance.

"Do I look like I'm kidding? Do I sound like I'm kidding? Do I give off some vibe that suggests I'm kidding?"

"No, not at all, but if your bid was higher, why didn't you get the job?"

"Yeah, that's the best part. One guy told me the board liked Reynolds better. Can you believe it?"

Crossing his legs stifling a laugh, he said, "Actually I can. You know you're not the easiest man to get along with, Henry. Not too many people like you."

"Then why the hell are you still hanging around?" said Hank spinning to confront Butler with white hot fire in his eyes. "And the name, as you well know, is Hank."

"It's a question I occasionally ask myself. I guess it's habitual. You know it started in seventh grade when you took the blame for spilling the ink on Miss Mueller's purse. You never did tell me why you did it."

"No, I guess I just didn't like the way the nasty bitch was tearing into you," said Hank quietly. There was more to it Hank chose not to reveal.

CHAPTER 3

Hannah's friends, Libby and Ted Reynolds, were headed to their backyard to relax and enjoy the view of the surrounding hills. Strung between two enormous red maple trees, an over-sized L.L. Bean hammock drew them in as surely as a trout to a fly. Ted put a tray of lemonade and ice tea concoction, popularized by the famous golfer Arnold Palmer, on a table near the hammock.

Sipping the drink Ted said, "You know what this Arnold Palmer needs?"

"More lemonade. I didn't put enough in, did I?"

"Some vodka wouldn't hurt either," he said.

"Not with company coming. I want you at your best, not half in the bag."

She added lemonade *sans* vodka. They lay back and enjoyed the much improved drink, even without the hooch, when her cell rang.

"Libby here," she answered.

"It's Hannah. Did I catch you at a good time?"

"Well, if snuggling with my Teddy in the hammock sounds like a good time, yes."

"Bordering on TMI there, missy. Dru and I just got to the lake house and wondered if you guys want to have dinner tonight to discuss your project.

"Hold on a sec, I'll ask Ted. They want to know if we want to sup with them."

"Gee, I don't know, hon, they only spent the whole day driving up here to talk to us. Ya think we should?"

"I heard that, Libby. I see he's still got his dry sense of humor."

"More snarky than dry, I can't seem to break him of it, so be prepared."

"Between Ted and Dru we've got a matched set, don't we?"

"Indeed, where do we want to meet?"

"How about the Harbor Hotel in Watkins? It's not far for you guys and it's just over the hill for us," offered Hannah.

"It's a date. Seven o'clock sound good?"

"Perfect, see you then."

* * *

"We have a date, huh? Feel like a swim?" I asked.

"Water's too cold. Now a boat ride sounds good though, how about it?"

The cottage, more like a full-fledged residence of post and beam construction, sits on the southwestern end of Keuka Lake, near the village of Hammondsport. Tied to the dock was Justin Powell's twenty-five foot wood hulled Thompson powered by twin fifty horse powered Evinrude motors, named *The Deal*. They boarded her and prepared to set off when Riley T. came bounding down the dock and leapt into the boat.

"How'd he get outside? I shut the door," I said.

"He's Wonder Lab. Surprised you didn't know that," said Hannah.

We leisurely cruised up the center of the lake, the three of us. Hannah drove while I hugged Riley.

"Who owns that beauty?" I asked, pointing to a spectacular cottage, more like a full blown estate. The name "Limbo" was written diagonally in black script across the middle one of three large brick chimneys attached to the main house.

Spectacular views of the vineyards, rising like columns of marching soldiers patrolling the mountainsides bracketed both sides of the lake. On the water, a few hearty skiers plied their skills nearby but mostly we had the lake to ourselves.

"Answer the question," I said with mock determination.

Hannah told how liveried servants tended to the needs of the gala party guests held at Limbo in the height of summer, back in the day. It still looked like it could be a magnificent site for such events.

"HELLO, that's not an answer. Who owns that beauty?" I asked.

"I'm not sure anymore. When I was a kid we were told the inventor of the eyelash curler built it. It was claimed the silly invention made him fabulously wealthy, as befitted the owner of such an alluring place," said Hannah.

"Was it true?" I asked.

"Who knows? I hope so," she said.

"Looks like F. Scott and Zelda would be right at home."

We turned back at the base of the bluff which forms the distinctive Y, for which Keuka was famous.

"It's known there are caves beneath the water line here at the bluff. Every once in a while, a disgorged body surfaces to give credence to the belief danger lurks beneath those waters," said Hannah.

"How deep is this lake?" I asked.

"It varies here by the bluff; I believe it's around 190 feet, though some places are only thirty. Its average is about 100."

When we entered the cove, which protected the Powell's cottage from periodic winter storms sweeping down from the north, I encouraged Riley to jump in and swim to shore. Riley beseeched me to join him with his deep throated yowling. I finally acquiesced, rolling into the water and gave out my own yowl.

I gasped, "You weren't kidding about the lake temp!"

"Brisk, isn't it?" she laughed.

"Brisk hell, its FBC. You know . . . freezin' balls cold."

Laughing harder Hannah said, "Welcome to the Finger Lakes."

After making shore, we ate on the dock. Over a simple lunch of tomato, ham and Swiss Panini sandwiches with Caprese salad, fittingly complimented by Bully Hill Growers Red wine from Walter Taylor's winery.

"Fill me in on your friends again," I said.

"The Cliff Notes version is Libby was our housemate at Cornell. She married Ted the summer after graduation. He was an All-Ivy baseball player with professional aspirations."

"What position?" I asked, as tomato juice leaked from my sandwich onto my lap.

"Pitcher, I think. His dream crashed when he tore a muscle in his back, rhomboid or trapeziums, maybe," she said. "Anyway, he went into commercial real estate in and around Elmira, Corning and even over to Binghamton."

"I guess he must be doing all right to think about a thing like this, huh?"

"Very successful, they have two kids at Notre Dame High School, an area private parochial school. I'm sure they're on their way to Cornell if Libby has her way. Ted played sports there— baseball and fall LAX."

"LAX?"

"Lacrosse, but his baseball passion was never fully extinguished. That brings us to the resurrection of the Pioneers which, by the way, is the first hurdle."

"There's a hurdle? We have a hurdle. What hurdle?"

"Libby told me the last owners are reluctant to relinquish the name 'Pioneers'."

"Why?"

"Who knows?" she rolled her eyes.

"We don't seem to know a whole lot," I mused, with what I considered to be the perfect measure of snark.

"Well, duh, what do you think the meeting is for, fool?" she said as she grinned like the Cheshire Cat and gave me a hug.

I thought proudly, Hannah does not take any shit—from me or anyone else.

"I guess I kinda deserved that," I said.

"No kinda about it, Bub," she said rising up to plant a big wet one on me.

"What about Libby? What's her story?" I finished the dripping sandwich and was now attacking the salad.

"Like I said, she was a roommate at Cornell. She had a swimming scholarship, was All-Ivy three years running. She's shortish, pretty enough, I suppose. Blond, blue-eyed and stacked as you guys are wont to say."

"How soon can we leave?"

"Down, boy, she's spoken for. And in case you forgot, SO ARE YOU!"

"Yes, ma'am," I said looking as a chastised one should.

"As I was trying to say, she won everything she ever competed in. She's got the same snarky, irreverent demeanor of all athletes, able to hold her own in any clubhouse. Sound familiar?"

Hearing Hannah's description, my eyebrows rose like two caterpillars crawling across a sidewalk to safety.

"In high school she was All-State in basketball, swimming and track. She can play near scratch golf but doesn't play much now. That's how she met Ted."

"How?"

"Beating the pants off him at an inter-fraternity/sorority golf outing. She was paired with Ted. He shot eighty and she had a seventy-six."

"Not bad," I praised. "Could she take you?"

"With practice maybe, anyway, Ted asked her out and fate took over."

Lunch complete, I decided to roam around the lake with Riley. With more than five acres to explore we set off. I often walked the boy when I wanted to do some thinking, as I did now.

I love getting involved in projects, especially to help people who face uncertainty. Due to family successes—as well as personal achievement—I don't *need* to work. But too young to retire, I like to keep busy.

But there's a catch. With other people's money and dreams riding, it puts me under a ton of pressure. Just like all real diamonds are formed. I'll probably end up in an engagement ring somewhere. It comes at a price. Even though as confident as an unopposed candidate I still fear letting people down. Good thing I can handle it... or at least I think I can, just like the *Little Engine that Could*.

CHAPTER 4

On their way to dinner, Ted pondered what to expect from the meeting. "I know your roomie Hannah's a PR whiz, and god knows we're gonna need one, but what's with her husband?"

"Former roomie, 'Sweet Lips,' you're my roomie now. She told me he's a genius at figuring out how to solve problems before they kill projects."

"Sounds like 'Wonder Woman' found her match."

"Let's hope," Libby said.

***

The newly built hotel, on the south end of Seneca Lake, boasted a fine restaurant with a patio overlooking the picturesque water. At roughly thirty-nine miles it's the longest of the Finger Lakes, with an average depth of 290-some feet. I was entranced by the serenity and beauty of the lake and surrounding hills.

"I guess there'll be snow here before too long, huh," I joked. Or hoped I was joking, it being the end of May. We arrived earlier at the Harbor House hotel hard by the south end of the lake, and after checking out a marina boatyard we made our way to the back patio overlooking said lake.

Just after settling at our table we heard, "Hey there, roomie." A pretty girl and handsome man made their way from the lobby.

"Hey girl," returned Hannah. After the introductions Hannah said, "To answer your first question, you've heard of the turnaround at National Motors, right?"

"Heard of? We bought two of 'em," said Ted.

"Well, you're looking at the man who was the primary reason for it," said Hannah.

I was embarrassed to take sole credit for my contribution to any endeavor.

Ted, looking directly at me, said, "I'm impressed."

"I can't take all the credit. It was truly a team effort and you know it, Hannah," I chastised.

"Go kiss your horse, man. We're not here for a modesty demonstration, Mr. Humble. I gotta offer some of your creds to these people. How else are you to impress 'em?" retorted Hannah.

"Yes, ma'am," I answered.

Ted and Libby looked at each other with a knowing smile.

"Hannah told me about your baseball career, Ted. I guess that's why you want to do this, huh?" I said.

"More like lack of a career. Injury precluded a real career but it didn't kill my love of the game and the desire to be part of it, Dru." I found myself liking Ted already.

"I get the love of the game... but why minor league baseball? Why not sponsor an amateur club?" I asked.

"I know it's a bit out there, but there's more to it than baseball. This area, Elmira, the Heights and all the other small communities around us have really taken it on the economic chin for a lot of years. In the last sixty years the population has decreased by over thirty percent."

"Wow," said Hannah, "that's a lot."

"It is a lot. It's a direct reflection of the economy here and in New York State in general. Companies have moved away, either to the south or offshore, taking their jobs with 'em. New York politics is killing the state. The taxes are punitive and rich people aren't putting up with it. They're moving away, as are the corporations."

I stood up to stretch, nodded my head and said, "Most people are trapped and virtually getting skinned alive. Nothing is being done to address the situation on a long-term basis. Sure there's a ten year no-tax inducement to lure companies to the state on the table. You're all afraid it's phony, right?"

"I figure if I can make a small difference in a small area it's what I want to do," said Ted.

I said, "I'm hearing this more often these days all around the country."

"Yeah it's a recurring theme in small towns. In my graduating class of 160, only about twenty still live here. Those who left did so, not because they wanted to, but because finding good jobs locally was tough."

Hannah nodded at Dru as if to say she agreed with this.

"People who still live here do so because they love the area and their families have deep roots. Many own their businesses. It's a great area to live in, aside from the economic plight."

"Sounds like the question posed to Mrs. Lincoln regarding the play," I said.

"Sure it's reeling but the people and scenic beauty are both positive attractions. I'd like to make a difference in life opportunities, in my small way, for employment and entertainment," said Ted.

"Where do things stand now?" asked Hannah.

"Ted's contacted Major League Baseball in New York to ask permission to contact all thirty clubs to determine if there's an opportunity for us. The response has been tepid, at best," said Libby.

"The most I could glean was a complete overhaul of the facilities and some kind of guarantee of solid profitable attendance would be needed," said Ted.

"The facilities, okay they can be upgraded, but how can you guarantee attendance?" I asked.

"Yeah, that's what I asked 'em," said Ted.

"And the answer is?" Hannah said.

"I'm still waiting for it."

"I heard you mention tax-free zones in New York State?" asked Hannah.

"Oh sure, comes under the heading of barn door closing," said Ted.

Hannah laughed. "As in after the horse already ran away, right?"

"Uh huh," said Ted.

"The ads are real, the state is offering ten years of tax-free status to any company moving or staying here. Sounds good, right?"

"So far," said Hannah.

"Yeah well, what everyone fears is the politicians won't give up revenue up front without a raise in taxes in other areas to cover the shortfall. Like property tax, school tax, sales tax, sin tax or any other despicable tax they can think of. Of course, everyone believes after ten years they'll return to taxing the bejesus out of companies again and send the economy down the tubes."

"Wow, you got some outlook there," said Hannah while she shook her head.

"Accurate though," said Libby.

"I was trying to remember statistics I recently read in a baseball magazine about the rise and fall and current state of minor league baseball. I thought the peak was just after WWII. But with several more leagues and teams back then, the total attendance nationwide was in the thirty million range compared to forty-one mil today. They may be up a bit right now.

"As for the major leagues they're currently enjoying great prosperity due to lucrative TV deals. The future looks bright. So it looks like baseball is stable and a good investment if operated properly. To the best of my recollection, television played a part in both peak and valley of baseball health."

"How do you figure, Dru?" said Hannah.

I explained, "After WWII people had more free time and discretionary income. Minor league baseball was affordable and fun for local people who wanted to spend time enjoying games and the festivities at the park. Every ballpark in small towns across the country put on shows to rival the old vaudeville circuits or circuses. Boxing, wrestling, barnstorming major leaguers in the off season and the like were all big gate attractions.

"Does anybody remember donkey baseball?" I asked.

"Sure," said Libby. "Our kid's school had a fundraiser a few years ago on our athletic field, it was a hoot."

"It used to be a staple at minor league ballparks in the fifties," I said.

"Hold it," said Hannah. "Is this what it sounds like, playing baseball on horseback or . . . donkey back? Musta been some article you read, Dru."

"Do I see wheels turning?" I asked Hannah.

"Maybe, was it one element of gimmicks used to gen up attendance in answer to TV?"

"What's TV got to do with it?" asked Libby.

"We can see almost all games today on TV, in any number of ways. Local stations, cable, satellite links, computers, tablets and smart phones. TV was such a novel idea back then people readily gravitated to it. When they started airing sports, baseball was among the first to be offered. For the first time a choice existed in the minor league towns. Why go to a local game when you could watch the famous stars in your own home, Guess what happened?" I said.

"Okay, so that's what started the decline of popularity, but what about being the solution today? What's changed?" asked Hannah.

"Good question," said Ted. "If I read the times right, people may be getting fed up with Performance Enhancing Drug scandals, greed on both sides of the ball, owners and players."

"And agents, don't forget the agents," said Hannah.

"Ah yes, the bottom feeders of all sports."

"Ted, the popularity is up about two percent over last year but it's been flat growth-wise for ten years. So again, why do you wanna do it now?" I asked.

Ted paused before answering, "I think people still love the game... although football and basketball have supplanted it with kids. The thing we gotta do now is win the kids back. We need to get the texters to rest their thumbs and get into active participation. We gotta make baseball cool. Provide equipment,

21

cool unis, nice fields to play on and sponsors for leagues. Build a better, fan friendly park, bring in fans by having events and attractions and of course, advertise."

"Promotional ideas, special discounts and fundraising events to lure customers can be just the beginning," offered Hannah.

"Don't teams do the same things now?" asked Libby.

"Sure, but do they all have a pro like Hannah?" I said.

"Do I detect a decision to join us?" asked Ted.

"Very astute, new friend, yeah, I think we'd love to get involved in this, if you'll have us?" I said glancing at Hannah for affirmation.

"Okay, great. Thank you. Do you guys really think we can do something?" said Ted.

"We do," said Hannah.

"But how's this gonna work? And why do *you* want to do this?" said Ted.

Hannah answered, "I want to do it to help Libby and you too, Ted. I grew up with baseball in Rochester and loved it. Our family was always going to games and talking baseball all year long. We'd welcome new players to town then follow former Red Wings as their careers progressed. Deserved or not, we took credit for helping launch their careers."

I could see Hannah's thoughts run across her forehead like the news crawl on the New York Times Tower in Times Square.

"When my mother or father and I were at odds, baseball seemed to buffer emotions and get us back on common ground. I'd like to be part of bringing those same buffers to other families. Dru, what do you say?" Hannah asked.

"Here we go again. Does this ring any bells?" I said.

Leaning forward with Ted, Libby asked, "Are we to infer it's good or bad?"

"No, it's good. Dru and I had the National Motors project work out rather well for all parties concerned. This is how it started," said Hannah.

I stood up again to stretch my balky back and said, "She introduced me to the people involved and we were off. So yeah, it's good. I love baseball too, played it, followed it, went to games all the time and I'd love to be part of this. I believe I can help."

"Did you play in college?" asked Ted

"No, I played football, blocking back mostly. The last year of high school I pitched though," I said.

"Not any good, huh?" asked Libby with a bear's shit eatin' grin. I could tell what Hannah meant about holding her own in the locker room and shook my head.

"He was pretty good. A pitcher, fast as snuff makes spit or so I'm told. Tell 'em the tobacco story," prompted Hannah.

"Yeah, okay. I was pretty good just not good enough to go further than high school. And I knew it."

"Don't forget about the tobacco story, Mr. Studly," said Libby.

"Okay, I was pitching against East Malcolm High on the Double-A field in Michigan. Worst locker room I ever was in, filth, mold, no hot water. Nobody showered there. Anyway, my shortstop introduced me to chewing tobacco so I took a chaw. Thought it made me look meaner to the hitters. In the third inning, the E. Mal. batter hit a bullet back at me. Immediately I swallowed the chaw. Oh no. I threw up my glove in self-defense, deflected the ball to our shortstop who threw the guy out at first. Out number three. During the play I went behind the mound and tossed my lunch, breakfast, and what was formerly the chaw on the ground in a pile of nasty. On the way back to the dugout, our shortstop ran up and said to me, 'I'm just tellin' ya, if a ball is hit through that shit I ain't pickin' it up.' "

Laughing hard, Ted and Libby said, "I can just see it."

"Not quite as funny then as it is now, I assure you," I said.

Ted and Libby were smiling and holding hands as I walked over to Hannah and gave her a big hug.

"Here we go again," I said.

She looked up and said, "I bet I know what's next, don't I?"

"Let's put together a murder board," I suggested. "Do we have an office or work space?" he asked.

"What in heaven's name is a murder board?" said Libby.

"I'm working out of my study in the back," said Ted.

I pictured a 12' x 12' room crammed with papers, books, printers, towers, modems, keyboard and supplies, in other words my messy office. Hannah and I exchanged questioning glances.

"It's not a play house or anything," said Libby spotting our reaction.

"Around here everyone is influenced to some degree by Mark Twain, including us. Ted built this replica of Twain's study in the back of our house. We have five acres so we have plenty of room."

"It's a replica with an additional area off to the side for meetings, storage and mini kitchen," said Ted.

"Okay, let's meet there tomorrow," said Hannah.

"Do you happen to have a white board?" I asked.

"Is that your murder board?" asked Ted. "I'll have one tomorrow."

CHAPTER 5

Finding Ted and Libby's house the next morning was easier in theory than actuality. Road signs seemed to vanish or change names for inexplicable reasons, causing our heads to swivel like Linda Blair in confusion.

"Where the hell did the street go?" I shouted with exasperation as we came to an intersection.

"You're still on it. It just changed names, is all," said Hannah exuding calm. "You know how Sixth Avenue becomes Avenue of the Americas at Franklin Street and it drives New York tourist's nuts? Same thing."

"Great, when are they gonna tell us?" I asked. Eventually we arrived no worse for the experience because we enjoyed the scenic countryside, if not so much the confusing signage.

Ted and Libby were waiting on their wrap-around front porch. They warmly greeted Hannah and me. As an added surprise, I introduced Riley T. Dog to the Reynolds.

"What's the T stand for?" asked Ted.

"See what happens?" I said looking at Hannah.

"Answer the man," she said.

"So glad you asked," I answered.

Ted laughed, Libby looked at Hannah and they shook their heads.

"Must be a guy thing," said Hannah.

Riley gave Ted the supreme compliment of accepting Ted's forearm into his mouth with a faux chomp.

"I hope he's not going to escalate this," said Ted.

"Nope, it's his way of including you into his circle," I said.

"How many in this circle?" asked Libby.

"Only everybody he meets, it's a very exclusive club," answered Hannah.

"Yeah, only because he hasn't met everybody yet," I said.

After a short stroll around the house down a flagstone path, we arrived at Ted's office. Hannah and I recognized the building as similar to one we saw last year at Elmira College, the Mark Twain study. From the clutter it was obvious Ted used it as his main office.

"I'll get the dollar tour out of the way, then we can get goin' here," said Ted.

"Dollar? Remember when it was a nickel?" I asked.

"Yeah, and I only charged you fifty cents for the tour of my place," added Hannah.

"But look at the view," offered Ted in his best circus barker's voice as he described the Architectural Digest-like features of the building.

We went into the side meeting room, and I noticed a newly installed white board and smiled.

Exiting a back door we stood on a pool deck surrounding an in-ground swimming pool that would do Hollywood proud. At the far end was a waterfall with boulders in a semi-circle and behind it a barbeque pit, and patio area, complete with dining table and conversation area. The whole of it was beautifully landscaped.

"All right, this'll do fine for our down time," said Hannah.

Libby mentioned they spent a lot of time here. Hannah and I could see why.

Back inside, Ted said, "Dru, you mentioned an agenda. Whadda ya got?"

"I call this the 'murder board' from a cop show on TV we enjoy," I said.

I moved over to the white board, grabbed a green marker and wrote TO DO:

Underneath I began jotting ideas with red bullet points.

- *Examine and secure the existing ball park or build a new one.*

- secure rights to the team name, if we gotta have it.
- Contact MLB to determine chance of getting a franchise and the hurdles entailed.
- Contact architects for plans and cost estimates for improvements to Dunn Field or designs for a new park if needed.
- Establish budget and secure financing
- Develop Plan B if we need to prove our viability to MLB
- Find out how to get players, staff, equipment, et al.
- Develop marketing plan
- set target dates.
- overcome unknown issues as they arise

"Wow, I believe this might be a record," said Hannah as she grinned at me.

I reacted with embarrassment. "Yeah, 44 minutes from drive in to now."

"What are they talking about?" asked Libby.

"Damned if I know," said Ted.

Hannah and I were both laughing at our friends' consternation.

"The last time he did this at National, it took him forty-eight minutes to come up with a plan," said Hannah.

"Yeah, I see what you mean," said Ted as he examined the list. "I don't see any holes," he continued. "How do you do it that fast? You just got here."

I looked at Hannah, then said, "Years of practice... and it's pretty basic stuff."

"Occam's Razor, right?" said Hannah.

"Yep," I said, leaving Ted and Libby even more perplexed. I explained Occam's razor was a logician's eponymous theory stating when faced with a decision with several choices, the simplest is usually best.

"What's our first step, Mr. Occam?" asked Hannah.

"I'd like to start with the ballpark. Can we get in to look it over?" I asked.

"Sure, I don't think it's locked, all the equipment and stuff is gone. Nobody is permanently assigned to look after it so it's probably open," said Ted.

"Uniform colors," said Libby.

"What about 'em?" asked Hannah.

"He didn't list them?" said Libby. Ted and Hannah stood speechless and I laughed

"Right you are, Libby. We'll let the major league affiliation tell us what we're responsible for," I said.

"Smart ass," said Hanna to Libby as she joined her in laughter.

Ted and I shook our heads and simultaneously said, "Women."

"Let's go," I said.

***

Dunn Field was about ten miles away and was, as Ted predicted, wide open. We entered through a gate between the main grandstands, where a door led us into what looked to be a clubhouse or a broom closet—hard to tell which. The lockers gave it away though. The room led directly to the field through the dugout.

"Wow, this is beautiful," I said admiring the diamond and outfield grasses.

"I know," said Ted. "I played on this in Small Fry, Babe Ruth League, high school and American Legion. That's about ten years altogether. I still get a thrill walking onto the thing."

"I can see why. I've visited Yankee Stadium and the Tiger's Comerica Park and this playing field is on par with them, believe it or not. The stands, no, but the playing area very much so," I said.

Ted filled me in later that Pat Santarone was the groundskeeper in Elmira when Earl Weaver was the manager, before joining the Orioles as a coach for Hank Bauer and later a Hall of Fame manager for the Orioles. He liked Santarone's work so well Weaver took him to Baltimore to transform a bad field into Gold Glove caliber. They carried on the tradition in Elmira for the players.

We walked the entire perimeter. We started down the first base lines past the home team dugout and bullpen in foul territory.

While in the bullpen, Hannah stepped up on the mound, "I didn't realize the slope was this steep," she said.

"It's maybe one of the idiosyncrasies of ball parks. The visitors' bullpen mound is dissimilar to the field mound. Sometimes it can cause a problem for visiting teams," said Ted.

"Why would that be?"

I looked at Ted giving him the okay to take the question sign.

"Well, when the pitchers warm up in the bullpen they sometimes have difficulty transitioning to the field mound. It might give the home team batters a slight advantage until the pitcher adjusts," said Ted.

"Wouldn't the same thing apply to the home team pitchers?" asked Hannah.

"No, because the home team is careful to make their bullpen mound as close to identical as possible to the field mound. The visitors' doesn't receive the same level of precision." I said.

"Doesn't seem fair, isn't that cheating?" asked Hannah.

"All's fair in love, war and baseball," was Ted's reply.

Hannah shrugged, muttering to herself. We continued our patrol around the outfield on the gravel warning track near the twenty-foot tall, wooden fence.

"Needs some paint here," said Libby.

"Needs some advertisers," Hannah and I said almost simultaneously. We noticed there were several unpainted areas where advertisers should be placing ads.

"Yeah, that's another issue, lack of community involvement."

We laughed and Hannah teased, "Carnak again, Mr. Carson?" I laughed and continued the tour. Fittingly, we finished at home plate.

"Let's go over and check out the dugout," I said.

"Watch your heads," cautioned Ted. "I about brained myself when I was in high school. I stood up when a teammate hit a two-run double and smacked my head hard enough to make me woozy." Hannah and Libby looked at each other and laughed.

"What?" said Ted. "You think it's funny?"

"No dear, but it does explain a few things," said Libby grinning like the village idiot.

"Welcome to my world," I said. "I put up with that sort of stuff for two years in Baltimore with the Cornell girls."

"That's right, you were with Kimberley, too," said Libby. "How're she and Justin these days? I've lost track."

"Just great, we'll give her a call tonight," said Hannah.

"I see what you mean about the ceiling, thanks for the warning," said Hannah.

"I'm used to having to duck and stoop in every dugout I was ever in growing up," I said checking out the view. "As usual, worst seat in the house."

"What do you mean?" asked Libby.

"Check it out," I said over my shoulder as I ran out to third base. "Show 'em, Ted."

When I was positioned as a third baseman would be, Ted said, "See how the infield looks like a turtle shell? That's mainly for drainage. The hump, however, makes it impossible to determine fair-foul or safe-out calls, down at third, or first base from either dugout. The manager has to take his players' word for those calls. If a player argues a call, the manager runs out to the ump to make sure his guy doesn't get tossed outta the game."

We went back into the short tunnel which led from the dugout to the small room we were in before. The girls asked what it was used for.

"Back in the day, circa 1940s through 1988, it was the clubhouse," said Ted.

"This? It's so tiny," said Hannah.

"Yeah, that's one of the reasons the club lost its affiliation," said Ted.

"What are the other reasons?" asked Hannah.

"Look around at the stadium, not the field, the stadium. It's small, run down, uncomfortable and just plain ugly. C'mon, I'll show you," answered Ted.

* * *

We made our way past the narrow passage I assumed was the concession area. Close together each section for the various selections was inadequate now—and probably was in 1950, too.

Making our way up the entrance ramp we eschewed the box seats for the middle grandstands behind home plate. Supporting poles limited view to certain parts of the field. Sure to annoy fans. The crumbling platform with its rickety seats made moving down the rows a hazard and screamed for a potential lawsuit. Satisfied, we made our way out the front gates, also open.

"Ted, do we even want to save it?" asked Libby.

Hannah and I looked at each other, and were noncommittal. The overall location served mainly only Elmira. Drawing from surrounding communities without some compelling reasons was problematic.

"Good question, Libby. How about it, Ted?" I asked.

"I've always envisioned it being renovated and brought back to life as it was," he said. "What do you guys think?"

"Since you asked, I gotta be honest. My initial thought is forget Dunn Field," I said.

"My, my, Mr. Blandings is gonna build his dream house, huh?" said Hannah referring to the old Carey Grant, Myrna Loy movie.

I took a moment to consider the downside of this location, facility, and the cost of renovation. "Maybe so. To get this project going we need to think differently than in the past. You said the population, from its heyday in the fifties, is down thirty-some percent. We need to build a state of the art stadium in a location convenient to more of the populi. What's east, Ted?"

"Binghamton's Mets draw from the east, so west or north probably makes more sense. This way we could draw from Corning," said Ted.

"How about Big Flats?" asked Libby. She was referring to the small but growing area west of Elmira. In recent years it had developed slowly with plenty more space to put a park. It could draw from Bath, Watkins Glen, maybe even the other lake areas like Ithaca.

"Maybe," Ted said. "I was looking at it a while back for a commercial development. Or what about north closer to Watkins and Ithaca but still near enough to Corning?"

"I think we need to study some data about the area," said Hannah.

"And land availability," I said.

"Now I see what they bring to the party," said Ted.

"Are we ruling out the south?" said Hannah.

"We're just a couple of miles from Pennsylvania. We could draw from their rural areas but the largest city, Williamsport, is over sixty miles away," said Ted.

"Okay north or west it is," I said.

We turned to face the front of the stadium and continued to be underwhelmed. I would have been surprised if it ever *whelmed* anyone.

"Who's this guy?" asked Hannah. She was standing next to a bust on a white limestone pillar of Edward Dunn who, I assumed, was the namesake for the stadium and said so. Ted knew the answer.

"He donated the land to the city for this place and was an enemy of my father."

"Ooh sounds like a story to me," said Libby.

"Haven't I told you this story, Lib?"

"No, sweetie, I would have remembered. Let's have it."

"To preface, my father knew how to teach stuff to people. All people, that is, unless he was related to them. He could hit the hell out of a baseball, softball, golf ball. You name the ball, he could hit the hell out of it, even when he got older. He tried in vain to teach me. I was a pretty good hitter, not great. I coulda been better but Dad ran outta patience after five minutes. There was yelling involved. But a guy named Dick Edwards learned to hit from my dad, who spent hours with him. He got it, and I asked Dick what the secret was, and from him I got Dad's secret too. Not from Dad but from Dick. So when it came time to teach my mother to drive, Dad decided to ply his teaching technique and skill and again— total lack of patience for family. Job's brother Arnold had more patience than my dad."

"Job had a brother named Arnold? I never heard of him," said Libby.

"Of course not, he had no patience," said Ted. We laughed.

"We were expected to hear it, love it, do it, period from the git-go. My mom was forty-somethin' when she finally got a learner's permit, at my urging. After the third one expired she got the penultimate one. She had it all down but the parallel parking. So Dad got a couple of orange cones and took us out to Dunn Field to practice. The large octagonal curb forming the platform for this statue served as a parking space. Dad placed the cones at either end of a turn and told my mom to fit the car between 'em.

"Dad told her, 'Pull your car up so your steering wheel is even with where the car you're goin' behind's wheel would be. Then slowly reverse while turning the wheel gently to the right until your front bumper is a hair past the imaginary rear bumper and cut the wheel hard to the curb.' All of a sudden she gasses the car. My father yells, 'Cut, cut... STOP!' *Bam!* She didn't cut, she didn't stop. What she did was jump the curb and slam into the monument, taking out the rear bumper. I howled. My father bent over holding his head and shook it back and forth as if a scourge had befallen us. Mom got out of the car and walked home."

"Dad said, 'Get in. I'll take us home.' I shook my head and said, 'I'll go with her.' We didn't see him for a couple of days."

"Did she ever learn?" asked Hannah.

"Yeah, a few years later I had my license, thanks to driver's ed. I taught her. She was forty-eight years old."

Hannah and I smiled and nodded, Ted had enough stuff to see this thing through.

The next day Ted contacted the County Clerk to inquire about land and received disturbing news. The large dormant section of land in Big Flats had recently been looked at by Hank Lewis. Hank and Ted had been rivals for years. Hank, older by a couple of years than Ted, seemed to resent Ted's success—which often seemed to come at Hank's expense.

"What's the story with this Lewis guy? Should we be concerned about him or what?" I asked.

"It goes back a while. When I first started acquiring and developing commercial property, I obtained a section in downtown Elmira. It was mainly because the owner didn't trust Hank and told him so. He always believed I poisoned his reputation to gain advantage. I didn't need to, he did it to himself."

"If you meet Hank you'll get a clearer picture of his personality," said Libby.

"Or lack thereof," said Ted. "The first time I met him, to be polite I asked how he liked to be addressed—Henry or Hank. He said anyway I liked. I chose 'Henry' and failed the first test. Turns out he prefers Hank."

"He mumbles most of the time, too. Says he has a reason," said Libby.

"You're kidding. Whatever could it be?" I asked.

"Get this, he says when he speaks quietly people pay closer attention and it pleases him." said Libby.

"Pleases him? It actually pleases him?" said Hannah.

"That's nuts," I said.

"Uh huh, isn't it? I think he just likes to manipulate people," said Libby.

"Tell us more about this guy," said Hannah.

"You're gonna love this stuff," offered Libby rubbing her hands quickly together.

"Okay, you asked for it. He's in his early forties, tall, skinny but sinewy. He smells like foul tobacco and musty clothes. He's bent over, shuffles along like an aged, infirm geezer and has a nose patterned directly from a John Deere model. His arrogance knows no bounds. He won the gene lottery, due mainly to his successful father, when he was born."

"A familiar story," said Dru as he glanced at Hannah.

"Of course, but it's how he handled it. As Ted often says, Hank was born on third and acts like *he* hit a triple."

"Good use of a baseball metaphor, my compliments," I said.

Hannah and I both chuckled.

"He's both impatient and unreasonable. He was raised with the silver spoon approach, mainly by his socially prominent mother, who really is the exact opposite of his reprobate father. Hank mistrusts everyone and worships at the altar of the almighty dollar. And he's universally disliked. One of the big reasons he distrusts people is a few years ago he invested nearly everything in his daughter's company. Lost it all due to unforeseen economic downturn. Ensuing scandal, similar to Enron—and everyone in town knows it," said Ted.

"Don't forget the wife," said Libby.

"Rumor has it, the love of his life, his college sweetheart at Colgate cheated on him with a fraternity brother after Hank married her. With all the other events, slights, slurs he thinks he's encountered through the years, it's molded him into the malevolent man you'll see," said Libby.

"Wow, I can't wait for the day to arrive. Does that mean he's going up against you if we want the Big Flats parcel?" asked Dru.

"I guess so, if the rumors are true," said Ted.

"If so, what's plan B?"

"I'm not sure that's plan A. It was just the first place I thought of. I'll do some more research. If I can help it I'd just as soon keep away from Whisperin' Willie—that's what I call him."

"If we find another place I may have an idea of how to out-fox Mr. Lewis when the time comes," I said.

CHAPTER 6

"Next order of business, let's contact the owner of the name 'Pioneers.'"

"Who owns it, do you know?"

"Oh yeah."

"So we'll talk to him," I said.

"I already did a few months ago. His name is Rance Butler. Insisted he wants to preserve the Pioneer heritage, so I don't think he'll sell," said Ted. "After making the call, I wondered how someone like Butler could become such a pompous asshole." Libby laughed at the memory.

"I've known him since we were eleven. Played Small Fry football with him for three years, played a little bit against him in high school football, even though he didn't play much."

"What's Small Fry?" I asked.

"It's like Little League but with real basketball, baseball and football rules. In Small Fry baseball a good catcher is vital because you can steal. That's the major difference from Little League. It's a local thing. We had a Little League in West Elmira but Small Fry had the best players—or so we thought. When it came time to pick the team to vie for the Little League tournament team to represent the area not many from the Little League teams made it but Small Fry's best players all did."

"Was Butler any good at football?" asked Hannah.

"Good? He was great, a real star. He maxed out there though. Oh, he played a little in high school but wasn't as great as when he was twelve."

"Why is he so arrogant then?"

"To make up for the last twenty-eight years, is my guess."

"So what's your real opinion?" said Hannah.

"Schmuck comes to mind. Did you buy that crap about wanting to save the heritage?" I said.

"I take it you don't," said Ted.

"Ted, if you offered him some cash he'd sell out the heritage in a heartbeat," said Hannah.

"So let's offer, whadda ya think is fair, Dru?" said Ted.

"That we let him live with it, that's it. Screw the name. We're gonna start our own new heritage, blow his outta the water, we'll make people forget all about the Pioneers," I said.

"I don't know, let me think about it."

"Ted, why is the name so important to you?" I asked.

"It's gonna sound silly but when I was a kid I had severe scoliosis. My mother and uncle, who lived with us, would rub my back and legs every night to relieve the ache. Uncle Bud, just got out of the army and stayed with us until he got married a year later.

"When I got better, after a chiropractor literally straightened me out over the next five years, my uncle took me to ball games to see the Pioneers. Later that summer he got me a uniform jersey from the visiting Binghamton Triplets, a Yankee affiliate. At the time, uniforms were handed down the chain of minor league teams from the major league clubs to save money. So I had a real gray Yankee away uniform. It was number six, my first number in baseball in Babe Ruth League ball... we didn't have numbers in Small Fry. So I guess I'm hung up on the memory of that as much as anything."

"That's sweet. Who was number six for the Yankees?" asked Hannah.

"Most prominently my all-time favorite, Mickey Mantle," said Ted.

"I thought he was number seven, and you're too young for him to be your favorite," said Libby.

"That was his number in 1952, his second year. The first year, 1951, he was issued number six. He got to wear seven the next year, that's the one he made famous and the one, after his All-World career, the Yankees retired. Mickey was my dad's favorite and he used to tell me stories of his exploits, so I just adopted him," said Ted.

"Dru, did you know that?" asked Hannah.

"Of course, he was my all-time favorite, even though I only saw him play on film. He was my dad's favorite too," I said.

"Okay, you guys I get all the history and memory stuff, but if we're moving the venue don't you think we need a new name?" asked Hannah.

Ted thought a bit and nodded his head. "I guess it does make more sense. We'll create new memories for kids, huh?"

"I think so. Now let's come up with a new name." They agreed to all think, but I had one in mind already. Hannah had her own ideas.

Next item on the list was contacting Major League Baseball but the pennant races were winding down and playoffs would soon be in full swing. I thought it would be wise to hold off contacting them at such a busy time.

Horse before the cart should be a simple concept but rarely seems to work out that way. Team first, then place to play. Recent baseball history though has favored place before team. To move a team you obviously need a place to go, or somewhere to build. The where is what makes it possible.

"I think we need to focus on land. I don't want to deal with Mr. Lewis either," I said.

"Ted, what about that land near the Domes of Elmira College? You know, the old farm land?" said Libby.

"It's worth looking into. If the college owns it they may want to dump it for cash. I'll check tomorrow."

"Who's hungry?" asked Libby. We agreed it was time for food... off to Morretti's for a relaxing uneventful meal. After dinner Hannah and I drove back to Keuka each with our own thoughts. The nighttime provided no distractions. I'm not sure what Hannah was mulling over, though I'd guess promotional ideas were crashing around her brain cells like ping pong balls in a mouse trap filled room. The ensuing explosion emptied every trap.

For myself, I couldn't help but fear letting these nice people down. I include Hannah, of course. My heart would deflate like a poorly constructed soufflé if I disappointed her. I was also wondering if I bit off more than I could swallow. Chewing was easy... getting it down would be easy. Ah... but keeping it down? Aye, there's the bitch.

I'd feel like a jerk if the plan failed after my forty-four minute murder board concoction. I'd made this plan comparable with a walk in the park. But they weren't. And I knew it.

CHAPTER 7

The next morning at breakfast, Hanna put in a call to Kimberley Powell in Baltimore. She told Libby they'd do it last night, but things ran longer than planned. Neither Hannah nor I could abide night driving, especially on dark winding hillsides so we drove carefully. Arriving at the cottage we decided to put off the call 'til morning and filled the void with other activities that seemed to disturb Riley. But we didn't care. Like I said, let 'im get his own girls.

"Kimberley Powell," answered Kimberley Powell.

"Hello, Mrs. Powell, this is your maid-of-honor. How ya doin', old married lady?"

"As well as can be expected, what with a wonderful husband, great friends and a thriving business. Whom did you say this was again?"

"Droll, dearie, very droll."

"How's the lake, Mrs. McKenna?"

"Couldn't be better unless we owned this house."

"Cottage, Hannah, cottage," chided Kimberley.

"Oh that's right, I forget you Lake Folk have your affectations. By the way, you're out of bread."

"That's it, eat us out of house and home."

"So you admit it's a home and not a cottage?"

"Yeah, yeah, yeah, I talked to Libby last night so I was ready for this morning's onslaught. I hear Dru's doin' his thing again?"

"Set a record too. Forty-four minutes before the bullets came out."

"I know, Libby and Ted were flummoxed. Does he really have a handle on it?"

"He does, or at least the complete outline of the plan." They chatted for a few more minutes and Hannah invited them up to their own house, but Justin was going out of town so they took a rain check.

***

I checked the murder board, solidifying the decision regarding the Pioneer name. At the M/T office, Ted and I figured, since he'd already been rebuffed by Butler, I'd take a turn at bat... so to speak.

"Why do I feel like a teenager calling for his first date?" I asked.

"Yeah, I'm sure you had lots of trouble getting dates," said Hannah over her shoulder as she left to join Libby in the kitchen.

"I noticed she didn't even try to hide her snark," said Ted, while a grin spread over his chiseled visage.

"Okay, might as well get this show on the road." I dialed the number Ted gave me. We sat in Ted's study for this epic moment. *He's right, this view is somethin'.*

"It's ringing," I said.

"Hello," answered someone.

"Mr. Butler?"

His mellow voice filled the office since I'd put him on speaker. "All day long, who is this? And by the way I'm not in the market for anything."

Ted stifled a chuckle as he brought his hands together in a silent clap.

I said, "No, no, Mr. Butler. I'm not selling anything. I'm the one who may be in the market for something you have though."

"Call me Rance. I don't believe I have anything for sale but you've got my attention."

"Okay, Rance, what I'm talking about is the Pioneers. Or to be precise, the name Elmira Pioneers."

"The baseball Pioneers? We went down in flames years ago. Right after Baltimore threw us away."

42

"I know, but you retained the rights to the name, I hear." Detecting an edge to Rance's attitude, I let it slide, for now.

"Until the day I leave this mortal coil, as they say."

There it is, I thought. *Edge confirmed.* "But why?" I asked.

"Young fella, I don't see what business it's of yours. Now if you'll excuse me I'm going to hang up."

I looked at Ted with a bemused expression and said, "He hung up."

Hannah and Libby came in with a coffee service complete with Danish and stayed to eavesdrop.

"How about that," said Ted shaking his head. Picking up his phone again I hit redial.

"Hello, for crissakes," the now familiar voice answered. I put him on speaker again.

"Rance, before you hang up on me would you please tell me why won't you sell the Pioneer name to me?"

Libby and Hannah moved closer to the speaker Dru was holding up to hear both sides.

"I can see I'm not going to get rid of you until I do, so here it is. My family was involved with the Pioneers ever since we were affiliated with the Brooklyn Dodgers back in the forties and fifties. Like Tommy Lasorda, we all bled Dodger blue. Then the traitorous, bastard, O'Malley chose to chase the almighty buck out to LaLa land. We built Dunn Field for them and they left us holding our dicks."

I rolled my eyes toward the others as Butler rattled on.

"He's giving a history lesson, Butler loves to do it to everyone," whispered Ted to the women.

"My dad died in those stands. I thought I'd go the same way, you know, watching the Dodgers farm club at Dunn Field. But that boat sailed on O'Malley's yacht. So I'm not going to sell for any price to anybody, got it?"

"Yes sir, Mr. Butler, have a good day and thank you," I said.

"What for?"

"For making my decision a no-brainer. Now I don't have to feel bad about not having the Pioneer name."

"What did you want it for?"

"Well, Mr. Butler, I don't see what possible business it is of yours, and I'm the one who's gonna hang up now."

"I guess that's that, huh?" said Ted after I'd disconnected.

"I should have realized when he said his name was Butler," I said. I looked over at Ted's quizzical expression and said, "It's a long story, I'll tell you some time."

"The funny thing is, you seemed to predict his reaction, didn't you, Dru?" asked Ted.

Hannah countered, "Don't be too surprised, guys. That's another arrow Dru seems to have in his quiver."

"You caught that, did ya? I'm going to start looking out for them from now on. I wonder if they're related?" I asked.

"Okay, fill me in on what I'm missing," said Libby.

"Yeah, me too," said Ted.

"Good luck getting him to tell ya, guys. I've been trying for two years to get him to tell me about something else," said Hannah.

"It's not a secret. Years ago I was helping a friend when a shit-bird named Butler tried to steal my friend's business away. Reminded me a lot of this Butler, only his name was Blake, not Rancid," I said.

"That's it?" asked Libby.

"More or less," I said as Hannah shook her head while I grinned.

"So do you still think we've gotta have the Pioneer name, Ted?"

"Dru, I just liked the tradition of it, I suppose. But the more I think of it, what with Dunn Field's stadium condition and location, I think a clean break with the past does work better. What do you think, Lib?"

"Yeah, I think a new name would be a good way to start this thing off, how about you, Hannah?"

"I think a new name would add significant promotional value as soon as we get the project off the ground," said Hannah.

Ted looked at Libby and said, "I see what you meant when you said they make quite a team, hon."

"Kimberley told me what you guys did for her and Justin at National Motors and quite frankly they're in awe of you both."

"Libby, nice to hear but you know how Kimberley is prone to hyperbole," said Hannah.

"Sounds like you told Libby what've you got in mind," I said.

"I promise I'll let you know when it's time, big guy. Unlike some I could name, I keep my promises."

CHAPTER 8

"Before we talk to the MLB people we need to get our local geese in a row," I suggested.

"That would be ducks, dear," corrected Hannah.

"Just as long as it's not a 'fowl ball,'" I said.

"That's a punishing remark, even for you, Mr. McKenna," chastised Hannah.

"As my aim was true, my goal just and my heart pure, I'm pleased with the outcome," I said, grinning like a happy chimpanzee with a banana.

Hannah groaned as Libby and Ted shook their heads, neither for the first time nor the last. We realized this project would be complicated, fraught with twists, turns and pitfalls. Hannah and I had been through similar last year with our National Motors project and were confident of success. Ted and Libby less so.

"Dru, you were saying you had a plan for dealing with Hank Lewis. Wanna fill us in?"

"It's quite simple, really. Let's call it the old misdirection play. Your old friend, Hank, doesn't know me from Adam's off ox so it's better if you confirm you're interested in the Big Flats property. After all it's you he wants to thwart."

"By thwart you mean have my head on a pike, right?"

"Couldn't have put it better my own self," I said.

"Meanwhile with your guidance, Hanna and I will look into the college land on Route 14."

"Yeah, I get it," said Ted.

"I've been in the auto parts distribution business for years, done rather well too. The name McKenna carries some weight there. I'll employ McKenna Automotive as my cover for the interest in the land, but make sure the owners know I'm not desperate, just exploring a number of options, Route 14 being one of several."

"So while Hank is focused on my interest in Big Flats, you'll get things moving up north, right?" said Ted.

"Clever, Dru. You think it'll work?" asked Libby.

"I do, but both of you must stay completely away from there and the deal. We can't let Hank or Butler tie us together, let alone the details of the baseball part. And yes, you can trust me on this," I said.

Ted and Libby both laughed, "Kimberley said you could read minds, Dru," said Libby.

"I never doubted it," said Ted a little sheepishly, "at least, not now."

"Let's get moving on our land deals, folks," I said.

After a few phone calls to the records people and a trip down to the records bureau it was ascertained Elmira College did indeed own the property just north of an existing distribution area known as the Holding Point. I scheduled a meeting with the college administrators for the next week.

Meanwhile, Ted contacted the town of Big Flats to inquire about a parcel large enough for their needs. Those included space for a ball park, amusement center, picnic area, hiking trails, horseback riding, and a dog park. It took a bit of time but the town found some land they could cobble together from parcels already up for sale by four different owners, none of whom were Hank. *So far so good,* I thought.

***

That night, back in our borrowed cottage, Hannah and I discussed what we were getting into.

"How do you feel about this thing?" I asked.

"A lot like I did last year. I like the people we're involved with, I think the overall plan is sound and worthwhile. There's doubt galore, caused by enemies known and unknown. There's bound to be hurdles ahead but I can't wait to get my hands on promoting this deal."

"So, you're up for it, huh?" I said.

"You bet I am. Until last year, for me, business was all about other people's success or failure. Me, I got paid either way. A successful campaign added glory and earned me a solid reputation but it wasn't like I had skin in the game."

"And now you do," I said.

"And now I do. I like this feeling of being involved with the outcome on a gut level. I think I better understand why you do this."

"You're right. I do get a sense of satisfaction and take pride in my part of it, but I genuinely like helping good people overcome the odds."

"What about the bad guys?" she said.

"Yeah you got me. I especially like sticking it to the bad guys. Arrogance is the most heinous sin a person can commit."

The next day Ted went to see the honchos in Big Flats. When he returned he gave me the run down.

"Dru, he was a shade over five feet, smelled like Cherry Blend pipe tobacco and Bay Rum."

"Sounds like the shortest honcho ever, maybe a honchlet, or maybe one of the Keebler elves, but he was very helpful, huh?" I said. "Greatsinger seemed to already know about our plan even though he wanted Ted to spell it out."

"Did you stick to the script?" I asked.

"Yep, played it close to the vest. Said I'd check with my financial people and get back to him." Ted smirked like he was holding something back.

I refilled his whiskey glass and urged him to continue.

"Guess who was parked across the street when I left?"

"Arnold Palmer," I retorted.

"More like Benedict Arnold. I circled back around the block to see Hank Lewis sneaking in the building I'd just left."

"So Hank's on to us," I said.

"Apparently, Dru, you called this one on the nose."

"So *Henry* bought it?" I grinned.

"Like the proverbial bridge in Brooklyn."

* * *

The next couple of days Hannah and I hung out at the cottage. She liaised with her New York staff, while I fished and went into Hammondsport to shop for our next few days' meals. While in town, I picked up a 'Things to do in the Finger Lakes' magazine. *We might do some of this stuff,* I thought.

While strolling around the quaint village I found myself standing at the marina as if drawn by a spirit force, Indian perhaps. Looking out toward the bluff, a random thought rocketed through my consciousness, quickly disappearing into the recesses of my mind. Immersed in the retrieval process, I fished for the gist of the thought when suddenly it broke the surface. Tangentially, I thought, *A fitting analogy in this place, where many a fishing expedition was launched.*

Did I think this project could be accomplished, or were unseen forces lying in the weeds waiting to pounce, thereby thwarting us? I didn't often search deep within myself but when I did it usually brought more help than hindrance. *I only wish I knew Ted and Libby better,* I mused. I think we're in for a bigger battle than it initially appeared. I thought of Hannah and was comforted by the thought, *I'm so lucky she's in my life. I need to ask her for her take on this deal.*

Turning from the lake and walking up a slight incline I gazed back at the lake and town below. This could have been captured in a Christmas snow globe from Thomas Kincaid, so quaint and old fashioned.

Back home, I found Hannah in her commandeered office. It was actually a spare bedroom overlooking the pool and lake in the distance, a beautiful view. I find it hard to focus for long before the vista would steal my attention.

"I had a thought walking around town. This thing is going to get more complicated. I know we can do it but it's going to be a lot harder than Ted and Libby fully understand," I said to Hannah.

"Sounds to me like you're asking if they can play *hard ball?*"

"How well you think you know me," I answered shaking my head.

"Well, am I right or what?" she demanded.

"Of course, you're right. I'm thinking Hank and Butler and maybe Greatsinger are all in cahoots. Small towns all have movers and doers. I wouldn't be surprised if these guys are those guys."

"What's that mean for us, Dru?" said Hannah.

"I always think it's better to have information than not to. I'm not ready to worry about how to combat these bozos until we know what we need. At this point just knowing where enemy positions are can help us outflank them down the road. My concern is Libby and Ted may not be up for trench warfare. These small towns can be enclaves of intertwined labyrinths of self-serving ego trips full of malevolent evil."

"Wow, that's some rant you got goin' on there. Where's it coming from?" asked Hannah.

"From a long line of family lore and personal experience. You saw it firsthand last year with Ian Steele and the oil folks," I reminded her.

"Yeah, I guess I did, huh? But we handled it okay."

"Yeah, I know but if you recall, we got very, very lucky, Mrs. McKenna."

" 'Luck,' a baseball man said, 'is the residue of design,' " said Hannah.

"Branch Rickey, GM of the St. Louis Cardinals and Brooklyn Dodgers, back in the day of Jackie Robinson," I said.

"I just knew you'd know that. The fact remains we did get lucky, persevered and won. We'll do it again, I can feel it," said Hannah.

"In your bones?" I said.

"You betcha, big guy."

I hope you're right, but we might share with Libby and Ted what we may be in for," I warned.

"We can do that. I think it's a good idea to get 'em accustomed to the way you think, plan and act in the heat of the fray," offered Hannah.

CHAPTER 9

We began the next day with breakfast at the Reynolds' hacienda at eight a.m.

"So you really think this is going to get down and dirty?" said Libby.

"If money is an issue I'm sure it will. Small town or megalopolis, it doesn't matter. People always want to win. Money is how they keep score," I said.

"I suppose you're right, especially with Hank. I just didn't figure on the others," said Ted.

"Start figuring. I'll be surprised if our boy Hank isn't the leader of this group but don't be shocked if there aren't others. In the end though it's Hank who'll be calling the shots," I cautioned.

"What's next?" asked Libby.

"I think we should inquire about more land in Big Flats to add extra diversion to the scheme. We need to stall while we move on the north property," I said. "In the meantime, I want to find out about successful small town franchises. We need to make plans for the size of the ballpark. Too small is no good. We never want to turn away fans. Too large and the place will seem empty and unsuccessful. We don't want to appear unpopular. Let's do some research."

"Libby and I can handle that," said Hannah.

"Murder board says we need to go to MLB next to get some info," I said.

"I'll take care of that," offered Ted.

I agreed. It was only fitting he should be the face of the project to MLB. After all I had no desire to stick around after it becomes real. It'll be Ted and Libby's baby to run.

The newly formed team got down to business.

"Hold it, we all have something to do except you, Dru McKenna. What's up with that?" asked Hannah.

"No flies on you, are there, dear?"

"I should say not, and don't try that sleight of tongue with me, Buster. What're you going to be doing?"

"Me, I'm going to play with my dog," I answered over my shoulder and headed for the car and back to the lake house to play with Riley, and most important... to think.

* * *

After spending the afternoon exploring the hills above the lake, Riley and I left to meet the team at Morretti's in Elmira. Calling Hannah's cell I told her we were on our way.

"Are you sure they'll let Riley in?" she asked.

"If they want..."

"Yeah I forgot McKenna's immutable law: 'Take me and my dog or neither of us,' right?"

"Right, Kiddo."

Over dinner Ted said, "You guys aren't gonna believe this. There's a team in Las Vegas up for sale."

"What league?" asked Hannah.

"Pacific Coast," replied Ted.

"Whoa, Ted. That's Triple-A," I said with a pronounced frown.

"I know, isn't it great?"

I looked at all of them then said, "You know the buy-in for a Triple-A team is about twenty mil, right?"

"Yeah, but with that we get instant affiliation, support for player and coaches' salaries and half the equipment costs," said Ted.

"Who's the parent club?" asked Libby.

"That's the best part, Hon. It's the New York Mets," Ted announced proudly.

"Wow, that would mean we'd be at a higher rank than Binghamton," said Libby with an ear-to-ear grin.

"Hold on, folks, we gotta work this out. Doesn't final approval of a sale and move need the Mets approval?" I said.

"Probably, not to mention MLB," said Ted.

"How the hell are we going to get that?" said Libby turning toward Hannah.

"Who knows? I've ridden this wagon before and all I know is we'll figure out somethin'," said Hannah. "Right, Dru?"

"Sure, lay it all on me," I answered with a smile replacing the frown.

Riley, who had been quietly lying next to me seemed to sense the meal was finished. He roused to see if he'd get his customary "last bites." He did and we returned to Ted's study to make plans for a bid on the Las Vegas 51s.

* * *

The next morning, I harbored a worrisome notion. I think if I put my brain on the edge of a razor it would resemble a BB on a four-lane highway. I need an idea but looks like I'll have to steal one.

I knew Hannah could tell I was worried, mainly because she said, "Dru, I know you're worried."

No flies on her or me, I thought.

She let me off the hook... for the moment. I took Riley out for his morning ablutions and asked the spirit guides for an answer. With coffee in hand I stood on the dock and stared out at the lake. I was still agonizing over what in God's name we could do to pull this off. *Maybe nothing*, was my fear.

Triple-A, how did I get involved in a business like this? I was fairly certain we couldn't get approval from either the Mets or MLB, but we'd soldier on and try. Helping out friends, sure I can do that. Overcoming small town petty grudges, conspiracies and the potential to fail beautifully, I'm pretty sure I can't do THAT too! Come on. Just let me come out of this thing with a scalp on my belt that's not my own.

On the drive to the Reynolds' Hannah knew I was still troubled. I was waitin' for her to nail me on it soon. True to form, I didn't have long to wait.

When we settled down in Ted's office, Hannah brought out her hammer.

"What is it, Dru? Something's bothering you and before you go Clint Eastwood on me with the tall, strong, silent bit I'm here to tell ya', Pilgrim, it ain't gonna fly, so don't try it."

I laughed. "You do know John Wayne said that, not Clint, right? Besides, he looked nothin' like a dame."

"Are we mixing movie references here or what? And don't think you're getting away with a patented McKenna distraction ploy, Bucko."

"I was thinking about Bloody Mary, hon," I said trying yet another distraction ploy using *South Pacific,* which she wasn't buying.

"I just bet you were. C'mon, what gives, or do I tell one of the most embarrassing moments of Dru McKenna's life?" she threatened.

"Wow! Okay, I was thinking today we really need to finesse this gambit of misdirection perfectly or we'll blow Ted's dream out of the water. I'm not gonna dismiss Hank as a small town yokel. I don't fear him but I respect him as the malevolent evil rat bastard I know he'll turn out to be. Revenge is a dish best served cold... but freezing him out might trigger some vengeful plot to thwart us. It's a delicate balance."

"Come up with a plan of your own, did we?" she asked.

"I believe I have, Mrs. McKenna."

"My hero," she sighed while gazing upon me with moon-calf eyes. "Whatcha got?"

With the unexplained plan in the middle of the room, we were joined by Ted and Libby who were finished seeing their kids off to school. Based on the looks of them, executing the plan for D-Day was easier than getting a seventh and eighth-grader off to school.

"What'd we miss?" asked Libby.

"Dru was about to share an idea," said Hannah.

"How does this sound? First we hide in plain sight," I said having received an answer from spirits, guardian angels or from somewhere out there.

"Like a needle in a haystack?" she asked.

"More like in a stack of needles," I answered.

"What exactly does that mean?"

"Well, the idea of the diversion is sound but I want Hank to think like a Steele-type hump might think."

"What's a steel hump?" said Ted.

Ignoring him for the moment so as to not lose my brain train o' thought, I continued, "In fact I'm counting on him to do exactly what I hope he'll do."

"Why do you hope he acts like Steele?" asked Hannah.

Perplexed, Libby turned to Ted with eyebrows about to threaten her hairline. "What's steel got to do with this?"

"Here's the deal. I just don't believe subterfuge will be fool proof in a town this size. There's too many accidental contacts, where a word here or there may jog someone's memory... and poof, the plan is up in smoke."

"As in the jig is up, Mr. Holmes?" said Hannah.

"Exactly, Mrs. Watson, just like that," I said.

"You believe Hank'll catch on?"

"Maybe not right away but when he ponders a while he could put the pieces together even if he doesn't know about us. He knows Ted is up to something, just not the whole agenda. People like Hank and Ian Steele believe they're the smartest most clever person in any room they're in."

"Who's Ian Steele? What the hell is going on here, Ted?" said Libby.

"Libby, I have no idea. They won't tell me. How about it, Dru? What are you guys talkin' about and who's this Steele guy?"

"Sorry, last year in Baltimore, one of the malevolent creatures we had to deal with was Ian Steele. He betrayed my godfather, Jon

Fallon, and was directly responsible for his death," I said, bringing them somewhat up to date.

"Wow! Jon Fallon was like a Warren Buffet type guy, wasn't he?" asked Ted.

"He was, even advised Warren from time to time," I answered.

Ted looked at Libby and said, "We are in rarefied air here, hon."

"And you're hoping Hank acts like Steele?" questioned Libby with a perplexed look still in place.

"Not the dangerous part but the treachery. I, er, we can deal with that," I assured them.

"We can?" said Ted.

"Here's my idea. What say we go to Hank and bring him in on part of the deal? Not the baseball part but the amusement park part. Ask him to join in the project financially. I don't think Hank will accept Ted's overture at face value, still it may keep him preoccupied enough to keep him away from the Elmira College land and keep our baseball deal secure."

"Okay, but how do we conceal the baseball part?" Libby asked.

"I've got an idea for that too. We do what any self-respecting man does when faced with a troublesome situation. We come up with an expedient lie."

"I knew it. I've always felt that believing everything a man says is dangerous. So what's the lie?" asked Libby as she cast an evil eye toward Ted.

"We tell 'em we went to Butler for the Pioneer name because we want to use it for the amusement park as a connection to a popular time in the area. I know we talked about calling it Eldridge Park but they've already started to resuscitate Eldridge in its original location on a small scale so that's out. We found we couldn't buy the Eldridge or Pioneer names so we'll need to change it."

"What if Butler, since he's in cahoots with Hank on other deals around town, offers to sell the Pioneer name after all?"

"We'll let him, but not to us. If Hank really wants to stick it to Ted, he'll end up with the name, the land, the whole enchilada."

"So it's not really a lie after all," said Libby.

"Not entirely, but it serves a purpose."

"How's that gonna happen, if Butler is the one selling the Pioneer name?"

"I'm sure Hank will instruct him to sell to Ted, which he will. After all, how much could he ask? Ted in turn will give it to Hank as the first step in the offer of an olive branch," I said.

"What if Hank turns the gesture down?"

"Then we go to step two," I said.

"What's step two?"

"Offering Hank a piece of the Big Flats land deal to go with the name."

"Holy cow! You've got Ian Steele down pat. You worry me," said a grinning Hannah.

"As well I should, dearie. I've been through it before."

"Doesn't Butler know it was you calling about the Pioneer name?" she asked.

"I never gave a name. I only said I was calling on behalf of Ted. Caller ID will show Ted's office number since I called from here. So as far as Butler knows the call was made by some minion of Ted's."

"It sounds audacious enough to work. What better way to keep your enemy close, eh, Sun Tzu?" said Hannah.

"Precisely. In addition, even though Hank ends up holding the bag, so to speak, nothing prevents him from profiting from a development program of his own. The whole idea is not to hurt Hank and his crew necessarily—but to prevent him from hurting Ted, which, I'm sure, is Hank's main goal."

"It's amazing how your mind processes these problems," said Hannah.

"Yeah, how do you do it, Dru?" asked Libby.

"Someday I promise to share the whole of it."

"Including how Red got his name?" asked Hannah.

"That and much more. I think you'll find it as fascinating as I do."

The rest of the day was spent mapping out responsibilities: the amusement park for the women, baseball for the men, and where Team McKenna's mascot dog would go on his next walk.

Back at the lake and after Mr. R.T. Dog's nighttime ablutions, the boys joined Hannah in the cave.

"How was the perambulation?" she asked.

"Quite satisfactory and you'll be glad to know the hood is secure, and we can all sleep in tomorrow. He's had a busy day."

"As we all have," she said, trying unsuccessfully to stifle a yawn.

* * *

Awakening to the delightful aroma of fresh brewed coffee and biscotti straight from the oven, I rolled over and soon was accosted by a leaping hundred-pound Lab who proclaimed it was the best day ever. Riley offered a morning faux chomp on my arm by way of a greeting. We horsed around until Hannah entered with a tray of goodies and the papers.

"What's going on in here? It sounds like you were fighting."

"Riley was just telling me what a great day this is, and alerting me to your arrival."

"Yeah, as if the delightful aromas emanating from the kitchen didn't already deliver that message," she said.

"You're right, it does smell scrumptious. Let's eat."

"And good morning to you too, fine sir."

I laughed as Hannah placed the tray on the nightstand and pulled her down to me. Seems breakfast would be delayed a bit.

* * *

After a bit of fooling around, we were in the middle of breakfast and the papers when the strains of *The Good, the Bad*

60

and the Ugly signaled an incoming call. A wave of dread washed over me. The number of times a phone call informed me of disaster looming was legion. I looked at Hannah with fearful eyes, as if to say, 'Not again.' In spite of myself, I took the call.

CHAPTER 10

In Hank Lewis' office the phone rang, he answered and said, "What?"

"It's me, Hank. I was talking to Bob Crandall at the college and according to him some big deal auto parts company is investigating building a regional distribution center over by the Holding Point," said Rance Butler into his cell as he drove.

"Really, who did he say it was?" said Hank.

"McKenna Associates, ever hear of 'em?"

"Holy shit, this could be huge. They're the largest and most successful aftermarket auto parts business on the planet. Who contacted Crandall, did he say?"

"A guy named... hold on, I wrote it down. Here it is, Dru McKenna."

Hank was lost in thought trying to figure out how to use this info to his best advantage.

"What chance does Crandall think this has of happening?"

"He's not sure yet. He's checking with the college now to see what's available. He knows the school needs funding for expansion so he's confident they'd love to do it."

Hank was lost in thought again. He sat mulling over ideas when he realized Rance was still there.

"Rance, I need a favor."

"What is it?"

"Go check with the college about any land in that area and see if we can buy it up now for cash on the barrel head."

"We?" asked Reynolds.

"Of course, you brought this to me so naturally I'd include you," said Hank. "I'll even overlook you calling me Henry. You know I hate that."

"Sorry, Hen... er, I keep forgetting. I'll get right on that and get back to you. Are you thinking of grabbing some land and selling it to McKenna?"

"Rance, sometimes you surprise me. That's exactly what I'm thinking. I've dealt with these kinds of hot shots before. If they want something bad enough they don't let anything stand in their way. It helps that I know of him but he's clueless about me."

"Good thing," muttered Reynolds.

After getting the news from Butler, Hank put in a call to his banker, Austin Coleman.

"Austin, how you doin'? Hank here."

"As if I didn't know. I put the volume on high after caller ID warned me," said Coleman laughing. "Doin' great, what's up?"

"I'm not sure, but I may be buying some land soon and wondered what I could comfortably commit to."

"Hank, you have enough collateral to float a loan for the whole county," Coleman exaggerated. "How much are we talking about here?"

"Not exactly sure yet, I'm just covering my bases. But I may have a figure in mind soon, maybe even today."

"Just let me know and we'll work it out, Hank."

"Thanks, Austin."

Later that day, Hank's cell intoned the theme from *The Godfather*.

"It's me, Rance. Looks like Reynolds has no interest in the college land."

"We already know it's the McKenna guy, so why are you calling?" asked a surly Hank.

"Just confirming. The good news is there's forty-five to fifty acres that's privately owned but the owners may want to sell. Crandall can't promise it but he thinks it's likely. It wouldn't block the sale of the parcel but its value might go up significantly being adjacent to a project of this apparent scope.

Hank rose and began to pace as Butler continued, "Crandall also mentioned an overlooked piece of land right at the entrance of the plots he forgot to tell McKenna about. It's an old piece that ran in front of Brown's Pharmacy—you know they had the best lemon ice cream when I was growin' up. Anyway when train tracks were laid years ago Brown's never sold this plot and it's been overlooked for decades. Crandall didn't think to tell McKenna about it. If you want to move now you could buy it. The Browns have no use for it and since the college really needs the money you can get the forty-five acres from Crandall. It's not sure McKenna will go through with the deal anyway, so for him it's a bird in the hand."

"Sorry I snapped, Rance. That was good thinking about Reynolds and terrific news about the Brown's land."

"Thanks, Hen, er ah, Hank. Are you willing to go on a flyer and buy this tract?"

"Yeah, land is never a bad buy. Even if the deal folds we may be able to do something later, and I have another idea in mind," said Hank.

"Anything more I can do, Hank?"

"Indeed, Rance, I want you to buy that land today. I'll call Coleman and authorize a check made out to the college to be picked up by you and delivered to Crandall."

"For how much, Hank?"

"That's for you to find out from Crandall. I'll meet his price. I gotta move fast."

Chapter 11

"Ted, what's wrong? You sound awful," I said.

"He found out about the college land," said Ted.

"Ouch! I knew small towns were tight knit but this is tighter than a duck's ass—and that's waterproof. How'd you find out?" I asked.

"I got a call from Steve Greatsinger. He's worried I'm gonna be more interested in the land up there than Big Flats. He sees our project as being a real boon to his area."

"Why did he think you were interested in that other land?"

"I'm not sure, but I know somebody was checking. Maybe it was Butler or maybe Greatsinger himself being squirrely," said Ted.

"Well, no matter, it sounds like we have you firmly entrenched as being interested in Big Flats," I said.

"So now it's time to contact Hank with an offer to join me, right?"

"Soon, but not yet," I said. "First, we need to get the ballpark plans together, investigate the Las Vegas deal, and get a firm quote on the land in both places."

"You guys comin' over tomorrow?" asked Ted.

"I'm sure we can, but I'll check with Hannah and call ya."

Over dinner, I filled Hannah in on the happenings of the day.

"Seems you were right about small town intrigue, huh?"

"I expected no less, Hank and Butler so reminded me of Steele. I couldn't help but be on guard."

"Anything we can't handle?"

"No, don't forget we're clever and resourceful people."

"I couldn't if I tried. You keep telling me every day."

At that point, Riley, who had finished his last bites, instructed me it was time for a walk. And so we did.

* * *

While the boys were walking Hannah called Libby and invited them up for the weekend for an old fashioned New England clambake.

"We were going to have you guys down, but I love the lake and a clambake tips it. We'll be up. Hannah, what do you think of this whole Hank deal?"

"Libby, I know I keep saying how good Dru is at this stuff but it's really true. I've never been around or even heard about someone with his instincts for solving issues that pop up in any project. It's like a sixth sense for finding the correct path in strange woods. It's uncanny how he always senses true north. We won't get lost in this mess, believe me."

"Funny, that's what Kimberley said. I can't wait to see how it unfolds," said Libby.

"You ain't seen nothin' yet. Wait 'til it really gets hairy," said Hannah.

"You mean more than it already is?"

"Oh yeah, probably as hairy as Chewbacca's butt."

* * *

On Saturday, Ted and Libby rode up to the cottage to visit Hannah and me. Of course, Riley, who greeted them as long lost friends with mock chomps and wagging tail, was assured he was the true reason behind their visit.

I was holding sway at the grill on the patio. I'd pre-cooked the chicken thighs and downed a Sam Adams Ale while waiting for the charcoal to heat. After greetings were out of the way, I brought out my version of a New England clambake.

"What's a Michigander know from New England clambakes?"

"I'm from a long line of New Englanders. I grew up on this stuff."

As we sipped our beers, Ted asked me how much baseball I played.

"I started in Little League, went to Babe Ruth League, then high school and American Legion. I played one year in college but wasn't good enough to go any further."

"What's your greatest day?" asked Ted.

"It happened in Little League. We had a terrific red-haired pitcher, Rusty Hatch, who threw hard and most times had good control."

"That usually means wins at that level," said Ted.

"Right, but we also had other very good players. We had Joe Kostelnek at first, Skip Johnson behind the plate, Gary Leak at second, George Olivetti at short, and me at third. Those were the All-Stars. Our outfielders were good hitters and fair to middling fielders."

"You got some memory. Are you still in contact with those guys?"

"Not a one," I said.

"I bet they didn't have many chances with that fireballer on the mound, did they?"

"Not many, usually weak grounder balls or pop-ups to boot. We were playing the other undefeated team in the league for the championship. In the bottom of the seventh we held a 2-1 lead. I remember this like yesterday. Three more outs and we'd celebrate at Lovell's ice cream parlor. Their leadoff hitter inexplicably walked on a bad call. Next guy, a lefty, hit it down the third base line swinging late on Rusty's heater. I was shaded over there because not many got around on Rusty. I easily scooped it up and threw to Leak for the start of a 5-4-3 DP."

"Not bad for kids, what thirteen?"

"I know, right."

"This sounds like it might not end well," said Libby.

"Very prescient, there are two outs, none on. I could see the trophy in our hands and was as excited as Christmas mornin'. Next guy got a perfect bunt base-hit down first, a tough play, base-hit. The next guy got walked on two of the worst called pitches I've ever seen. I know how that sounds but after all these years I still believe it. During the game I got three hits and drove in both our runs. Now I was thinking of the MVP but knew Rusty would probably get it... mostly because he deserved it."

"What happened?" asked Libby excitedly.

"Well, the rest was in slow motion. Our best outfielder was in right field over toward the right field line. 'Cause a right-handed batter was up and they swung late too."

"Did he?" asked Libby unable to stifle her enthusiasm.

"Just as if we planned it, which we did, the batter popped up the first pitch right to Corky Kramer, just a can of corn. We all watched the arc as we inched toward the second base side of the mound for the upcoming celebration. We never took our eyes off the ball. Corky yelling 'I got, I got it,' as we were taught to do on all fly balls. He didn't *got it.*"

Ted laughed and Hannah rolled her eyes at Libby who also laughed. I didn't find this painful memory all that amusing,

Hannah asked, "What happened?"

"The ball hit him right on top of the head and stunned him. He promptly fell like a wounded buffalo. The ball rolled a few feet away and the runners ran like they'd stole something. Corky just sat there dumbfounded. The rest of us were jumping up and down yelling 'pick it up!' He remained inert. Gary Leak ran out to retrieve the ball and threw home but way too late. Both runners scored. Corky later said he lost the ball in the sun but when we looked up all we saw were clouds. I'll never forget that moment, we lost 3-2. End of story."

"If that was your best day, what was your worst?" asked Ted.

"Same day."

We sat silent a moment as if grieving the loss of a loved one. Then laughter rang out and doubled them over. Each apologizing, but I too joined them in glee. I guess it was funny, after all.

"That's some memory, hubby dear," said Hannah.

"I think anybody who has competed in anything at any level has similar memories. Some can handle 'em and others not so much," said Libby.

"You're right on the money, Libby. As I recall, someone blew a short putt for a team victory in college golf," I teased.

"Never mind, Bub, now I know your underbelly, so watch what you say, Mister Loser," said Hannah.

After the tale of my disappointment I resumed assembling the next ingredients to go in the bake: corn on the bone, lobsters, sausage, potatoes, all on the grill carefully watched until done. Accompanied by Naylor Wine's Gris, it was a veritable feast.

They all loved it and complimented the less than humble chef.

"Where did you get this recipe? It's delicious," said Libby.

"I stole it from Bobby Flay, courtesy of the *Food Channel*," I said.

"What about the authentic New England Clambake from generations of McKennas?" asked Hannah with an impish smile.

"Perhaps I embellished a tad," I said.

After dinner, while we wallowed around the pool Ted asked, "Where do we stand with the ballpark designs?"

"Hannah and I did some research on attendance levels and the size of successful Triple-A clubs and there's a study by the Economics Department of a Maryland college that said the size recommended for Triple-A stadiums be a 10,000-seat capacity. That's probably optimal. Only twenty percent of teams of that level sell out so they concluded that smaller parks may be better than some current ones."

"There are a number of variables to consider like population pool, positive promotional activity, team's playing ability, and the new-stadium honeymoon among them. I think we need to think about our chances of being approved by MLB first and foremost. I believe there's a good chance if we don't meet the minimum it will be held against us," said Hannah.

"I can see what you're sayin', but what can we do to convince the Mets and MLB to take a chance on us?" said Ted.

"I think I have an answer. We build a pro forma to detail our C.V. including financial position, our business acumen and our promotional plans including the entire entertainment facilities, and past success," I said. "Also I think we should size the thing to be a 12,500-seat facility with twenty-five to fifty luxury suites and sky boxes—some not all, on season ticket basis, but we'll figure all that out later."

Discussion turned to cost of land, building the field and stadium, scoreboard, sound, team acquisition and operational expenses. We adjourned to the cottage, since the nights were getting chillier.

"How about the money, Ted? What's your plan?" asked Hannah.

"Well, we need to delve into the costs Dru just mentioned and get some numbers together so we can figure out the financing."

"Okay, some of us have marching orders, right, ladies?" I said. "I have a standing walking order from my dog. Tomorrow I'll return to the college to move the land deal forward. Ted, you can touch base with Hank and put that part of the plan in motion."

With that we bade goodnight and looked forward to the next steps.

When R.T. Dog and I returned from securing the 'hood, Hannah asked if I thought this project was doable.

"Providing we get approval from the Mets and MLB we should be A-OK. I have a feeling Triple-A may be one A or two beyond our reach and therefore hard to get acceptance for… but if we put a plan together that impresses them enough we may be in line for a lower classification. I believe it's a more realistic goal, given this population pool and all the variables like demographics connected with something like this. We may be better off at the Double-A level but we'll see how it shakes out. In any event we'll be able to swing it. Hell, I can swing it myself. Or I should say *we* can swing it."

"Are you sure you want to get that deeply involved?"

"Remember your husband and his family has done pretty well for ourselves over the years. Don't forget the inheritance from Jon Fallon. Actually, we'll use Fallon's money for this, but I want Ted to chip in up front and as always in these deals, I'll structure it as an internal loan he'll pay back. I have no intention of full time team management."

I stood up to give me time to mull this over. Am I sure I wouldn't mind running this show? It was appealing but there'd be a lot of tension and dealing with disagreeable humps that would turn me into a hump my ownself. Who the hell wants to be a hump this side of a camel on Wednesday? After my quick bit of introspection I answered, "Guess whose name will be on the stadium?"

"Ian Steele?" guessed Hannah.

"You really are a wise-ass, aren't ya, sweetheart?"

"Always and forever. Why don't you tell me whose name now?"

"Jon Fallon Stadium. I want to pay tribute, and I figure invoking his name with the powers that be in MLB won't hurt us either."

"You have more angles than a pool table and my geometry classes," she said, "and remember I went to Cornell not Ohio State," chided Hannah.

"But Michigan is where the donkeys go."

"Oh ya, I forgot. Goodnight, dearie," she said kissing me goodnight.

CHAPTER 12

"Are you sure we can handle this, Ted?" said Libby.

"Sure? No. But, I haven't been this amped for anything in my life. Have you noticed how everything seems to be falling in place? And I believe, in Dru, we are associated with the most skillful project architect in the world."

"He is amazing. I can't wait for what Hannah has in store for us. According to Kimberley, she's the Princess of promotion."

"What, the 'queen' was busy?" Ted snarked.

"You know you share a lot of the same qualities as Dru. For one there's the smart ass side to both of ya."

"Thank you dear, I live for recognition."

***

"How surprised will the little piss-ant be when he finds out it's me going up against him?" asked Hank. He and Rance Butler were sitting in Hank's office enjoying the Irish whiskey Hank favored.

"He's bigger than you, Hank, and I'm not sure he doesn't already know," answered Butler.

"Only by size," grumbled Hank.

"Steve seemed to think he knows about your interest," said Rance completing his update.

"Yeah, but Steve wouldn't tell him anything. He plays his cards close to those paisley vests of his. He ain't that sharp either. Oh, he may wonder a bit because of our past run-ins but we haven't crossed swords in a while. I know what he's up to but I'm betting he has no clue what I'm up to."

"What exactly is that, Hank?"

"First I want that Big Flats land, then I want to rub Reynolds' nose in it. Then I can be free to develop the thing any way I want."

"So you don't really have a plan."

"Yeah, I do, it's to stick it in Reynolds' ear, smart ass. You're being pretty smart-mouthed today. What's got into you, Butler?"

"I'm not sure it's a good idea to underestimate Reynolds. After all, he did eat your lunch quite a few times in Binghamton, and every time you two have competed."

"Yeah, sure, but I was distracted with the lawsuit with the Ex. I'm going to meet with Steve on Friday and get this deal movin'."

Ted answered his cell and was mildly surprised to hear from Steve Greatsinger.

"Hi, Steve, what's up?"

"Ted, I just wanted to let you know Hank is coming in on Friday to discuss the land you're lookin' at."

"I'm surprised he's looking at it. Did you mention I too was lookin' at it, Steve?"

"I wouldn't last too long if I spread intel like that around, Ted. No, I didn't." Ted thought about it. Since Steve was telling him about Hank's interest, he concluded Steve didn't much care for Hank either. No surprise, not many did.

"The reason I called is to say, if you really want this land, you better move soon."

"Thanks, Steve, I appreciate that. And I am interested but I haven't got the financing in place yet. What did you decide the freight is?"

"Thirty mil, Ted."

"Yeah, that seems okay but I can't make an offer until my ducks are rounded up. I'll commit to thirty mil to discourage others, but if you get a better offer, take it. Thirty is probably my limit."

"Okay, if you're sure. I'd give you last look if you wanted, but you'd have to beat the high card, Ted."

"I understand, and thanks for the heads up, Steve."

Hanging up, Ted's first instinct was to call Dru. It looked like the plan was coming together nicely.

* * *

At home that night, I told Hannah the news of my misgiving. I wondered how Hank had found out about Ted's interest in Big Flats so quickly. "Should we be worried? It seems to be working to plan."

I told her, "I don't think worry is what it is. For now to be wary should be enough, but if we stick to my script we should be fine. Or maybe we should be scared witless."

CHAPTER 13

The whirlwind of the next several weeks flew by. Design plans from three architects and three contractors for the stadium were submitted. It took several days to decipher then run comparative analyses between the various sections. Seating, restaurants, restrooms, offices, mechanicals, HVAC, field turf, clubhouse, concessions and completion time for all of it were totaled, analyzed and discussed. Several rounds of clarification meetings took place with the aim of finalizing a decision. The decision was truly a collaborative effort as we all weighed in on the items of most concern. The bids for each portion of the project were scrutinized, compared and finally decided upon.

After those meetings we reached a consensus on a design and picked a contractor. Baseball Partners from State College, Pennsylvania, were chosen to build the stadium based on the designs of Geiger Limited Partners of East Brunswick, New Jersey. Both firms had vast experience in design and management of sports building projects for football, baseball and basketball venues, for over twenty years.

Now all our attention could be focused on land acquisition, securing ownership of the Las Vegas team—or more likely an expansion team—then finally winning approval from MLB and the Mets or some other team. The most important of these was convincing MLB and the Mets that our company, Regional Baseball Partners, was the best candidate for their approvals.

"Now that we have those details established I think we need to discuss our approach to MLB and the Mets," I said.

"That shouldn't be so hard, will it?" asked Libby.

"Hold on, Kemo Sabe, Let's discuss financing first. I've been so caught up with land and the stadium and Hank and all his crap,

I haven't done anything. We still need to finalize the North land deal. Where do we start?" asked Ted.

I started laughing, "I was wondering when you would get around to that. I, on the other hand, am all over it. This ain't my first at bat and I've got a strategy."

"Well I'm glad somebody's on the beam. Whatcha got?"

I go over to Hannah, bend over, give her a quick kiss and sit down beside her and say, "Hannah and I discussed this... and we're gonna finance it ourselves." Ted and Libby look like moose ready to knock off their antlers. Okay, I guess it's Ted who looks like that. Libby looks like she's about to see her first child off to school... that is if moose even go to school.

Hannah and I grin and start laughing and I wonder if she can read my offbeat, inane moose analogy. No, of course not, so I continue, "And you'll repay the loan at a modest interest. Deal?"

"Are you serious? I can't believe it. I figured to hock my eye teeth. We can't accept this. It's too much," says Ted with a stern look on his face.

"Hannah, talk to him. We didn't ask you down here for this kind of thing. We wanted advice, not a hand out, please," said Libby.

"Hey guys, listen closely to what he's proposing, okay? This is no charitable event. Nobody's manning the phones ready to take pledges. We've been blessed with some fortunate bequeaths giving us an opportunity to help others. We did with Austin and Kimberly with National Motors last year. This year it's your turn so shut up. We've got work to do."

"So this is a real deal, huh?" said Ted.

"Real as wet rain, we can do this. My godfather was Jon Fallon, and he left us a rather substantial inheritance. He also asked that we use it, at our discretion, to fund worthwhile causes, programs or ventures. This one seems to qualify on a couple of levels. My lawyers will draw up the details and we're good to go, if it's okay with you two. If it's not, then we'll walk away. What do you say?"

Ted said with strain evident on his face, "It's okay but I feel guilty accepting it. I don't know what to say. I had no idea you could do this or would, for God's sake. I'm stunned."

Libby moved into Ted's arms with tears streaming and said, "Of course, it's okay. Thank you."

Ted and Libby looked like the weight of the world was now somebody else's problem, no longer theirs.

"So I guess all systems are go, huh?" I said.

"Seems like it. Where are we on the college land?" asked Hannah.

"Well, I got back to Bob Crandall to set up a meet tomorrow. I told him I have two other bids, one in Binghamton, one in Rochester."

"That oughta get his attention," said Libby.

"Sharpen his pencil a tad, as well," said Ted.

* * *

That night on the cottage deck overlooking Keuka Lake, Hannah and I sat quietly taking turns rubbing our dog's back and belly. The boy was in reverie. We now knew Ted and Libby had the sand to see the project through to completion despite obstacles presented from Hank Lewis, Rance Butler or anyone. What was unknown was MLB and if they were of a mind to play ball with us or not.

* * *

Ten a.m. the next day, I entered Bob Crandall's office on the Elmira College campus, admired it sufficiently, chatted a bit, then got down to business.

"Judging from what you told me on the phone, you've been busy. Those locations have definite pluses but also some negatives. We, of course, have only pluses," said Bob Crandall with a big grin and twinkling eyes. I was taken with the man and hoped my assessment would prove to be accurate.

"Dr. Crandall, you're right. I have been busy, and maybe I haven't been entirely fair here."

"Please, call me Bob. In what way haven't you been fair?"

"Please, call me Dru, Bob. I'm afraid my other choices are farther along in the process. I have pricing, tax relief, and an immediate sale can be achieved in both places quicker than expected."

"Dru, I'm prepared to show the land I have available. It's a little under 550 acres. There's a wedge on the northern boundary that is privately owned, but I believe the owner would sell if you need it."

"Bob, that would be enough but how big is that privately owned parcel?"

"Around forty-five acres, give or take."

"Can I rightly assume they're looking to sell?"

"The guy who owns it has another party interested in the property. He would prefer not to sell to him, but he needs money, so the college bought it. If this goes south I'll step in and buy it myself from the school."

"What's that story about? Why didn't he want to sell to this other party, Bob?"

"Yeah, how can I delicately put this?"

"Forget delicacy, just put it, Bob."

"Well, the guy's a dick head. I'm afraid he got wind, somehow, of interest in this land, and his ploy would probably be to hold up any possible project for ransom."

"I take it this is no close friend of yours?" asked Dru smiling.

"Dru, I can honestly say I don't know a single person who is his friend. He's tried to vanquish everybody with whom he's had any dealings. He leaves a sour taste in everybody's mouth."

"May I ask something?"

"Shoot, Dru."

"Is it possible this guy is Hank Lewis?"

"Holy shit, how'd you come up with that name? I know I didn't say it, did I?" said Bob with a worried expression on his patrician face.

"Relax, I am just now becoming aware of Mr. Lewis and his rep, and I gotta tell you, I hate humps like this guy sounds. Has he approached you about buying the land? I think I can suggest a strategy that would be a win/win for all."

"Let's hear it, Dru."

"How would you feel about raising the price to him by as much as fifty percent?"

"I take it you don't want the land?" he said.

"No, it's not that. I do want the land, but at the price you quoted. Not at the price this hump would have to offer me to make what he wants to make. If he buys it thinking he's gonna screw me over he'll have another think comin' and you'd make some money for the college. Mainly I'd like to turn the tables and stick it to him, if you're willing."

"Would you be interested if he turns down the whole thing?"

"What are you crazy? Not at those prices, Bob." We both started laughing.

"Dru, tell you what, if you decide to build here I'll gladly sell to you at the original price."

"Bob, I think we can do business and I'm going to enjoy the whole thing. Now about that price..."

After discussing what I wanted and giving the parameters of time and availability it was decided I would have to wait for Bob to develop a plan to price up that much acreage in the best interest of the college. I was warned there might be purchase of homes necessary to add any additional pieces of land which would drive up the price. I told him to investigate and get back to me. Bob Crandall was so excited by the potential windfall for the college—not to mention himself—he put his troops to work immediately.

"I'll call you about Lewis when I know."

* * *

Ted wasn't sitting on his hands either. His meeting with Steve Greatsinger gave him an opportunity to commit to forty million bucks.

"I stretched it as far as I could and maybe I could squeeze out a bit more, but if it goes to forty-six mil I'll be out."

"I'll get back as soon as I can, Ted," said Steve.

* * *

"Hank, the bid is fifty million," said Steve Greatsinger through the phone. After a measured pause he let slip, "I don't think Ted can go any higher."

Hank was now pacing his office floor, a sure sign he was intent on nabbing his quarry. "What, I'm bidding against Ted Reynolds? Okay Steve, my offer is fifty mil," he said, smiling so wide the corners of his lips nearly touched his ears.

"Consider this a done deal. I'll have the paperwork to you ASAP."

* * *

I was pleased to hear from Ted the plan was proceeding on track and schedule. I headed down to meet the others at the M/T study. Ted had just arrived and the distaff side of the project began filling in us on the status of things.

"Guys, Libby and I were discussing ideas for marketing the team and drawing up the list for other attractions for the amusement portion of the project."

I said, "This oughta be good, Ted. Be on the lookout for Whack-a-Mole." First was a recreation of the old Eldridge Park components. They decided on a roller coaster, followed by a merry-go-round, bumper cars, fun house, and tunnel of love started the process. Then midway games like Skee Ball, photo booth, and her personal favorite, Whack-a-mole.

"There it is, Ted. I told you never let her get behind you with a mallet."

Ignoring me, or trying to, Hannah soldiered on, and listed all the modern arcade games and of course, the stage and bandstand gazebos came next. Their job would now be to source them. We agreed to leave for the lake for dinner and down time since we've been at it hammer and tong for two days. But before I joined the others on the dock I had one call to make.

Under the name McKenna Automotive I reached out to the New York Mets to discuss terms for buying the Las Vegas 51s. They told me I'd have to pass financial muster but they were sure it would be a mere formality so I was authorized to contact the owners of the 51s.

Ted stuck his head in my office at the cottage to tell me I was up to bat at the grill. It was six p.m. while I was on the phone with Vegas. Dinner time at Keuka Lake meant it was only three p.m. for the workers in High Roller town. I told Ted I'd be there after this call.

"Yes sir, I am the owner of McKenna Automotive, and I've been looking for two things. One, to put our name on a high profile professional sport to keep it in the public eye, and two, to become involved in a project to satisfy my love of the game of baseball. I am aware of the stadium situation there, and will be prepared to address it if and when we own the team. So when would you like to meet, and where?"

I was mildly surprised they agreed to see me so easily. What I didn't know was MLB was exerting great pressure on them to hear me out. *Here I thought it was my skill and charm that won them over.* A meeting was scheduled for the next Friday in New York of the minor league clubs in the Mets chain.

Celebratory dinner that evening was a specialty of Chez McKenna née Powell at the cottage... pizza from Morretti's.

* * *

"I can hardly believe this is really happening," said Ted on the flight down the next Friday morning.

"Believe it, and wait 'til you guys see the bona fide Chez Connelly-McKenna abode," I bragged.

The rest of the week was spent preparing my presentation to the owners of the Mets, and the 51's owner who asked to attend the meeting. We decided no reference to moving the team would be made, even if the Mets took me aside and point blank asked my intentions. My party-line answer would be that ownership must be secured before any plans could be made.

In the interim MLB received a Triple-A rating of my financial picture. The Mets owners wondered if I had designs on the parent club. In a tense pre-meeting call they even asked me about it point blank.

I assured them I didn't.

* * *

Hannah catered breakfast and dinner for the four days we spent in NYC. Her House Manager, Ivor Thompson, acted as tour guide for Ted and Libby, even though they had been to the city on numerous occasions. They thoroughly enjoyed his docent-like expertise regarding the history, restaurants, cultural events available and specifically his company.

On our last day, I was invited to lunch at Citi Field by the Mets owner, Joel Leonard.

"Okay, Dru. I've done my due diligence and your record of accomplishment speaks for itself. What I... we... want to know is what are you going to do with the 51s?"

"What would you like to see happen?" I asked.

"To be honest we're hoping you get 'em the hell outta there. It's too far away. Too hot, too distracting for players and too much temptation for them. We need 'em focusing on baseball, not bimbettes. As far as the stadium goes, it's abominable, we want a state of the art facility."

"Well, we'll see what we can do," I said.

* * *

"How come you didn't assure him by agreeing to do it?" said Ted.

"I never count chickens nor divulge plans prematurely."

"So you don't trust him?"

"Ted, I don't know him. For all I know he's got an ace up his sleeve. Right now I trust, but need to verify. We've got power because only we know about the plans in Elmira."

"When do you think we'll have their decision?"

"Less than a week, I guess."

* * *

And so it was. Four days later Joel Leonard called with the final decision. The 51s were now mine—step number one completed. I honestly was surprised they would be so eager to sell. The hard part would be selling them on movin' the 51s to Elmira. If they agreed to that I would be astounded. I concealed this belief from Ted and Libby so as not to cause them untold stress and worry. But I did tell Hannah.

"This has been in your mind all along, right?" she said.

"Pretty much. Look at it closely. Why would the Mets move a team to East Jabibee with such a relatively small pool of fans to draw from and with a Double-A team already in Binghamton?"

"You could tell 'em about Mark Twain," she said with a snide grin while sipping an Arnold Palmer. "What do you think will happen?"

"I'm not sure but I'd like the opportunity to pitch Ted's plan for a shot at Double-A ball."

"Isn't Binghamton, New York, the Double-A franchise holder?" she asked.

"It is.

"Are they not doing well?"

"No, I think they're doing okay. That's not the parent team I have in mind, my love."

"Dru, whadda ya have up your sleeve? What Major League club are you zeroing in on?"

"I couldn't tell you right now."

"Couldn't or *won't*?"

CHAPTER 14

"Henry, you're a baseball fan, right?" asked Rance Butler.

"Hey dip-shit, how many times I gotta tell you the name is Hank, huh? Hank, got it?"

"Yeah okay, Hank, I keep forgetting. I just saw on-line the Mets are selling their Triple-A team in Las Vegas."

"So what, I'm a Red Sox fan. What do I care about the stupid Mets?"

"I was just wondering who bought 'em is all," said Rance.

"You do that. Lemme know how it turns out," said Hank with sarcasm dripping like a dip stick at Jiffy Lube.

"Where's the land deal stand, Hank?"

"Seems about wrapped up, I meet with Crandall at the college in the morning."

The phone, with strains of *The Sting,* signaled a call. Caller ID warned him.

"Hank Lewis, here. Oh, hello, Ted. What the hell do you want, a loan?"

"Maybe, Hank, just maybe," answered Ted. "I'd like to meet with you today or tomorrow. How 'bout lunch, my treat?"

"I never turn down a free meal. Where?"

"Let's say Horrigan's around 12:30 today, can you make it?"

"Let's say," he said then abruptly hung up.

* * *

"Okay, that's done," said Ted.

"Hung up on you, didn't he," I said.

"How'd you know?"

"Easy. You didn't say goodbye. He's really a first class jerk, huh?"

"Absolutely, top shelf, bottled in bond."

At lunch time, waiting in Horrigan's restaurant, Ted Reynolds looked at his watch. 12:45. He knew Hank would be late. *Typical Hank,* he thought, *gotta jerk ya around.*

Horrigan's, an old-fashioned bar/restaurant, simple décor, simple food, simple to find, is a perfect lunch spot.

At one o'clock, Henry Lewis strolled in. He spotted Ted, sauntered over and bumped into a frazzled waitress who was in his direct path. He nearly caused her to drop the full tray of food she was delivering onto a nearby table. Without so much as an apology, Hank pulled out a captain's chair and plopped down. In keeping with his well-known rudeness, no apology for his tardiness was offered either. Politeness was obviously not in the man's makeup.

"Okay, Ted, what's this about?"

"So much for small talk, eh, Hank? Let's order first."

As they waited for their lunch, Ted began, "Hank, I know you want to ace me out of the Big Flats property. Do you know why I want it?"

"No, I have no idea and less interest," said Hank.

"Well maybe you should, and maybe you should think of joining me in my idea."

"As if you'd ever want me to join you in anything. What's up, Teddy?"

"Okay, Henry, here it is." Ted noticed Hank blanch at the use of Henry. He knew full well how much Hank despised the use of his name in such a manner, but he was just countering his being called Teddy which he didn't care for either, as Henry Lewis knew well.

"Some of my fondest memories growing up are the times I spent at Eldridge Park. I miss it and want to recreate it and expand on it in Big Flats."

"That's very touching. So I'm stopping you, huh?" said Hank grinning like a player drawing the needed ace from the river.

"I suppose you could, but why not join me in the venture?"

"What exactly does this park adventure entail? And, of all people, why pick me?"

"I know we're not bosom buddies. I suppose we've had our differences over the years, you and I, but this is something that could really benefit this area. I can't swing the whole thing myself so I thought of people who would be able to help handle a project of this scale. It's a short list and you're at the top. Obviously, we're not friends—doubt if we ever could be—but this area needs an economic shot in the arm. A project like this could do wonders for the economy, boost everyone's morale and perhaps stimulate like-minded people with ideas of their own to follow, some of which we might be able to capitalize on ourselves."

"What keeps me from just taking over the whole thing and cutting you out?" said Hank.

Ted acted as if he were thinking of this angle for the first time. He wasn't, of course... knowing Hank as he did. Finally Ted said, "I suppose nothing really. I knew it was possible you'd think like that but I figured we would put your name on the thing from the git-go. You take the credit and the bows. I'll do the grunt work."

Hank looked like he was actually considering this then said, "I still don't get why you came to me. I can name several people with the wherewithal to get into this, so again, why me?"

"Okay, listen, I thought it was time to bury the hatchet and not in each other. It's as simple as that. Sometimes people who are at odds can agree to do something for others without the prerequisite attached strings you seem to be looking for. Let's face it, not many people can stand you, Hank. They don't know you, except by rep, because you've never been accused of doing anything to help anybody else, so they figure from the way you treat people you're deserving of neither respect nor friendship. Maybe something like this could help change your image around town."

"And why are you so concerned about my image?"

"Actually I'm not, but it's true that this could help. But if you don't care about that... well, I just thought I'd throw it in."

"Uh huh."

Ted knew Hank smelled a rat but couldn't figure out what Ted's angle was. The plan was moving along just like envisioned.

Their food arrived, and they ate in complete silence. Hank stood without a word and abruptly left.

"Not to worry, Henry, I'll get the check," said Ted to the empty chair.

***

"How'd it go?" I asked when I received Ted's call.

"Pretty much like we thought, he's wary but maybe interested. I gotta tell you, the deal did sound good when I offered it."

"How'd you leave it?"

"I don't know," said Ted.

"What the hell does that mean?"

"Just what I said. After we ate he got up and left without a word."

"Wow, he is amazing. I'd say his personality needs work, but it doesn't seem he has one."

"I can honestly say I've never met a more disagreeable creature... ever. He smells a rat but can't figure out where I'm coming from. But I expect he'll be in touch. How are the girls coming with their sourcing project?" asked Ted.

"Libby has turned into a dynamo. She's found a carousel maker in Wisconsin, a bumper car and roller coaster company in Ohio, midway booth designers in Albany and a company that builds lakes in Florida."

"That's terrif but what do we do with a lake in Florida?" snarked Ted.

"The most interesting possibility is a place in Florida that Libby says claims they can do all of it. They'll be doing some kind of travelling the next few months but my company's jet will take good care of them," I said.

"So what have *you* been doing, big guy?"

"Mostly, playing with Riley at the lake. That and working on the college land deal. It seems Hank upped the ante on me. He found out it's McKenna Automotive that's behind the land acquisition. A part of me wishes we could let him have this one too and find another place. Cost him a bundle."

"We could but it would have to be another city and probably another state," said Ted.

"I know but there's more at stake than smiting Ol' Henry. I'm seeing Bob Crandall tomorrow to discuss what we can finalize immediately. I'll meetcha here after the meeting."

I explained what Bob Crandall was going to offer Hank as a selling price for the north forty-five acres. Ted doubted Hank would go for that even if he thought he could pass on the higher price to me. I told Ted part of me wanted Hank to try that just for the sheer pleasure of turning him down flat and leave him holding the bag.

Ted expanded. "What I'd love to see is Hank fork over at the higher price, you stuff 'im, and his only recourse is to sell it back to Bob at the original price. That would give the college a handsome profit. And give Hank a nice loss."

"My, still waters do run nasty when provoked, eh?" I said.

* * *

The next day I met Bob Crandall at Elmira College's faculty dining room. Bob was his buoyant self and after getting the pleasant chit-chat out of the way, we got down to cases.

"Dru, I'm afraid someone has let the cat out of the bag. Hank found out McKenna Automotive is behind the land purchase. I'm sorry."

"Don't sweat it, Bob. How'd he find out?"

"I don't know. I don't recall telling anyone but the board you were interested. But I'm not sure somebody wouldn't brag about knowing something other people don't, human nature being what it is."

"All too well, Bob. It really doesn't matter."

"I do have good news. I got him to way overpay for his section."

"Good news for you, maybe, I'm not sure this is where I'll build yet."

"The good portion of the news for you is not that we got Lewis, odious man that one, to pay more—but we reduced your price ten percent."

"Okay then, now you're talking. Bob, I appreciate your help on this so I'm going to advise you not to take what you see and hear in the news the next few days too seriously."

Bob sits at attention itching to become privy to some inside dope. Or maybe it's just a rash.

"When I sense a wolf closing in I take defensive positions."

"Is that all you can tell me, Dru?" Bob is practically ready to leap into my lap as his curiosity builds.

"For now, but I won't keep you twisting in the wind. At least, not for long."

The fact was we weren't in dire need of the extra acres. It just would have been nice to have them.

In the recesses of my mind I was uneasy. I feared something out there was circling like a hawk after its prey... lurking but unwilling to show itself, still a threat all the same. The image kept me awake wrestling with what else could go wrong.

CHAPTER 15

"Dru, for god's sake, what're you saying?"

Ted was now on his feet with no place to go. He was waiting for me to explain what catastrophe had befallen us now.

"Ted, I just got a call from Joel Leonard owner of the Mets, it turns out MLB has denied my right to own the Triple-A franchise."

"Holy shit," was Ted's eloquent reaction.

"My very thought," I said.

"Did Leonard say why?"

"He was calling prior to takeoff on a plane to Vegas so he couldn't go into details."

"What do you think it could be?"

"I have no earthly idea," said a very somber and confused man. I couldn't imagine being turned down for any reason. I have the wherewithal to swing a deal like this. I'm a fairly adroit businessman and not a bad dancer so I am stumped. "I'll call you later. I've gotta think."

* * *

Hannah and I spent the evening watching *The Godfather*, which somehow seemed *apropos*.

"I feel like Sonny after Vito got hit," said Hannah.

"And look where that got him."

"I know, I'm just sayin' it makes me mad. Is every project a roller coaster ride like this is?"

"Pretty much. Every once in a while during a project ya have to go to the mattresses. Ya got a fight on your hands and it might get tough. It's one of the reasons I do this stuff."

"You gotta be crazy. This is so frustrating. To feel like you're close enough to touch it only to find out it's a mirage. To feel you're this close and get rocked back. To feel the hard part is solved, and it's all downhill from here, only to find an abyss around the next bend awaiting your arrival."

"I know it appears that way, but the challenge of overcoming pitfalls makes the success taste so much sweeter," I said.

"If you ever get to taste it."

"Oh, we will," I said with more confidence than I felt.

Finding a knowledgeable contact proved to be nothing short of a stroke of genius. I was proud of the fruit-bearing idea that could possibly save the day. I was prouder still, since it was Hannah who came up with it.

"Call Justin, he knows that baseball guy. You know, the former Oriole?"

"Have I ever told you how great I think you are?"

"Not nearly enough," said Hannah blushing a bit.

"Justin, Dru here. You gotta minute?"

"Lemme see. Do I have time for the guy who saved my ass, how many times?"

"That would be four... but who's counting?"

"Apparently you are. What can I do for you?"

"I need a favor. I've been rejected from buying a Las Vegas Triple-A baseball team by MLB and I don't know why. I know you're friends with..."

"You mean Cory Yeager?"

"Yeah, couldn't come up with the name, thanks."

"Yeah, we still go to a game once in a while, usually the Nats. He lives in Fairfax or Burke, somewhere near D.C. His brother Andy pitches for Elmira or will, he's told. Why?"

"I need to find out who dropped a dime on me and why, and what I can do to resolve it," I said.

"Oh, is that all?"

"I know it's not an easy thing but it's fourth and long and the clock is running."

"I thought it was baseball we're talking about," said Justin.

"The donkeys in college thing again, really?" I said. "I know why donkeys don't go to college. I guess you didn't learn that at William and Mary, did ya?"

"I guess you would know since you had some in your classes at Ohio State, right?" said Justin.

"I'm not surprised you became a smartass, and for your information it's Michigan that accepts donkeys. They can't get in OSU."

"I'll talk to Cory and see if he can find out something. Probably have to bribe him with a look at next year's car models, though."

Man will never change, I thought.

Meanwhile I called my old friend, Raymond St. Cloud. "Hey, Bro, what's going on?"

"What's this Bro shit? You white men trying to upgrade your image?" said Raymond.

"If I were upgrading, I'd be calling you... why?" I said.

"Pointers, my friend, pointers on how to act and think. What are you involved with now?"

"Baseball, Raymond. Hannah's got a friend who wants to reintroduce the game professionally back in his home town. I should say the friend's husband wants to do it."

"With Hannah?" said, Raymond feigning a shocked reaction.

"None of that, Raymond," I cautioned.

"Couldn't help myself, sorry," said Raymond, stifling his chuckle.

"So what can I do for you?"

"I'm not sure but when I find I'm stuck I usually call on my blood brother who never ceases to amaze me with his knowledge, contacts, ability to gather intel, and who's the soul of discretion."

"We Indians are always wary when you pale faces start buttering us up. Let me go put my wallet in the safe and I'll come back on the line in a minute. So what does my pale friend want now?"

"I tried to buy a Triple-A baseball team in Vegas, and after passing credit checks and everything short of a rectal exam, MLB turned me down, and I need to find out why."

"And they won't tell you?"

"Not yet."

"Vegas, you say? I know a guy who may be able to help, but he's costly, Dru."

"I was hoping you'd know a guy. And I figured he'd come dear, being you don't know any cheap thugs, just the costly ones, but what can he do?"

"I don't know yet but let me inquire and see where it leads. You game?"

"Indeed I am. So what've you been doing?"

"My tribe wants to cash in on this casino action, and I'm the point man. Can you believe it?"

"Believe it? I'm not the least bit surprised. Your tribe has wise leadership."

"Thanks, I do look forward to it."

"You're the leader, right?"

"As the turn into my driveway."

"Raymond, doesn't the turn depend on which way you're coming on your street?"

"I forget you haven't been to the new house. I live at the right hand side on a one way street. I'll call when I hear something. My best to Hannah."

I felt like an anvil had been removed from my chest. Speaking with Raymond always inspired fond memories of great times including the time our grandfathers performed the blood brother ceremony on two young lads destined to achieve great things many years ago.

That's all I could think to do, so I went to find Riley T. Dog. It didn't take long. He was on the bed upside down, all four legs in the air having what looked to be a racing dream. Chasing bunnies or squirrels, I could only assume.

"Hey, Rile, wanna go out?"

Without a moment's hesitation I had his answer as my 100-pound waggy-tailed friend sprang from the bed landing on all fours and displaying eagerness for the aforementioned outing.

Hannah and Libby were putting the final touches on their travel plans for the amusement park portion of the project. They were planning to be gone for two weeks in the first phase of the schedule, selecting vendors and contractors. They planned to spend another two weeks on phase two, which was choosing the midway games. Using McKenna Associates corporate jet, leased from the Fallon Group Charter Service, eased the tedium of their travel plans. Hotels and ground transport were all arranged to the nth degree. Eisenhower would have benefitted from their expertise during D-Day. They were to lift off at seven a.m. on the next Monday.

In bed for the night, I brought Hannah up to speed on the contacts made today, and she me on the travel plans.

"This is going to sound silly," I said, "but I'm gonna miss you."

She laughed. "Sweet, not silly, and I feel the same way. We haven't spent too much time apart the last couple of years."

"That's the way it should be," I said.

"I hear people on TV talking about spending too much time together, but I don't buy into it. You're my best friend too, and I enjoy hanging widja."

"Ditto," I said.

"Ah, my glib emotive lover, how well you put it. Ditto indeed."

Riley chose that moment to nuzzle his way between us and settle in for a nighttime snuggle betwixt his people. Eventually he would become too warm and shuffle sleepily off to his sheepskin covered bed under our bedroom window.

During the night I slept fitfully, trying hard to grasp a thought dancing in the recess of my mind which refused to come forward.

I knew its emergence would eventually happen but the anticipation was driving me nuts. Somehow, I believed when this wispy thought manifested I'd have a pathway to follow. I've had this feeling many times and trusted it. It had never let me down before.

CHAPTER 16

Raymond St. Cloud called Monday morning.

"I wonder who that can be," said Hannah knowing full well who'd be the only one to call at six a.m.

I said, "I have an idea," in a semi snarky early morning manner.

She picked up the phone to answer, and I grabbed for it and missed.

She glared at me through slits for eyes and said, "As if you didn't know. Hello, Raymond. Dru isn't here, wanna come over?"

"Ah, the lovely Miss Hannah, if only it were true," said Raymond.

"Yes, and I see you're the same suave debonair gentleman I recall, Raymond. How are you?"

"Here, dear, here, you can't see me."

"Hannah, gimme the phone before you miss your flight. He'll keep on for hours, especially if you encourage him." I lunged at the phone and missed again.

"Hold on, Buster. I won't be rude to any man who has the good taste to call me lovely. Besides without me there is no flight, thank you. Raymond, now here is Dru."

"Got you up, didn't I?" asked Raymond.

"Only because you casino rats haven't been to bed yet," I said.

"Get yourself some fully leaded coffee, you're gonna need it."

Alerted by the tone in Raymond's voice, I thought, *this is serious.*

"Whatcha got, Raymond? This doesn't sound good. Is someone out to whack me?"

"Been watching too many cop shows on TV, have we?"

"No, I found out the scoop about your blackball from MLB, and it's nothing more sinister than political greed. No hits out on you... that we know about."

"Whadda you mean political greed?"

"It seems some local office holders don't want to lose the Triple-A team on their watch. They're hoping to petition MLB to move maybe the Mets, Rays, Athletics, somebody, anybody to Vegas. They don't want the stigma of a town that loses a Triple-A team hung on them. They've already threatened MLB with costly lawsuits to keep the 51s out there."

I shook my head and said, "Didn't see that coming. Wow! Makes this a horse of a different color. What are the chances of Vegas moving up to major league class?"

I could hear the smile in Raymond's silence as he listened to the inner workings of my mind.

"According to my sources, it's a popsicle in Death Valley. Being close to gambling makes MLB nervous—think of Pete Rose. MLB went as far as they did with Triple-A because of the threatened lawsuit."

I sagged back into the bed. I could feel the energy drain down my legs and onto the floor.

Feebly I muttered, "Got any ideas?"

"Maybe, but not over the phone," he said.

"Right, feel like a swim in cool, clear lake water?"

"Does it have fish in it?"

"Sure, you wanna fish?" I said.

"Does a hobby horse have a wooden dick?"

"I take that as a yes," I chuckled. I could feel the energy creeping up my legs and knew I'd be okay. Although the siren call of the pillows beckoned a powerful message, I resisted with great difficulty.

"Affirmative, I'll see you day after tomorrow."

I took Riley for a walk, and called Ted to fill him in on the news and warned of Raymond's arrival.

"What do you mean you're warning me?"

I laughed and said, "You're in for a treat. Raymond St. Cloud is a bona fide original. He says he has an idea or two on what we can do to get what we want."

Riley and I were on the dock sharing a burger and corn on the bone when Hannah called. I scraped a bit of corn for him and Riley was most grateful, I could tell by the ferocity of his baseball bat-like tail pounding on the dock with exuberant wagging.

"You wouldn't believe the detail work they put into the carousel horses they build and restore. They've got a wall full of plaques and other awards for their work around the world. We picked out the design we want. It's a fifty-four foot diameter beauty. The colors of the horses' and tigers' sleighs will take everyone's breath away."

"Sounds delightful," I droned, "but may I ask the price of this beauty?"

"Of course, we got a deal. I haggled and saved $29,000."

"So the out of pocket is now what, exactly?"

"$1,150,000 not including installation."

"And here I was afraid of overspending. Silly me."

"Dru McKenna, you know damn well we gotta make this a focal point of the park or not bother with any of it. The carousel must be our *piéce de resistance*. We'll have one of the finest examples on the east coast. These guys are the only manufacturer with in-house capability to design, build, ship, install... all in one-stop shopping. We saved a bundle by coming here, believe me."

"I do, I was just yanking your chain."

"Seems like that sums up my life with you, McKenna."

"As if mine is so much different, Mrs. McKenna."

"Ask and it is given, right?" I said.

"You betcha."

"We spent the day detailing the animals, chariots, all the aspects of the ride. We listed as much as there is, including motors, platforms, lights, music, brass fixtures, the works."

I interrupted, "Including the brass ring dispenser?"

"Including that, and I placed the order. I'll send you pictures. They also told us of a friend, in Findlay, Ohio, who does the bumper cars. We're going there tomorrow."

"Sounds like you girls have had a full day," I complimented.

"Yowza, now if we can get you guys to work out your little baseball thing, we'll be up and rolling."

"That's my girl, always got my back. Or are you *on* it?"

"Both," she said. "So, what do you think Raymond's got hold of?"

"I just hope it doesn't involve some kind of criminal activity, what with Las Vegas' rep and all that."

"How's our boy doing?"

"He misses you almost as much as I do."

"And how much would that be?

"You know all the billions and billions of stars in all the galaxies in the heavens? Add all the grains of sand in the world and you have a tenth of the amount he misses you."

"And you more so, Dr. Sagan," Hannah laughed.

"Almost, sweetie, almost. Say goodnight, Gracie."

"Goodnight, Gracie," and she hung up.

I sat on the dock and reflected on Raymond's cryptic admonition. I wonder if the politicians are involved in drugs, smuggling, money laundering, or any of the like. A chill ran over me at the thought. *Is this the time I fall flat on my face? I've never failed before.*

***

Raymond showed up at lunchtime and was welcomed by Riley's traditional faux arm chomping, reserved for closest friends. After paying tribute to the amiable animal, who was bounding around, wagging his Louisville Slugger-like tail, and begging for affection, Raymond shook hands with Ted and me. "What's for lunch?"

"You're in for a treat now, Ted. You're not gonna believe this show," I gleefully said.

"Ignore him, Ted. I'm just a growing boy," said Raymond with a thunderous laugh.

Ted was indeed impressed with the mountain of picked clean rib bones piled up in front of Raymond's empty rib plate at the end of the meal.

"You're slowing down, Raymond," I said. "I doubt we could even build a four-bedroom house from the meager pile of bones in front of you."

"Well, you said this was only lunch. Didn't wanna seem like a hog."

Ted chuckled and wiped his mouth with a linen napkin. "You know I'm getting used to this stuff, Dru. Everybody around you seems to be a character."

"Including you?" I asked.

"Oh yeah, especially me."

Ted had already picked up an essential aspect of my personal self—namely the ability to attract the most interesting and skillful characters. It was my relationship with these people which enabled me to achieve such success. I couldn't have done it without them and was grateful.

"Okay, Raymond, what gives? Is the mob's goon squad out to whack me or what?"

"I see your vivid imagination's running amok again. I told you it's nothing nefarious, just political nest feathering."

"Somebody's using this to secure an election?" I asked.

"That's the gist, but it's far from simple. We're talking a U.S. Senate aspirant here. For this dude it's potentially a path to the presidency. He seems to be one of those guys who won't let anything or anybody get in his way, particularly over something as politically insignificant as baseball. All he had to do was call a friend who knew a friend that knew a guy inside MLB to kill your purchase of the team, Dru."

"How'd you find out so quickly?" I asked.

"The guy his friend called, called a friend of another friend who just so happens to be my friend. He told me what he did on John Brewster's behalf. Not too many people could resist making a friend of a potential Senator... let alone a President, you know."

"Let me get this straight," I said, "This Brewster mook wants to be a Senator, so he wants the glory of first, keeping the Triple-A team in town. Then he'll apply to MLB to buy an existing major league team and move it to Vegas. I assume he'll build a dome too, is that it?"

"In a well put nut shell, yes."

Ted pushed back from the table. "Holy shit, when I started with this idea I had no clue where it would lead."

"Welcome to Dru's world, Ted. I've known him for twenty-some years and never in all that time have I known him to get involved with anything that turned out to be simple. Nothing's even remotely simple. But take solace, my new friend. In all that time I've never seen him fall flat on his face either. You're in for a helluva ride. You might as well buckle up and enjoy it because he won't quit now. With or without you, for him, it's now personal."

Ted just shook his head, "Kimberley told Libby we wouldn't believe what we were about to see. I guess she hit the ten ring." While Ted enjoyed the praise being given to me by my friend, hearing me praised, it turns out I really don't feel comfortable with this kind of accolade.

***

I spent the rest of the day contacting friends who feel allegiance to me. It's totally unnecessary, but I can't convince them of it. Another odd but still valid example of "ask and it is given." First, I asked for background information on John Brewster—his family, education, job history, finances, the works. Then I asked other people to check on character issues just to see if anything popped.

I didn't really expect anything but got a stunning surprise. Turned out John Brewster's father was in the Marine Corps with my father in the Middle East. The name Paul Brewster rang a bell with me, so I pulled up from my computer my father's file, which held the commendation the McKenna family received detailing the events leading to Thomas C. McKenna III's being awarded the Silver Star for heroism.

Trey, as he was known, was in the process of dragging Paul Brewster and two others away from sniper fire when he was wounded the first time. He went back to rescue three other trapped Marines before taking out the sniper—thus completing the rescue of six men—before being killed himself.

Riveting twist, I thought. I wonder if John Brewster's dad is still alive.

Hannah convinced me it was time to call Paul Brewster.

"What can I possibly say and not look like a groveling weasel? I'm not a politician. I can't trade on my father's heroism by asking him to help me foil his son's quest for the U.S. Senate," I said to Hannah. We sat in the dwindling light of dusk on the patio discussing this.

"No, I'm afraid you can't do that. Let's think of other options. How about Raymond? That's his part of the world, maybe he knows somebody for this, too."

"That's not a bad idea, glad I thought of it," I said with an innocent expression.

"Yeah, Mr. Quick to blame, Mr. Slow to give credit... but always Mr. Ready to take it. My, you are clever."

Hannah and Libby planned to leave in the morning to start sourcing suppliers for the midway attractions.

I spent the rest of the evening out on the dock communing with the stars. I always marveled at the clarity of the heavens away from the intrusion of urban electric brilliance. Clarity of purpose I had. Clarity of vision I had. Clarity of game plan was still a bit murky. I hoped our plan would succeed, but the unforeseen variables could lay waste to the whole magilla. Boy, I sure didn't want to be the author of a revolting development... but I could be!

***

After taking off on the flight to Ohio the next morning, Libby asked to see the preliminary itinerary again.

"I agree our first stop should be Cassidy's Games. From their brochure it looks just like Eldrige Park in the early fifties," said Libby. "I'm concerned that if we're not careful we could make this *too* old fashioned, ya' know?"

"I don't see a problem as long as we mix old and new... and appeal to geezers, boomers, Xers, millennials, and untitled little kids," teased Hannah. "We can't ignore technology, and by adding those together we can offer something for everyone. I'm hopeful we'll have some crossover."

"You sound confident, Hannah."

"Experience and my gut, Libby, I hope the Cassidy people will have some guiding ideas for us, too."

"Just so they include Whack-A-Mole, right?"

"Absolutely."

CHAPTER 17

Near Sedona, Arizona, Raymond was enjoying a late lunch while he sat poolside at his hacienda. First time visitors expecting a Spanish motif were pleasantly surprised by the modern stone, brass, glass and wooden structure. Its modern post and beam construction would not have been out of place in New England or the Pacific Northwest. But set in Arizona it stood out, much like Frank Lloyd Wright's Taliesin West did down in Scottsdale. Oddly, however, it blended quite well with the environs.

Raymond loved the east and was very comfortable emulating the culture of that part of America. Not one who strove to immerse himself in local conventions, he always chose his own path, usually unconventional, always unique.

Answering the phone, Raymond, assisted by caller ID, said "Hello, Dru, what can I do for you?"

I filled him in on the situation and begged for ideas to help get the politicians off my back. "A guy named Paul Brewster was in Syria, Lebanon, all over the Mid-East with my father and other places. Dad saved Brewster's life. As you know his son has thrown a monkey wrench into our baseball project and..."

At this point Raymond interrupted, "You'd like me to speak to Paul on your behalf, right?"

"On the button, my friend. I can't openly trade on my father's heroism. I'm just not comfortable doing it."

"But if I somehow remind Paul he owes you one that would be okay?"

"Boy, hearing it out loud sounds as smarmy as it feels, doesn't it?" said Dru.

"Let's examine this thing," said a very lawyeresque Raymond.

"Yes sir, counselor," said Dru.

"Wise ass. I may not be an attorney, but I can offer some insight and wisdom from time to time."

"All right, watcha got?" I asked

"The approach you conjured up should be the last resort, not the opening gambit," offered Raymond. "What I propose is a substitute target for John Brewster to focus on."

"Such as?"

"The most pressing issue in Nevada—namely water—is exactly what we need Brewster to zero in on. Without the Colorado River supplying Lake Mead, Vegas dries up, literally. So what we do is encourage him to come up with a plan for California to develop more desalination plants to ease the demand on the Colorado and thereby build Lake Mead's supply back to original levels. It's eventually going to come, so let's put young Brewster in the vanguard of the ultimate solution now before disaster befalls the western states."

"I see you've put some thought in this. Any chance you have a financial interest in desal plants?"

"As God intended, my friend, I'll get in touch with John Brewster and remind him of the seriousness of water, and ask why they're focusing on frivolous baseball issues to make a centerpiece of their campaign. In this case we'd be on the side of the angels, don't you agree?"

"I have one question. What could a Senate candidate from Nevada do to influence California to help?"

"That, my brother, is the beauty of this. Right now John Brewster's name recognition quotient isn't very high. Becoming involved as the spearhead to solve the western water issue would change his image. Or more precisely, give him nationwide notoriety, not just in California and Nevada. From there the press will do your job for you. He'll forget about baseball until the World Series."

"You amaze me with how your mind seems to work. This is a terrific idea. I may join you in this desal thing."

"One thing at a time, boyo," said a smug Raymond.

I thought about Raymond's idea and the more I did, the more I agreed with it. I was glad I didn't have to use my father's deeds to pave the way. Not for the first time in my life was I grateful to have a man like Raymond with me.

The next day I brought Ted up to speed at his Mark Twain replica study.

"I can't help but admire what you've built here. It's almost like Twain's presence is looking over us," I said.

"I've had the same thoughts from time to time. I hope it's not too pretentious."

"Don't worry, I think it's a fine tribute to one of the world's most important authors—one with a local presence to boot."

"Thank you for that, Dru. I appreciate the sentiment and besides it is a very functional design for my office, and I love the view."

"It is relaxing. But we don't have time for that relaxing stuff. Let me tell you about Raymond's idea. I believe it's a good one."

I gave Ted the whole plan. An agreement was quickly followed by the question as to what would come next.

"We'll let Raymond do his thing, and believe me, he's the most persuasive individual I've ever encountered. When he's finished I'm betting MLB will have a turn around, and I may have my next project lined up, we'll see."

"As for me, Dru, I agree with the girls' park plans and Raymond's desalination diversion. I'm ready to approach Hank again."

"Just be careful. He impresses me as a master button pusher. Don't get caught off guard and let anything about baseball slip," I cautioned.

"Don't worry about me. The eye is on the prize. And I'm not bad at button manipulation myself," Ted said, twirling an imaginary handlebar moustache.

The first clarion call came from Raymond. Not only did John Brewster jump on the idea, but he volunteered to put the baseball initiative to rest if his father could invest heavily in Raymond's multi-plant desal project. John, for the record, would be a silent partner.

"As we figured he would, John Brewster believed if he came up with a solution to the water issues confronting the western states he'd be a shoe-in for the Senate seat and possibly more. He's probably correct," said Raymond.

I couldn't help but laugh as Raymond related how Brewster had immediately embraced the idea as his own.

"Remind me never to take you to a hypnosis stage show. You'd have the whole crowd opening their wallets to you."

My next move was to contact MLB and the Mets to rekindle their fire. Thanks to Raymond, life was lookin' good once more.

Why did I so fear the future?

* * *

I scheduled a New York meeting for the next week and made arrangements to take a $250M letter of credit with me. My grandfather was fond of saying, "Money talks and bullshit walks." I knew which one I needed to have.

Riley and I drove down to our house in the city. The pooch's reunion with Ivor brought tears of joy to Ivor's face, along with sloppy wet dog kisses. The fierce wagging of Riley's tail signaled his mutual feelings about the reunion.

Ivor administered the requisite noogies to the beautiful boy dog, gave him a treat and escorted us into the house.

"News of the sale of the Mets' Vegas farm team is all over the news, Dru. Wait 'til you hear who's buying!"

CHAPTER 18

Ted was startled by the strains of *Eye of the Tiger,* his ring tone. He was more startled by who it was. He was most startled by what Hank Lewis wanted.

"When can we meet to go over your ideas? I've been thinking it over and maybe instead of burying the hatchet in each other we can attack something together. Whadda ya say?"

"Hank, I never set out to bury a hatchet in you, you just took it that way, and that's the truth," said Ted.

"Yeah okay, so you said before. When do you wanna meet?"

"You pick it, and I'll be there."

"How about 2:00 p.m. today, too soon?"

"Nope, I'll be there. Your office, I assume?"

"Sounds good, see ya then."

"Is he coming?" asked Rance Butler.

"He is," answered Hank.

"Does he suspect what he's in for?"

"How the hell do I know? Do I look like Kreskin? All I know is I want to hear his plan, and figure out how to hijack it while he's thinking we're joining forces," said Hank with a malevolent sneer Simon Legree might envy.

* * *

When Ted showed up at precisely 2:45 p.m. he fully expected to be kept waiting. To his surprise he was escorted immediately into Hank's office.

"Good of you to come. We get you anything?" No mention of being forty-five minutes tardy.

"No thanks, I'm good," said Ted.

113

"Let me say first, I am aware we've been at loggerheads for many years, and I must say I'm tired of getting my ass handed to me. I figure if I can't lick 'em, join 'em."

"Hank, I'm glad to go into this with you but only if you agree to be up front about where we are at any point. If you have an idea, share it. I'll do the same, okay?"

"You bet, Ted. Right now you want some land in Big Flats. I'm looking at the same property. We've been bidding against each other on every other deal we've competed for, and that has surely driven up the prices. I don't know what you want the land for. As for myself, I want to develop the first phase of a Columbia, Maryland, type community. I don't need a partner to accomplish it. You came to me wondering if I'd be interested in joining you in your venture, but I haven't got a clue what it is you're looking to do. Why don't you fill me in?"

"Hank, I've never intentionally gone after any project with the idea we were in competition. I know it worked out that way sometimes but never was a stated goal of mine to defeat you. I develop ideas on my own, and act on them. Some see the light of day, others don't survive the sunrise. This is a case in point. You want to develop a small town, or at least a large neighborhood and I want to develop an Eldridge Park 2.0. I want rides, games, play areas, picnic areas just like the old park in its heyday."

"You're right. That is completely different from my intentions. At this point we have to choose which path to follow, don't we? If we don't agree on a partnership to control the land price we'll be going head to head once again. I propose we both think what it is we want to do in Big Flats and meet again soon to discuss our intentions. Sound good?"

"Yeah, I'm good with that. That wasn't so hard was it? We should have done it several projects ago. Coulda saved a few bucks, maybe more than a few," said Ted.

"You're right, I let my desire to win control my brain. Let's take a week and think."

"Sounds good. I'll call next week, we'll do lunch," said Ted.

* * *

At home Ted said, "Libby, I'm going out on the patio to hose off the slime I'm covered with now."

"What are you talking about? I don't see any slime."

"I just met Hank, and he agreed to share thoughts with me and actually sounded sincere. Then it hit me. He wanted to find out what my plans for the land were. He intends to steal it."

"The snake," she said.

"You said it. We got any Arnold Palmer tea?"

"No, but I can whip some up easily enough. I'll squeeze the lemons and meet you by the pool."

"Good idea. If it's warm enough for a dip, wanna join me?"

"Sounds like more than a dip you're thinking about."

"Can't blame a guy for trying, you've been gone ten days."

"Yes, I have and I don't blame you. I'll be out with the tea."

After they enjoyed a swim in their heated pool and each other, they toweled off coming out of their cabana. Sitting poolside they discussed their latest adventures. Ted was amazed at the progress the ladies made, and the speed in which they did it. As for Ted's less than excellent adventure with Hank, his conclusion was agreed with.

"Have you told Dru yet?"

"No, he's in NYC trying to sort out this Triple-A club business from MLB's end. We're going to talk tonight."

CHAPTER 19

While on my trip to the park with Riley, I immersed myself trying to figure out the latest curve ball I'd been thrown. MLB was buying the Las Vegas 51s for them. Raymond's plan had worked perfectly for the son, but MLB's move poleaxed me. I was thrown for a loop. I felt awful, like the flu. Everything ached. I almost hoped it was the flu.

The Good, the Bad and the Ugly ringtone got my attention.

"Raymond, I assume you heard the good news?" I answered.

"Yeah, all I can say is you white men are sneaky bastards."

"May I remind you of Custer's demise?"

"We were just trying to redress the balance for the good guys," said Raymond.

"What can we do to overcome this?"

"I need to think on it for a while. Figuring stuff out is supposed to be your forte. I solved the first part by getting the son off it," said Raymond.

"What I'm hearing is you didn't see this twist coming either, huh?" I said.

"At least I'm in the trenches with somebody I can trust, so I've got that going for me. I just hope the damn thing doesn't collapse on us. Buried alive is not what I envisioned for a solution to our problem," I said.

"Yeah, that's never good," said Raymond.

"I'm going to speak with Ted tonight and tell him what's happened. I'm sure he'll be less than thrilled. I'll call you after that."

Ted and Libby enjoyed a light lunch, made plans for dinner and discussed the overall scheme of things.

"Hank really is a despicable human being. If you're correct and he intends to steal your plan, and go forward, I could almost come to loathe him," said Libby.

"No need, he can't help it. It's the scorpion and frog thing, it's his nature."

"When he finds out you have been onto him the whole time, and were acting as a stalking horse to protect the real project, he's going to go Vesuvius on you."

"I think even Hank will feel like a winner because he put one over on me, finally. I'll never reveal the actual plan. I'll just make him think I got lucky with plan B."

"*If* we get lucky," said Libby.

"Yeah, and I'm afraid it's a big *if*."

"What are you thinking of doing?" said Libby.

"I'm going to strongly suggest Hank take it and continue with his planned community idea. I'll float some of the numbers for the park equipment and hope to scare him off by the enormity of the costs. His pockets are nowhere near as deep as McKenna's."

"Did you know about Dru's inheritance from Jon Fallon?"

"How the hell would I know about it? It's not something you spew forth even to friends," said Ted.

"Hannah hadn't mentioned it either. Before Dru told us I had no idea."

"I looked it up. It's in the financial reports on the McKenna Associates website. Fallon was Dru's godfather, and he had several billion. Speculation is that Dru's share was north of at least one of those billions."

Libby cleared the lunch dishes, and Ted rinsed them and loaded the dishwasher.

"My god, that's enormous. No wonder he doesn't worry about costs," she said.

Ted rolled his eyes and smiled, "Don't you believe it. He knows where every penny goes... and controls all of it."

"Hank's gonna wonder how you can swing the financials, you know?" she said.

"I think I'll come up with a sugar daddy my own self. In fact I may be lookin' at her."

"Maybe Dru has an idea."

"Maybe he does."

* * *

For some apparent reason I drove down to NYC to confront MLB in person the next day. Why I chose to drive had to be a brain cramp because as scenic beauty goes it can't be beat, but too often it's monotonous. I made an executive decision to fly from now on.

At the moment, I wasn't focused on anything but baseball. Of course I cared about the skirmish with Hank but the main goal was to distract Hank and get a baseball team under our control.

Finally some leg room, I offhandedly thought. I was going downtown in one of the new van cabs for a meeting with MLB in NYC. It gave me satisfaction to see the van was hydrogen powered.

Arriving at the MLB offices, after greetings were exchanged, I brusquely asked, "Guys, what's going on? I thought the funding was approved for my group to take ownership of the Las Vegas team."

"Relax, Dru," said Joel Leonard. "This was a preemptive strike to stop gambling interests in Vegas from enjoining any sale of the team. By taking control first, MLB prevents that."

"What happens if MLB decides to relinquish control to a new ownership group? Won't they enjoin that effort?"

"Dru, you're very astute. We do face that possibility. As of yet we haven't got a solution."

"I may have an idea," I said. "The Mets, being on the east coast, would naturally prefer to have their team closer to Citi Field, right?"

"I would think so, yes."

"How does 200 miles away sound?"

"That's why we're in Binghamton, did you not know?"

Chagrined at my lapse, I meekly said, "I forgot."

Chapter 20

I called Hannah and filled her in on the meeting.

"Did they bite, or are you still casting bait?"

"My, aren't you the poster girl for L.L. Bean? But you're right, MLB is doing exactly what I expected. I know they must have an overall strategy but I don't think it's fully in place. Call Ted and Libby and set up a meeting at the cottage for ten tomorrow morning. I'll drive home tonight. Love you, see you guys soon."

I dug my car out of our garage and headed back to Keuka after dinner. It was a moonless night and once out of the bright city lights I was bathed in blackness. Devoid of breathtaking vistas, the ride home following the white ribbon could hypnotize a driver. I love driving especially when I've got some heavy duty thinking to do, but when I drove on I found the thinking goes south as well as alertness... which scares the hell outta me.

The next morning, at Keuka Lake, we got right down to business.

"Let me get this straight," said Ted. "Initially they bought the whole idea but now something has changed, huh?"

"Ted, I think that's it, but we can't be deterred." I told them about my *faux pas* with the 200-mile thing and Binghamton but rallied and said, "We gotta keep moving forward or we'll be dismissed from any consideration. There are a lot of details to work on but mainly we need to finish off the land deal, park building designs and park plans and all the rest. We need to show we're a viable choice, not sometime in the unforeseen future, but now."

"We're already on that path, Dru," said Libby. "We've got event schedules and completion dates for everything," referring to the To Do chart on the Murder Board.

"Folks, we gotta get up to warp speed now. Libby, you and Hannah finish the work on the park, Ted, you the baseball stadium. I'll finish the land acquisition. We need to get this done sooner than soon, so let's get moving."

* * *

The next three days were a flurry of activity from phone calls, outside meetings, inside meetings, all to finalize our plans. At the end of the week we met at Morretti's to unwind and catch our collective breath. As we were finishing our meal, in walked Hank Lewis, Rance Butler and Steve Greatsinger. Hank spotted Ted and Libby but had no clue as to the identity of me and Hannah. Steve Greatsinger knew me somehow and nodded hello.

"You know that guy, Steve?" asked Hank.

"Sure that's the guy whose picture was in the Times as inheriting Jon Fallon's money, or a portion of it. If he's involved in this deal with Ted, I'll tell you right now his pockets are much deeper than yours."

"So who the hell is he?"

"He's Dru McKenna, of McKenna Automotive."

"Holy shit! Did you know about this, Rance?"

"Why would I? I didn't know you were doing anything outside of Big Flats. What's up?"

"Up? I'll tell you what's up! We're up to our asses in fire and we're about to get burned. That swinging dick Reynolds is playing me... us... for suckers with subterfuge. C'mon, let's get out of here. I know what's going on now."

In the parking lot Hank stomped over to Butler's car, and in a rage, kicked the passenger door hard enough to leave a sizeable dent, chipping the paint in the process. Then he got in and slammed the door as hard as he could. The sound of door parts rattling around inside got Butler's attention.

"Hey Hank, whadda ya doing kicking my car?"

"Fuck your car, dick head, we need CPR—Complete Program Reversal. Reynolds doesn't want the Big Flats property, he wants the college land. Isn't that right, Steve?"

"Hank, Ted hasn't talked to me in months. I haven't seen him in longer than that." Steve left in bewilderment.

"Well it's clear to me. Reynolds cooked up this deal with Big Flats to trick me into looking the other way while he sent this McKenna schmuck to work with Bob Crandall at the college. I'll bet baseball is still the goal. I'll bet he's the one who told you to stick the Pioneer name, remember, Rance? I bet he's trying to start another team up, but how? We need more info."

"And where're we gonna get that?" asked Butler.

"Now you're going to see how it's done in my world, oh clueless friend."

When Hank arrived at his office, donning his charming persona, or what passed for one, he placed a call to a "friend"— Phil Malozzi—who was a sports reporter in New York.

"Phil, Hank Lewis here. Got a question for you."

"That's the same old Hank. Whadda ya think? I've been sitting here just waiting for your call, for what now, five years?"

"Yeah, good one, Phil. Look I need to know if there's been anybody sniffing around looking to put a baseball team in the Elmira area."

"Why?"

"Phil, let's say someone owns some land. Land somebody else wants to buy and put a team on it. Let's say the price of that land may go up if this baseball thing is real," said Hank.

"Somebody would stand to make a bit more than the current asking price. Is that the gist?"

"Yep."

"Let's suppose somebody does find out about this, would there be a finder's fee involved for the information?"

"There could be."

"I'll get back to you," said Phil.

Hank hung up, looking like the proverbial cat with canary feathers stuck in his teeth and said, "And that's how we do it in this neck of the woods."

***

"So do you think he saw us?" asked Hannah.

"Judging by his about-face retreat, I'd say yes," I said.

"Who was that with him?" asked Hannah.

Ted said, "The sandy haired guy was Rance Butler of Pioneer name fame. The other one was Steve Greatsinger of Big Flats."

"That's right. He's the guy we've been in contact about the land there. I'm surprised he was with Lewis. You told me he doesn't like him much," I said.

"Hardly anybody does, not even Butler, if the truth be known," said Ted.

"Well folks, the cat's out of the bag now," I said.

As we left the Reynolds place after dropping them off, Hannah saw concern etched on my face.

"Is it bad, Dru?"

"Bad enough. The trouble with dealing in a small pond is it's tough to hide a deal of this magnitude without word leaking. Everybody knows everybody else and their business. Now things will get a bit hairy, I'm afraid."

Hannah didn't say anything the rest of the way to the cottage, nor did I. The possible ramifications of this chance sighting could spell serious trouble for the whole project... maybe kill it.

"I'm going to stay up a while and think," I said.

I poured two fingers of the Creature, in this case Middleton Reserve, and went out on the dock with Riley to review the day's events. For one of the few times in my career as Mr. Fixit, problem solver extraordinaire, I was flummoxed. What seemed to be a very clever ploy had blown up in my face. In the back of my mind I knew the possibility existed, but got so wrapped up in the plan, its execution and the time line I pushed it into one of those mental arroyos of my mind.

"Riley, I'm afraid your daddy has stepped in it now. Why the hell do I take on things that could ruin other people's lives if my ideas don't work?"

I feared Ted and Libby could lose everything if this deal failed. I was deeply bothered by my role, if that happened. Riley put his head in my lap and looked up as if to say, "Buck up, private, you'll figure it out." I seemed to know my dog's thoughts or, more likely, I was projecting mine onto him.

"I better, Rile. It's just, people are counting on me, maybe counting too much. I don't want to let them down, especially since they're Hannah's friends. Most of all, I don't want to let Hannah down." *God what a mess*, I thought.

My dog and I sat looking out over the serenity of the lake and the twinkling bejeweled sky above.

* * *

At eight a.m. Hank had still not gone to bed. All night he sat up devising plans to slay Ted Reynolds' dragon. He ran various scenarios from beginning to end until he could barely think. Then out of nowhere came the realization it wasn't Reynolds he should focus on but McKenna, who was the real target.

He spent the rest of the night researching Dru McKenna. The list of projects he successfully was involved in was beyond impressive, the latest being saving National Motors in Baltimore. Hank mused, *I'm driving National's Eagle model myself.*

Despite his admiration for McKenna's resume, Hank was savoring the idea of taking him apart, and in the process taking

Ted Reynolds with him. In another place and time, the term would've been "vendetta."

At the core of it Hank was blind to the jealously any competent shrink would spot. Hank thought of it as justification for addressing perceived wrongs maliciously done to him. *A pound of flesh won't cut it*, he thought. *I want the whole carcass strung up on the Joshua tree.* Nothing less could lead Hank to the promised land of success and acclaim.

Not familiar with the incoming caller's ID Hank initially ignored it, but inexplicably had a change of heart. "Who the hell is this?" answered Hank with his usual charm.

"This is Sister Marie Raymond of the Notre Dame orphanage. Am I speaking to Mr. Lewis?"

"Yes, Sister, you are. And please forgive my rudeness," he said while standing up beginning to pace. "I've been harassed lately with unwanted calls and I'm a little testy, I'm afraid. What can I do for you?"

"Mr. Lewis, I was reluctant to make this call since you've been so kind to us in the past, but I've nowhere else to turn."

"Quite all right, Sister. What is it you need?"

"I'm afraid we're in a lot of trouble. The facility here needs some major repairs to the roof, plumbing, miscellaneous equipment and kitchen appliances. We failed a recent health inspection and our accreditation with the state is to be revoked in thirty days."

"Is that all?" Hank knew there was more, much more probably.

"Well our buses and cars are in sad shape too, but that really is the list."

"Okay, here's what we're gonna do, so listen up." Hank was pacing in his office now. He had the call on speaker so he was free to roam about, as was his habit while thinking. With a smug smile he rubbed his hands together as he spoke.

"I'm gonna give you a list of things I'll need from you, and another separate list of things I'm going to do for you, okay?"

"Okay," she said.

"First, e-mail me the complete list of all the things you need and who told you they were needed. Second, I need a deadline for all this work to be completed by. Third, I need the contacts at the various agencies involved. Fourth, any additional things you can think by the end of today, got it?"

"Got it," Sister Raymond seemed to know that Mr. Lewis had not been educated in the parochial school system as he was not the least intimidated by the clergy as many are. He may not even be a Catholic, *odd* she thought was his willingness to help.

"Now, this is what I'm gonna do, Sister. I'll have my contractor out to inspect your place tomorrow. On his recommendation I'll attend to the roof, plumbing, and kitchen up grades. This means cabinets, floor, appliances, wiring, granite counter tops the works."

"Oh, Mr. Lewis, I don't know what to say," said Sister Raymond.

"Call me Hank. Mr. Lewis was my old man, and he wouldn't a done any of this. This isn't a loan, and it's not to be ever mentioned to anybody where it came from. Agreed?"

"Is that a deal breaker?"

"Definitely."

"But why, I feel it's the least we could do. This is going to cost a fortune."

"Don't worry, I have a fortune. A few of 'em, in fact. As for athletic equipment, beds, linens, and infirmary items, anything else... just ask, got it?"

"Mr. ...Hank, I can't thank you enough."

Hank smiled. He had a soft spot for kids in need. He'd been one. His father was a drunkard; his mother died giving birth to him. An aunt raised him, and she and her second husband treated him like a slave. He left at age sixteen and began figuring out how to make a fortune, any way he could.

He could now afford to reach back and help others, but only on the QT. He didn't want anyone to know about his largesse. People had used and abused him his whole life and he wanted no acclaim from any people... ever.

CHAPTER 21

I finally crawled into bed at four a.m. At eight a.m. I was startled awake by *The Good, the Bad and the Ugly*.

"Rise and shine, sleepy head," said Hannah.

"Who is this?"

"You know damn well who. See you on the dock anon," said Hannah as she abruptly disconnected.

Now up, showered, powdered, and dressed, I descended to the dock where I found my lovely wife, and faithful, brave and steadfast dog. By the looks of it, a breakfast spread fit for a king, a queen and jester, was spread out on the table.

"This looks good," said me, the hungry man.

"I should make you wear it," said Hannah feigning petulance.

"Just like a woman. Wake a man from a sexy dream and expect him not to be confused."

"Was I at least the star of your dream?"

"One of," I said to a pair of eyebrows heading for the hairline.

"And who may I ask is the other?"

"That would be me, dear."

"Droll. Did you figure out what to do about the baseball project?"

"In a manner of speaking."

"Call Raymond, right?"

"You know me so well. Or *think* you do."

"I'm not guessing here, Bub. I've watched you do it many a time."

After breakfast I did as Hannah thought and called my longtime friend. I didn't know if the call would help but as my mother used to say about the therapeutic benefits from chicken soup, it couldn't hurt.

"I've been wondering when I'd hear from you."

"Raymond, I'm stuck for ideas. I need some of your Injun wisdom."

"Who, if not your blood brother would you come to for Injun savvy? What's bothering you?"

"I can't figure a way out of this baseball mess. MLB threw me a curve on this one."

"No pun intended, right?"

"Raymond, I've told you before, I mean all my puns."

"Yeah, here's what I know. They don't like being involved in Vegas with the gambling and all. They keep a major league franchise from moving there though by already having the minor league team in place. They control its operation in conjunction with the Mets."

"That much I know," I said.

"What you *don't* know is there's talk of expanding each league by one team."

"Whoa, when, where, who?"

"You forgot why," said Raymond.

"I know why. Greed, of course."

"I don't know the time frame, but if I were you I'd be heading to New York pronto."

"Injun savvy, huh?"

"You got it, Kemo Sabe."

"Raymond, I'm always amazed at what and who you know. Thanks."

"You're welcome, it's what brothers do."

On my late afternoon walk with Riley, I ruminated over what Raymond had to say. This area was too small for a major league team, or even a AAA team. Going after an expansion team was an untenable strategy for Elmira and environs.

What if we went back to the original idea of bringing a lower class minor league team to the region, maybe AA? I thought.

"Good idea, Riley T. That just might work. And a helluva lot cheaper too."

When Riley heard his name he came running over to me and seemed to ask if it was chow time. It was. You could set your watch by him. His body language was unmistakable, as if he was never fed and ravenous. With all the leaping, barking and searching for a plush animal friend to accompany him to dinner he hardly took notice of the full bowl of chow in his raised eating station until the moment it was there. His race to the station was akin to the start of a hundred-meter dash.

The next morning, Riley and I were pounding down Route 17 bound for New York City. The four and a half hour drive gave me ample occasion for reflection. I had resolved to fly down from now on but the leasing company, Fallon Aviation, informed me routine scheduled maintenance was due. Ergo, back on the road.

Using the windshield time to mull, I devised a strategy to convince MLB to allow McKenna Automotive to own a AA franchise. Plans for the new stadium were in the works. My financials had been vetted so I had a strong base from which to pitch our idea. Much, however, was contingent on the location of the expansion franchises.

Another idea shot across my mind so rapidly I couldn't grasp it. That was beginning to be annoying. *Either give me the damned idea or not, but quit screwin' around.* Maybe later, I sighed, Riley picked up his head. Thanks to the miracle of Blue Tooth I pressed the button and answered Hannah's call and filled her in on my meeting with MLB. I planned to meet, then head home since she was leaving the next afternoon.

We decided I'd call Ted in the morning and find out where he stood with Hank and the land acquisition ploy in Big Flats, if it was still alive. Hannah reported on the schedule Libby and she planned for wrapping up the amusement park plans. I walked Riley, and then hit the hay.

CHAPTER 22

Breakfast at the Mark Twain replica study was once again a distinct pleasure for Hannah and me. Riley and I had returned in the early morning from the City after leaving in time to hear the crack of dawn along the way. The pastoral 270-degree view from the study, the cozy confines and sumptuous meal made the trip well worth it.

"What's up with MLB, Dru?" asked Ted.

"As it stands now, Vegas is out."

A veil of doom descended upon the room. All four of us were silent as we explored unknown labyrinths, each in our own way. Ted was despondent, Libby was angry, Hannah wracked her brain for a solution.

Me, I was comfortable with it. I never really thought we could get a team classified higher than AA. I still had great concern to even get that approval. To pull this project together we had to develop a failsafe plan to entice MLB to play ball with us—or more to the point, let us play ball with them.

"This is final?" asked Libby.

"Right now I don't see them changing their minds, but we may have an alternative," I said.

"Without the baseball part the whole project goes up in smoke. I've done something I regret," said Ted.

All eyes snapped toward him.

"Ted, what are you talking about?" asked Hannah.

Ted found it difficult to make eye contact with any of us. He sorta hemmed and hawed, gathering voice for a confession.

"I'm afraid I made a grievous error. I really screwed up."

"C'mon man, out with it. What'd you do, for crissakes?" I impatiently asked.

"Easy hon," said Hannah, "let him get it out."

"What do ya think I'm waitin' for?"

"Dru's right, here goes. I was talking to Steve Greatsinger, and I implied I was going to drop out of the bidding on the Big Flats property. Then we see him with Hank. He must have told him. It's probably why they did the quick about-faced exit."

I looked at Ted and thought carefully before I spoke.

"Ted, we don't know that for sure. In fact I can't see Greatsinger going against the grain and aligning himself with Hank. Think about it. Why would he be the only one this side of Rance Butler to do so? What I'm more afraid of is Lewis connecting the dots that lead to Rance Butler. Remember I told him to stick the Pioneer name? I probably shouldn't have done that. This size town, a project of this magnitude, everyone knowing everybody and their business, it was a heated cauldron waitin' to bubble over."

"Is Hank that intuitive?" asked Hannah.

"Oh yeah, he's sharp as a hat pin and as conniving as an ex... partner," said Ted very carefully.

"Don't worry, Ted, I've never been married before," I said chuckling realizing Ted intended to say ex-wife.

"Good to know," said Hannah.

"You don't think it's a big deal?" asked Ted.

"Not yet, Ted. I think Hank may have figured out some of it, but putting the two parts together may take him a while."

"What can we do about MLB? You said you may have an idea?"

"Actually it was some info Raymond gave me. He got wind MLB may have expansion plans. If they put a team where I think they might, McKenna Automotive makes a lot of sense for them."

They all were paying close attention to what I was saying, processing what it could mean. For my part I had a smug "I know something you don't know" expression.

Hannah surely recognized it. "What do you have up your sleeve, an ace or something?"

"In a manner of speaking, yes. It's my opinion than MLB may be expanding by two teams, one East, one West. If I'm correct it would make sense for the western team to use Las Vegas as their Triple-A or expand the league there, and dissolve or move the 52s closer to the Mets."

"So you think we could still lure them here?" asked Ted.

"That's a good question and I don't think MLB will ever think of this area as the proper fit for such a high classification as Triple-A. I think we were overshooting our target. The population pool works against us, even on a regional basis."

Silence reigned as they continued to process it all. Libby got up and prepared snacks: guacamole, corn chips, Arnold Palmers and sufficient napkins unto the task.

"So what do you think they'll do?" asked Hannah.

"This is just my gut talkin' here, but I think I'll go back down to New York and put my two cents in for what McKenna Automotive can propose. I'll fly out in the morning."

"And what would McKenna Automotive be offering?" said Ted.

"I will share with them how cool it would be to bring baseball back to Brooklyn, that's all," I said.

All heads snapped around, even Riley's. Of course, he was just reacting to his people's excitement.

"Do you think they really are considering it? They couldn't be the Dodgers again, could they? Is it really possible?"

A cacophony of sound, these staccato bursting questions filled the air with hopeful glee. Riley was amped up to the point he couldn't contain his excitement and leapt on my lap, all 100 pounds of 'im.

After the laughter subsided, reason replaced euphoria. Silence pervaded the room. Deep in thought we mulled over what this news could mean. From the ashes of failure there arose a slight possibility the dream could live. Almost as if a stage manager cued the cast, each turned to me with unasked questions on their lips.

I cleared my throat and said, "Here's what I know for certain. MLB is considering expansion, period. Raymond, through his source, believes it's gonna happen and soon."

They all sat up on the edge of their chairs eager for me to continue. I did.

"Brooklyn has been mentioned but not officially. No decisions, preliminary or final have been made. As I said, what I'm thinking of doing is going to New York and throwing McKenna Automotive's hat in the ring to become an owner of a franchise but only here in this area. I know they find us appealing, but aren't sure what to do with us.

"Surely they'd want you to play any role you want," said Ted.

"Thanks for the vote of confidence, Ted, but right now their cart is before our horse. We have to turn the cart around, or put the horse in front. In this case, actually in every case the ass goes last, if ya git my drift."

"What in the world is that supposed to mean?" asked a bewildered Libby.

Laughing, I said, "Simply this, I'm going to put together a sales kit and pitch it. Yes, pun intended. I'm gonna pitch it to the MLB powers that be and sell 'em."

"Are you thinking of taking Raymond and maybe his source?" asked Hannah.

Dru put his head down for a second, then rose up and smiled at her. "You really can read my mind, can't you?"

"Not really. I've just learned how you think about some things. Don't worry, I have yet to uncover any of your darker secrets," she said.

Turning to Ted, Libby said, "Dark secrets? He has dark secrets?"

"We all do, dear, we all do," answered Ted with a grin.

"To answer Hannah, I'm going to ask Raymond to come along, and you too, Ted. I'll ask Raymond about his source, but I'd be surprised if he would want to include him—or even if the source wants to be included if we asked, but we'll see."

"Are you going to include the other plans for the facility in the presentation, Dru?" asked Hannah.

Libby said, "Oh, please do, Dru, I just know that when they see it they'll be reminded of good times from their pasts, too."

They all laughed at the conviction and passion in Libby's voice. She blushed when she realized how vehement her plea must have sounded.

"I really believe they will," she said with still the same intensity, but quieter.

They continued to chuckle as Ted said, "We do too, hon, we do too."

"In fact, I'm counting on just that reaction," I said.

"Ted, Libby," Hannah said, taking the stage, "Dru and I are very good at creating a sales presentation and making it, or in this instance Raymond making it. Libby, this is what you were really asking for when you called me. Now we get to work."

"I wondered when that was gonna happen. All this layin' around you guys have been doin' so far made me wonder what we were payin' ya for," said Libby in full snark mode.

"Pay? We're getting paid?" I asked.

Hannah gave me a lengthy look, shook her head and said, "Libby, thank you. I wanted Dru to see for himself your true nature. It's probably good for Ted to witness it, too," said Hannah.

"Believe me I've seen it too many times to count. It's how I know she's up to speed," said Ted.

Hannah smiled and said, "Amen."

The next few days were a blizzard of thoughts for the best order in which to make our presentation, what to include, highlight, minimize and finally organize and assemble. We discussed and made decisions on every conceivable point of sale. In the end we were satisfied the pitch was of major league caliber, including the glitz.

"There's glitz?" said Ted.

"Again, whadda ya think I'm payin' these guys for, if not glitz?" said Libby.

Hearing this byplay I said, "Is this what Cornell breeds? Girls like you, Kimberley and Libby?"

"Yeah, ya wanna make somethin' of it? Put up yer dukes," said Hannah with faux aggression.

"I'm so glad you called these guys, Lib," said Ted. "Thank you for all your work, we really appreciate it, believe me," Ted gushed.

"We're not done yet. The actual presentation is going to be every bit as important. We have to decide on how we present this to them," I said. "I think I have the perfect plan of attack."

"I'd like to say I don't believe I should be in on the presentation," said Libby. "I get nervous answering the phone, and I'm afraid I'd sink it. I'm a support type, I'm comfortable in that role. What's more, I like it that way."

Trying to be supportive Ted said, "Oh Libby, I don't believe that for a minute."

"Believe it, Ted," said Hannah. "Remember Mr. Gilvary's speech class freshman year, Libby? She had the distinction of being the only one in the class to start sobbing before she made her first speech. As I recall, she may be the only person to get a B without ever actually making a speech."

Libby, with head bowed shook it back and forth laughing at the memory of an example of the level of her greatest fear.

"It's true. I did that. Now you know why it would be better for me to stay away, PULLEEZE!"

Laughing, we realized how close we had become as friends. A group hug followed in which even I, who was uncomfortable with such displays, participated.

"Okay, here's the lineup for the presentation. Since I'm the known element to these guys, I'll introduce Raymond, Hannah and Ted, then I'll throw it over to Raymond."

"Whoa, hold the front door. Why Raymond?" asked Ted.

I laughed and made eye contact with Hannah. "You want to tell 'em, dear?"

"Guys, Raymond can sell cats to mice. I've seen him in action and it's truly a spectacle. I'll be surprised if he doesn't have them eating out of his hand at the end."

Libby looked at Ted and said, "Hon, that's high praise coming from Hannah."

"Okay, if you guys say so. I'll have to trust you. Raymond it is."

I continued, "He'll start with an outline of the overall plan including baseball, amusement park, riding trails, picnic areas and bandstand, complete with renderings and a history of baseball in the area. Next, Ted, I think you should do some background about the Dodger past affiliation with the area, and what it would mean to the town."

Ted began to strut as Harvey might if he were doing this.

"Easy there, big boy, don't get excited. Hannah has the results of our man-in-the-road survey she developed in NYC during our last visit. An overwhelming ninety percent of the sample was enthusiastic for the idea," I said.

"We shouldn't mention MLB expanding into Brooklyn unless it's already known they are," said Hannah.

"I completely agree," I said. "Raymond told me he heard they've been thinking of the possibility, but nothing definite has been decided."

CHAPTER 23

At this point we adjourned to the patio off the "Mark Twain" office to relax and have lunch. The freshly mown grass and lingering leaves were green as if in envy of the colorful fall flowers. The breeze tempered the sun's rays, making the early stages of afternoon comfortable.

"You know what we haven't done yet?" asked Hannah.

"Gee, I don't know, go jump in the lake?" I said.

"Close, but I was thinking about fishing," she said.

"I didn't know you fished, Hannah," said Libby.

"Sure you do, remember the trip to Taughannock Park our sophomore year? We thought we could show the city girls how it was done?" said Hannah.

Libby laughed and said, "Yeah, I got two sunnies and you got a blue gill, while the girl from Philly got a five-pound rainbow trout. I guess we showed her, huh?"

Ted and I glanced at each other, shook our heads and smiled. BLTs, potato salad and Arnold Palmers served and eaten, talk resumed of our upcoming presentation.

"When we go back in, let's wake up Raymond," I suggested. And we did.

"Raymond, guess who this is?"

"It's not my brother, Dru McKenna. He knows better than to call before eleven a.m.," said a sleepy sounding Raymond.

"It's really the only time I can be sure to find you, Big Guy."

"Bullshit! I can smell a white man's con a mile away. You think I won't be sharp this early, and can take advantage of the poor Injun again, huh?"

"Poor Injun, my ass. You and your tribe have money like you invented it and kept the rights to it. But you're right about one thing, we do need your help," I said.

"What again! I've been saving your ass since the day we met."

"Yeah well, we both know the truth about who saved whom, so stop showin' off in front of my friends, and roll the sleeves up your massive arms and pitch in, okay?"

"Pitch in? Good one."

"Thought you'd appreciate it."

Libby and Ted glanced at one another, rolling their eyes. They were getting too familiar with the interaction between these two close friends to be taken aback.

"C'mon guys, we've heard this act before. Dru, tell Raymond what you want him to do," said Hannah.

"She's got us, Dru. What can I do to help?"

"Just your presence and wits should do the trick. When can you get here?"

"Give me directions from the Hilton in Horseheads, and I'll be there anon. I flew in last night. Thought you might need me."

"Shoulda gone straight to New York if you were as omniscient as you think you are," I said.

When Raymond arrived we brought him up to date on the whole magilla including the rift with Hank Lewis.

That night the five of us flew to NYC in the McKenna corporate jet and made our way from Teterboro, New Jersey, across the GW Bridge down to Casa McKenna.

Upon arrival Libby and Ted were astounded by the upstairs of Hannah's, and now my, house.

"Hannah, this bedroom could be in a luxury hotel. It's breathtaking," said Raymond.

"That's because it's for my best clients when they stay over," she answered.

Raymond enveloped the doorway to Hannah's office as he maneuvered his six foot eight, 300-plus pound hulk through the door. They reviewed the aspects of the situation and began developing a strategy to compel MLB to include them on any future expansion plans.

"I don't think we should limit our interest to just Brooklyn, although it is an attractive concept. If they decide on another eastern team for the majors, we need to stress what we offer and why it's the best," he said.

"I concur," said Hannah.

We spent the rest of the day and night building our presentation brick by brick, only to tear it apart the next day. Raymond spent the night and we reconvened at nine a.m. providing enough time to feed Raymond. Pitch revision and reconstruction were repeated thrice more until we either got it right or got sick of trying. We weren't sure which.

Finished, we couldn't resist returning to 21 Club on the off chance they could match the cuisine at Hannah and Ivor's domain. Not the case, although it did come close. We resumed discussing the MLB plan and proposed schedule.

It was confirmed, I would initiate the meeting Monday at eleven a.m. which was the earliest MLB could see us. Raymond, Ted and I would attend with Hannah and Libby standing by with our surprise visitors. If needed to discuss the Eldridge Park 2.0 details, Hannah would handle that with Libby on back-up only if needed.

"Terrific, maybe we can catch a show or two in the meantime," said Raymond.

"Wow! I love this guy," said Ted, "here we are up to our eyebrows in the biggest deal of my life—which incidentally will result in either my financial success or catastrophic ruin—and he wants to hit the neon lights on Broadway. Sir, may I applaud your style?"

"Certainly," said Raymond, "my pleasure to share it."

"Are you people nuts? We need to focus here. It's fish or bait-severing time. We can't have distractions like this," said Libby. She had a look of utmost concern the likes of which Ted had never seen from his fiery wife. But he shared her view.

"I seem to recall a roommate of mine at Cornell, who on the night before an economics final went drinking at the Library bar just off campus, and had to be poured into bed at two a.m.," said Hannah.

"Sure, you would bring that up. I'll have you know I aced that final."

"Okay then, Broadway it is," I said.

Monday arrived cool and crisp with the last vestiges of spring. We were on our way to the offices of MLB to make our pitch when I grabbed Ted and Raymond and said, "Look! I just saw Hank Lewis getting into a cab while Bill Lattimore waved goodbye."

The three of us stood there like Lot, Pillars of salt. Well, two of us did. Raymond thought we were nuts.

"What's the matter with you guys?"

"Raymond, the guy getting into the cab is Hank Lewis," said Ted.

"Is that the guy you told me about last night? What's he doin' here?" asked Raymond.

"Precisely, what *is* he doin' here? Let's grab a cup o' Joe and give Bill a chance to get back to his office so we can find out," I said.

"Bill, Dru here," I phoned. "I just had a shock. We were on our way to your office and saw you saying goodbye to Hank Lewis. What's up with that?"

"Dru, I'm glad you called. We need to cancel your presentation today, in light of the meeting I just had with Mr. Lewis, okay?"

"Not really, what's goin' on?" I asked.

"Where are you guys now?"

"Coffee shop right across the street."

"Hold tight, I'll be right over."

I told Raymond and Ted with more dread than I thought possible. Just a few hours ago we were so confident. Now it was all likely to change. *Yikes*!

Bill came in and intros all around were made and we got down to it.

"What the hell did you do to that guy?" asked Bill.

"Whadja mean, Bill?" I asked.

"Okay, where to start?" Bill wrung his hands. "He told me you two guys stole a land deal from him by lying to some college guy, bankers, real estate people and now you're trying to buy a major league team for Elmira, New York. What the hell is he talkin' about, guys?"

"Bill, you have just met the most odious human on the planet. There's not a shred of truth in any of that."

I gave Bill the actual facts, answering his questions as they arose. Ted filled in the blanks while Raymond took it all in.

"So you're telling me you've competed with this guy, Lewis, for years on various real estate transactions and never lost to him. Do I have that right, Ted?"

"Bill, not only have I never lost to him, I can put you in touch with a guy who headed up a group selling a parcel of downtown property in Ithaca, New York, who told me I won the deal despite the fact Mr. Lewis had better numbers."

"You're kidding. Why would they do that?"

"They despise him and didn't trust him."

"Yes, I'll want to check him and your references out. Let's talk on Wednesday. Maybe we'll get back on track by Friday, sound good?"

I told Bill it did, and we all went home.

Hannah and Libby were on pins and needles. We milled around running scenarios while Raymond discussed Southwestern cuisine with Ivor. After all avenues had been examined we were left with the most difficult burden any of us could deal with, the need for patience.

"I have a poster on my office wall that shows two buzzards sitting high in a dead tree overlookin' a barren desert. One buzzard turns to the other and says 'Patience, my ass, let's go kill something,' " said Raymond.

Laughing I asked, "Who gave you that?"

"Ex-wife. It was a wedding present. She knew me a long time."

"What happened?" asked Libby.

"We got divorced," answered Raymond.

"Why?" asked Hannah.

"Ran outta patience!"

We sat there laughing in part because it was ludicrous, and part because it typified Raymond.

On Wednesday we heard from Bill Lattimore who had vetted us again and rescheduled the Friday appointment. We were elated but more worried than before. All except Libby—she was a total basket case.

Friday's weather was a duplicate of Monday and we were anxious to begin. As we neared the office Ted noticed several large semis parked in front of the building.

"Are they moving?" asked Libby, as we entered. Once inside we were captivated by the memorabilia displayed. I loved browsing the treasures featured on its paneled walls. Uniforms, signed balls, bats, various paintings, photographs highlighting the careers of the greats of the game—Hall of Famers all. Ted and I were enthralled.

Raymond, however, was content to sit and admire the beautiful receptionist. Upon seeing Raymond St. Clair, two of the officials fell all over themselves to welcome him and his friends. Turns out, a couple of years ago Raymond had steered them into land deals in Arizona which increased their net worth several times over. As people do for friends, they in turn shared the tips with two other board members.

The meeting was presided over by Expansion Committee Chairman, Bill Lattimore, who introduced in turn panel members: Ray Fielitz, Dave Coder, Jack Wright, Jerry Gray, Joe Geiger, Ed

Dirks and Frank Mitchell. These men were high ranking business and financial moguls whom Major League baseball found vital to their future.

"Gentlemen," Raymond began, "some of you know me as a shrewd judge of financial opportunities." Receiving head nodding from four of the seven panel members, he continued. "Rarely have I seen one such as this. In a financially depressed area a bold and captivating idea has emerged to not only bolster the local economy and provide much needed jobs, but bring joy to an area that sorely needs it. But it's not just about the locals it's also about MLB making a statement to baseball fans everywhere. MLB has a heart and is open to becoming part of the feel-good story of the century."

"A mighty bold statement, my friend. Can you back it up?" asked Bill Lattimore.

"I'll leave you guys to answer that, sir. We are about to engage you in the ride of a lifetime," intoned Raymond in the beginning of a spellbinding performance.

CHAPTER 24

Raymond signaled me to open the double doors to the conference area, and escorted two young buxom models into the room. To say they were scantily clad would be superfluous. All eyes were focused on the blonde and red-haired girls to the exclusion of all else—even, I believe, the Second Coming, if it were to occur at that moment.

Three porters entered, pushing large hand carts which contained the props for the next part of the presentation. There was a sound system and a screen was pulled down from the ceiling. A video system was hooked up behind the audience. The conference table was removed and the gentlemen in attendance were moved to the back center of the room. The men took their eyes away from the girls for a moment, then glanced with puzzlement, as if to ask Bill Lattimore *"What the hell's going on?"*

As all the items were installed, two full-sized carousel horses, complete with brass poles, were wheeled in and mounted by the girls.

"Oh, to be a horse," whispered Raymond in my ear.

Ray Fielitz said it out loud.

"Hold on, Mr. Fielitz," said Ed Dircks with a smirk.

Raymond signaled once more and a music and light show began. As befitting their audience, Hannah and her team selected music from the swing and big band eras, augmented with modern versions by Big Bad Voo Doo Daddy. Raymond had their undivided attention. The members were captivated by the sights of amusement parks, new and old, evoking nostalgic childhood memories from all on the screen.

Comments such as, "Oh, look there, I remember those," and "I loved those," were spontaneous utterances. Smiles revealed people who were thoroughly enjoying the experience.

Raymond read their reactions and skillfully guided their trips down memory lane. They went willingly. "Remember the brass ring, the cotton candy, the Whack-A-Mole?"

The frequent nods of agreement exposed their emotions as they conjured up individual memories. There was no fidgeting or fussing. Their rapt attention to Raymond's facts and smooth, easy manner of delivery were in concert with the slick visual and acoustic show. Supported by colorful graphs and pictures of the locale, including mentions of Mark Twain's home and grave site, Ernie Davis's grave and the grave of Hal Roach—producer of the Keystone Kops of early motion picture fame—caught their attention because none of them knew these historical factoids were indigenous to the area.

When it came time to dwell on the amusement park, the carousel horses and models were wheeled down close to the member's seats. The girls easily slid off their rides and gave each member a four-color brochure to examine. Stunning renderings and detailed scale models of the proposed facilities for the baseball and amusement parks, riding trails and picnic areas, were wheeled in on capacious tables. Invited by Raymond and led by the models the MLB men grouped around the displays, which gave them a close-up view of the project's scope and proposed impact.

Raymond expertly delivered this carefully crafted presentation. When he began compiling the activities available to choose from they were flummoxed. To think all of this would be contained in one ballpark area was hard to fathom. In an area of maybe 300,000 plus people, it seemed inconceivable. However, Raymond pointed out with tax breaks, efficient management to insure low operational cost, and virtually no competition its profit potential was astronomical.

These were people who were not easily taken in by *legerdemain* gloss and fru fru. They were bottom line people, period. But Raymond, by dint of his esteemed financial reputation, did indeed impress them.

By the end of his two-hour gig, he received a standing ovation, an unheard of tribute from this august body of accomplished men.

"Raymond, I've never witnessed a proposal I enjoyed as much as this one. Very few questions are left to ask," said Ed Dircks.

"Loved the music," said Joe Geiger.

"How about the scenery?" said Dave Coder, continuing to ogle the young ladies.

"Very thorough," said the chairman of the committee, Bill Lattimore.

"Thank you, Bill. We gave this a lot of thought and effort. But we wouldn't be here if we couldn't deliver on every facet of this proposal. In fact we guarantee it," said Raymond.

"Raymond, how do you propose to do that?" asked Ray Fielitz still with one eye on the young ladies.

"By every means necessary, gentlemen. We've got ample resources, excellent management people, proven experts in public relations, and an advertising pro that helped launch National Motors' sensational campaign last year. How many of you own a National car?" Six members raised their hand. Bill Lattimore was not one of them.

"What's the matter with you, Bill?"

"Raymond, I live in New York. I have a car service."

"Well, we here," a sweeping hand gesture indicating Bill's partners, "all drive 'em, and guess what? We highly recommend 'em, right guys?" asked Raymond.

"I'll just bet you do. Get it gratis, did ya?" said Ed Dircks.

"Didn't have anything to do with it... but yes," said Raymond with the biggest grin to be seen this side of Chief Wahoo, mascot of the Cleveland Indians.

"By the way, Dru, you were spot on by reducing your interest to the Double-A level. Even with all the expert advice and PR work, you can't increase the area's base population adequately enough to support the effort on the Triple-A level. It's been proven," said Lattimore.

"It flows nicely with the past history of the Dodgers in Elmira," said Raymond. The Pioneers were affiliated with Brooklyn and Baltimore in the Double-A Eastern League. It seems like a natural fit doesn't it? Where are you guys in your decision making process, if I may ask? I never miss an opportunity to close a deal," said Raymond.

"We read the papers, and are frequently surprised when so little of our deliberations are reported," said panel member Ed Dircks.

"Speaks well of your professionalism and security," said Raymond. "I'm reminded of Ben Franklin's homage to secrecy, 'Three can keep a secret if two are dead.' " Chuckles ensued and heads nodded in agreement.

"To answer, Raymond, we're wrapping up our decision now. Your presentation is timely and well-presented and, may I say, nothing like we've ever seen. We can't give you an answer now, though. We haven't consulted, but I suggest you make yourselves available in case we have any follow-up questions. I promise our answer won't take long," said Bill Lattimore.

Leaving, Ted patted Raymond on the back and said, "Good job, Raymond, thank you."

"It did seem to go well. Now all we have to do is wait to see if we're in or get blown outta the water," said Raymond.

***

Back at Casa McKenna née Connelly, we were served lunch by Ivor who asked how it went.

"It went well. Right guys?" said Hannah hopefully.

"Remember about the eggs and chickens?" said Dru.

"Or Yogi," she replied.

"It's not over 'til it's over," chipped in the Brit Ivor.

"My, my, you have come a long way in the assimilation process," complimented Raymond. "I wish my fellow tribesmen would do so well."

The rest of the day was spent reviewing possible questions MLB might ask. Preparation was the key to successful outcomes in any endeavor, so believed all of us.

Just a few ticks past four-thirty, we received a call from Bill Lattimore's assistant with an invitation to the 21 Club for dinner at eight that evening. The result of the afternoon deliberations was not mentioned. Not a surprise given the closed mouth reputation of MLB.

"But I don't think they'd buy us dinner at 21 if we don't got it," I chirped.

"Who says *they're* buying?" asked Raymond.

Arriving at the 21 Club and shown to our table, we were greeted by Bill, Ray Fielitz and Ed Dircks, all with beaming grins.

"It's not often we have the pleasure of delivering good news in person to people who come in front of us. We thought, why not take the opportunity to celebrate? What I mean to say is, we were completely sold on your proposal and want to officially—in private, anyway—welcome you to the world of professional baseball," said Bill.

"That's the best news I've had since I learned about June 25, 1876," said Raymond.

The facetious remark was met with blank faces, except for mine. I am well aware of the significance of the date. "You'll have to forgive Raymond's occasional flights of fantasy. He thinks he's a real Indian," I said.

"I am a real Indian," he replied with an indignant expression and tone.

"Yeah, I'm as much of an Irishman as you are an Indian," I riposted.

"Hold on fellas, what happened on June 25, 1876?" asked Ed Dircks.

Swelling up to his full six foot eight, 350 pounds, Raymond said, "Custer happened, sir. Or should I say Crazy Horse at the Little Big Horn, thank you very much."

They all laughed including Raymond, especially Raymond. Ted and I lowered and shook our heads marveling at the chutzpah my friend could get away with.

"Raymond, I believe you could tell us to go to hell and we'd look forward to the trip," said Bill Lattimore. "Am I to conclude this is a welcome bit of news then?"

"It is, sir, thank you very much," I said.

The MLB expansion committee members explained very carefully how important it was this news not be leaked. A year would pass before a formal announcement would be made. They also said Brooklyn was a serious contender but swore us to secrecy about it.

The celebration continued 'til almost midnight. On the jet back home, Raymond said, "I suppose I can go back home. Nothing can go wrong now."

I wondered why a chill ran down my spine, like all of the three blind mice running from the farmer's wife.

CHAPTER 25

Two weeks later Ted called with the spine-chilling explanation. Henry Lewis had filed suit against Ted and me for fraud. He claimed the deal in Big Flats was solely to make his inclusion in the Holding Point land acquisition impossible. He further claimed Ted misrepresented his interest in the Big Flats property and his interest in joining forces with Mr. Lewis—calling it a fraudulent ploy.

I was watching ESPN. "Turn on the TV, Ted! They're carrying the official announcement of the Major League Baseball decision to expand to thirty-two teams, one in each league."

The pleasant shock for residents of the state of New York, more specifically Brooklyn, was the return of MLB to the borough in the National League East Division. The American League entry would reside in New Orleans. They made no mention of farm teams or other organizational structure. The impact on the expansion cites would be enormous. Unsolicited seat requests flooded the MLB offices in New York since no addresses existed in Brooklyn or NOLA.

"Have you heard from Lattimore yet?" said Ted.

"Not yet. I'm gonna give it a day or two to allow things to settle. I'm sure he'll pass us off to the new owners. Anything more about Mr. Wonderful's threatened lawsuit?"

"No, and I'm surprised. I'm sure he'll try to prove *with malice*. We didn't promise him jack so why would any judge entertain such a frivolous suit?"

"I'm going to meet with Bob Crandall this afternoon and get the buy finalized. It will give me leverage in case Hank does sue or enjoins or anything else he devises."

"By the by, I may have a deal cooking for developing the Big Flats property. I'm stealing Hank's idea."

"A planned community?" I asked.

"Yeah, another real estate guy, a friend really, may want a part of it."

"Do I sense a buy-in type of deal there?"

"No flies on you, I need to get out from under this Big Flats deal to join you at the Holding Point."

"All in due time, there's no rush. We've got a lot ahead of us. Why not offer to sell Big Flats to Hank, in a formal written proposal? That might sit favorably with the courts and get you off the hook," I said.

"Not a bad idea, oh wise one," said Ted.

Hannah and I were on the dock enjoying steamed shrimp and Genny Cream Ale. I thought about all the details yet to be resolved.

People can get overwhelmed by complicated affairs like this and panic, but not me, thought Dru.

I reflected on the progress so far. *God, I do love this stuff*, I thought. Hannah filled me in on her meeting with Libby and the carousel people as we finished our snack.

"What's for dinner, darlin'?" I asked.

"You haven't finished your last shrimp yet and you're already worried about your next meal, as if the condemned man can't wait," said Hannah with an exasperated look.

"Just a bit of pre-planning, dear. Okay, here're the choices: either you cook somethin' or we go to Snug Harbor. You pick."

"Hmm, how 'bout the Harbor then snuggle later?"

And so it was.

The fall day dawned as expected. What was unusual for the time of year was the temperature. It was the third week in September and it was hot as wasabi.

I also had a surprise waiting for me.

I just didn't know it yet.

Hannah had scheduled an early meeting with Libby to review, yet again, details for the amusement park. My later meeting was with Bob Crandall at Elmira College for three p.m. I drove to the college with my mind on closing the land deal and getting Hank off our backs once and for all.

At his suggestion, we met by the Mark Twain study on campus. I saw Bob sitting on a nearby bench with an ear to ear grin, ostensibly to discuss the final terms of the college land sale but apparently not yet. It was then Bob surprised me with a treat.

"Dru, every once in a while we allow someone special to visit inside the study. Now is one of those times."

As we neared the entry I noticed ivy well on its way to enveloping the structure. Bob explained the study originally sat at Langdon farm on East Hill. Historical pictures showed a vine which wrapped around the whole building, except for the windows. When I entered, I was taken aback by how small it was compared to Ted's replica. To think the incomparable Mark Twain wrote large portions of Huckleberry Finn and Tom Sawyer on the very desk I was standing next to brought me chills and sent me into a reverie of sorts. When I visited the Smithsonian or other history museums I often had the same reaction then as I did now. I found myself immersed into a time of history where Mark Twain lived. I could visualize Mr. Clemens at this very desk smoking a cigar and writing.

Bob said something and I reluctantly slipped back to reality. Sweat pouring from my brow, I asked, "What'd he do in the summer? There's not a zephyr of air movement in here. It's almost October. What the hell was it like in July?"

"Precisely... hot." Bob said, "You have to realize, during his time the study was perched amidst the stately elms on East Hill at Langdon Farms. Breezes usually wafted through the open windows, which as you can see, encircle the structure. Together, with the shade from the enormous trees, they united to offer a modicum of relief."

I shook my head wondering how he could focus on his work in such conditions.

"In the winter, the stone fireplace behind the desk provided the only heat. The windows were a little tighter than now and easily sufficed."

I inspected the fireplace and windows, and with a curious bent I said, "Tighter then? How could that be, given modern materials, construction techniques and insulation today?"

"Well Dru, three reasons. One, we didn't add any modern materials in order to preserve the authenticity of this historic study. Second, we don't have the money even if we wanted to cheat authenticity and add insulation. Third, it's not like we get a lot of traffic through here, so there's really no need."

I nodded in understanding. As I stood there I relished the reverie conjured up again while Bob explained about whatever he was rattling on about. Once again I was back in the nineteenth century by my imagined time travel, just like I did in Edison's laboratory at Greenfield Village in Dearborn, Michigan, General Washington's headquarters at Valley Forge's huts, Patrick Henry's seat at Colonial Williamsburg's Capitol, and other historical venues I'd visited.

Snapping back I said, "Thanks, Bob, this is really special. I can't tell you how much an arm chair history buff like me appreciates this."

"Now, what's the final price?"

"Don't like to waste time, huh?" said Bob a bit surprised by my bluntness.

"I don't got it to waste. I know Hank wants to skin me and Ted alive—mostly me now, I'm afraid. If I own the land outright his suit will reek of malice, and what better venue for finalizing this deal than Mr. Clemens study?" I said.

"You're right. Well, we figured on fifty million. Sound okay?" He said this without blinking.

I, however, did blink but with only a slight pause, "I agreed to thirty million."

"Afraid that's a bit light, Dru."

"Look, Bob, I know the land's been appraised at twenty-five million and you know I'm in a spot. So I'll give a bit to thirty. You won't get anywhere near thirty around here and we both know it, so whadda ya say?"

"I say deal. Truth be told, I'd have taken the twenty-five."

"Hey, truth be known, I'd have gone to thirty-five."

We both laughed and shook hands, sealing the deal. I took a moment to glance around one last time before we left.

"Don't forget to lock up," I teased. Bob shook his head and we walked across campus to his office. I made out the check, and now Bob Crandall had in his possession the largest financial instrument he'd ever seen. He held it and stared for what, to him seemed like an eon, to me a nano sec.

On my way back to the cottage, I called Ted and filled him in. He and Libby were giving Hannah a lift to the cottage and were staying for a famous McKenna old fashioned picnic.

"Yeah, it's good news, Dru, but did you have to go so high?" asked Ted.

"Ted, when this goes to court—and I'm sure our friend is going to take it there—I want the college with us to fight him tooth and nail. It's important for the public to know what the cost to the local economy of finding in favor of Mr. Lewis would have been. It's worth the extra money now, trust me."

"Oh, I trust you, but that's still a lot of shekels."

I couldn't hold back a chuckle as I said, "Ted, it is a lot of money but I consider it a solid investment. Remember you're paying me back every blessed dime."

"Oh. Okay, so now I know why you can laugh. Risk, huh?" said Ted.

"I'm enjoying this whole deal, aren't you?"

"Sure, but... oh I get it."

The next week, just as I predicted, the presiding judge disallowed Hank's suit citing malice. The deal stood, and now all the pieces were in place. Yet I still had this uneasy thought that somethin' was amiss. No clue what it was, just a feeling.

But it still worried me.

CHAPTER 26

The next day, at high noon, Hanna and I sat over a lunch of BLTs with sliced avocado added—so technically they were BALTs—with Ted and Libby. We were discussing schedules for the next few days each involving our realms.

"I've got all the pieces built and ready to ship so we need to get on with the site prep, right?" said Libby.

"On the money, dear heart. We'll bring in enough crew to do both parks at once. With the plans for the ball park selected and the contractors lined up the only thing left to do is obtain work permits from the various government entities," said Ted.

"You've got a pensive look about you, hon, what's up?" asked Hannah.

"Just watching those thunder clouds. Probably gonna rain."

Looking up at the brilliant sun, a stunned Hannah said, "Dru, there's not a cloud in the sky. Tell me what's wrong, please."

Aware that I must have floated off to the planet Mongo, I noticed the concerned look on Hannah's face as well as Ted and Libby's. "I guess I just have the sense of some impending cataclysm. Nothing I can put my finger on, but similar to the way I felt just before we got the call about Jon Fallon's death."

I looked at Hannah with the same sad eyes she remembered from that day. My godfather, Jon Fallon, was targeted by his truly evil protégé and what was supposedly intended to be an embarrassing situation turned out to be the outright murder of three people.

"Oh, Dru, please don't go there. Everything will be okay," she said wrapping her arms around me.

"I know everything is going well, just sometimes I get these weird notions. You know the 'what else can go wrong' type. Sorry, let's finish our lunch. These sandwiches are terrific. Ivor told me about his discovery of adding avocados. Said I should try them. He was right."

I still couldn't help feeling the dire circumstance I feared was about to occur. And then it did.

* * *

The Chemung County Board of Approvals was withholding permits for the entire project, claiming approvals from all the departments were not yet submitted. I went nuts.

"What kind of horse shit is this?" I railed at the County Clerk after reasonable language and tone failed to impress him of the urgency of the matter.

"Sir, watch your language. We do not condone this type of behavior from our residents."

My head turned purple, as I yelled, "Condone! You don't condone! You're a group of myopic, bureaucratic, pencil pushing, red-tape loving, mouth breathin' knuckle dragging humps, who are holding up a multi-million dollar project that will provide a few hundred jobs to the area—to say nothing about boosting the economy! Where's the newspaper office around here? We'll see what the public thinks about this. Maybe the Mayor or Governor should know, too. Nitwits, all of ya!"

I stomped out of the office, slamming doors and cursing all through the parking lot. I sat in the car trying to regain my composure. I was holding the steering wheel so tight I feared my white knuckle grasp would bend the thing. The thought of explaining to the insurance adjuster how my defective steering wheel shattered finally served to calm me. The ensuing drive to Ted's house took no time at all. I was in such a fury I noticed not a bit of it. No scenery, no traffic, no nothing.

"Well my friend, I heard you made an impact of sorts at the Board of Approvals," said Ted as I entered the M/T office.

"News do travel fast in small towns," I said.

"It do."

"I couldn't believe they're holding up a project of this magnitude over red-tape bullshit. I just lost it. How bad is it?"

Ted was relaxed in his ergonomic, state-of-the-art executive chair and smiling gleefully.

"The next time you pull one of these fits of pique let me tag along. I don't wanna miss it."

"If there's a next time, you'll see it in on the evening news along with footage and a report from a CSI unit. It'll probably go viral on YouTube too. This is unbelievable!"

"Hold on, Kimmo Sabe. The Mayor and every ranking official in the state, this side of the Governor, maybe him too, has undoubtedly weighed in on getting this fast-tracked by now."

"Fast-tracked? That boat sailed my friend. This better be moving at warp speed or this state can kiss this project goodbye."

"You don't mean it, do ya?"

"Ted there are times—and I don't do it often—when I gotta swing the big hammer. Everything in my way, at those times, is a nail. I'll get this done, trust me. If they stall this thing too long we'll lose the MLB, NYC backing and we'll be DOA. So yeah, I mean it."

I went over to the mini fridge and grabbed a couple of Genny's. I gave one to Ted and sat down in the loveseat next to the sliders which opened to the deck.

"How long do ya think this will take before we hear from somebody?"

"Who knows, Dru. I've never been in this kind of situation, but I figure they're all trying to think of a way to calm you down and contain the damage. You're right. When the impact of what you threatened hits home, action will be taken." I was surprised how relaxed Ted seemed. He obviously had more faith in the bureaucratic cogs grinding away to resolve this crisis than I did. Oddly that made me feel better too.

"I'll give 'em an hour, then I'm going to war," I said.

"Funny, I thought you already did."

"You'll know when war is officially declared, trust me!"

"Now what have you started, Dear Heart?" said Hannah coming in with Libby. "I just heard about your scene at the Board of Approvals."

I filled the ladies in on the happenings, the ramifications and my plans to resolve the situation.

"Big hammer time, huh?"

"You got it."

"How long?" she asked.

"'Til war? About thirty minutes," I answered.

"Sounds right."

Twenty minutes later, Ted received a call from Jim Baxter of the Board of Approvals. He put it on speaker phone.

"Ted, I just found out about the dust-up here with Dru McKenna and your project. Unfortunately sometimes the cracks are bigger than they should be and big stuff slips through. No excuse for it really, but it happens. Barring any unforeseen problem you'll have your approvals tomorrow morning. I've talked to the inspectors and the findings are all in. It's just the written reports which need to be filed. That will happen by tomorrow. Your certificates will be ready by ten in the morning. Ted, I apologize to you and Dru. I don't have his contact info handy so if you'd pass on the message I'd be grateful."

"Hold on, Jim, Dru's right here," said Ted.

I listened with an amused look on my face while adding simple responses to Jim Brewer. At the end I gave him my cell number and thanked him for his prompt action. I did not, however, apologize for the outburst at the office.

"Well now, I handled that well, don't ya think?" I said.

"I think you'd better wipe that bear-shit eatin' grin off your face, Buster," said Hannah.

"Well put, sister. After all we have to live with these people," said Libby.

Everyone laughed and we filed the episode in the 'no harm, no foul container.'

The impediments overcome, it looked like all systems were a go. The team decided it would be wiser to build the amusement park before the baseball stadium since the team would not be assembled for two years. This meant Hannah and Libby were in charge of their portion of the project, leaving me and Ted free to deal with Hank Lewis, the politicians and MLB.

Libby had a bit of experience dealing with contractors, both prime and sub because her father was an engineer for a large architectural and engineering firm with worldwide projects. She assembled the contractors, laid out the schedule of events and sequenced their time frames. She consulted with her father on the companies best able to handle her various job requirements. Construction was scheduled to begin immediately and last at least eighteen months. To achieve it they had to begin before winter struck. After it did progress would be sporadic, depending on the vagaries of Mother Nature. To help inspire adherence to the stated goal, a built in schedule of bonuses for early completion was detailed. Correspondingly, a detailed assessment for lateness was also included.

"Never too early to hold contractors' and subs' feet to the fire," pronounced a feisty Libby.

"Libby, you look worried. What's wrong?" asked Hannah.

"Nothing, it's just so unnatural. My dad always told me to expect problems every step of the way. So far we're humming along without a glitch."

"You'd feel better with a glitch or two?"

"Maybe. I just wonder if I overlooked something, ya know? How about your end, Hannah, are all the suppliers on board and on-time?"

"Yeah, they are, even the carousel people. Who knew so many merry-go-rounds were being built every year? Their business is booming but they assured me when we're ready for them to deliver, they will."

"Now who looks worried?" said Libby.

"I wasn't 'til you shared your father's admonition. Thank him for that, will ya?"

The lightness in Hannah's voice belied her spoken fear. She was, in her own offbeat manner, trying to soothe Libby and allay her concerns.

Ted and I were in New York to meet with both the MLB execs and the owner of the expansion Brooklyn team. This was to be the formal acceptance of Ted and me joining the minor league program at the Double-A level.

The office was as interesting to me as the first time I visited it. Priceless memorabilia and pictures of the Hall-of-Famers provided a wonderful trip down memory lane for Ted and me.

Bill Lattimore was smiling broadly as he joined us. He spoke of the baseball history Brooklyn and Elmira shared.

"It was the best of times after WWII. The men were back home, at work, with money to visit the ballparks frequently. Attendance soared and prosperity reigned until the advent of TV. Ya know, it's ironic the very invention that sent pro baseball into decline is the very reason baseball's popularity is trending upwards now, especially since the revenue from all the sold TV rights are pouring in."

We were there to meet the new Brooklyn owners Adair and Ralph Meyers who were in Bill's office.

Adair Meyers, co-owner of the Brooklyn franchise with her brother Ralph, welcomed Dru and Ted into the family. Adair was a feisty five foot six inch ball of energy and wit. Ralph was a reserved patrician with an air of style and grace. They were charming, warm and gracious.

"My brother Ralph and I are so happy that someone from Elmira has stepped up to bring a team back home. I graduated from Southside High too many years ago, and I visit every year. We have a place on Keuka Lake we stay at in the summer."

With that Ted perked up and asked, "What side of the lake?"

"East side, why do you ask?"

"We used to have a cottage on the West side a couple of miles north out of Hammondsport," said Ted.

"I'm staying in a friend's cottage on the West side now," I added.

"I should say my daughter, Molly, and her husband Dave Adler and I really have the cottage. Ralph comes up for weekends when he can. He keeps so very busy with the real estate end of our business, therefore his free time is precious."

"I'm sorry to hear about the Southside thing, especially since I went to Notre Dame High, but we love being in cahoots with fellow Elmirans," teased Ted.

Smiling, Adair asked, "Dru, your participation in this project is curious given the parochial nature of the Brooklyn and Elmira teams. How'd that come about?"

"Easy enough to answer, Adair, my wife browbeat me into helping out her friend, Libby."

"Libby's my wife," explained Ted.

"You know, Dru, Joel Leonard was fearful you had designs on the Mets when he heard McKenna Associates was nosing around baseball," said Bill.

I raised my eyebrows in surprise and said, "Really? That's a surprise. I didn't know they were for sale."

"They're not, but there's been rumors," said Bill.

"To paraphrase Mark Twain, the stories about my interest in buying the Mets is greatly exaggerated," I joked.

"Have you picked a name for the team yet, Adair?" asked Ted.

Not yet. Ralph wants to go back in history and name 'em the Robins. I favor the Colonials. We'll have to fight it out, I'm afraid. How about the Elmira name? Are you going with the Pioneers?

Ted laughed as I answered, "We were gonna buy the Pioneers name from the last owner of the club, but he refused to sell it, then later tried to hold us up on the price... so we dumped him and his name."

Ted said, "Dru's wife, Hannah, came up with the idea for a promotional contest to let the fans vote on the name."

With a mirthful smirk, I said, "I hope we don't give birth to the Purple Spotted Owls."

"The uniforms might be cool, but then again who could you get to wear 'em?" said Adair with eyes twinkling.

Meeting over, it was off to nearby 21 Club for lunch.

***

At Keuka Lake, Hanna was focusing on the makers of the games, carnival attractions, roller coaster, bumper cars and carousel, while, in Elmira, Libby was knee deep in the fight to keep the contractors in line, on time and on budget.

"How's it going, Lib?" asked Ted as he called the M/T study while perched on a loveseat in the McKenna house.

"Okay so far. I talked to Hannah earlier and mentioned my dad's advice about being prepared for the other shoe to drop."

"I bet she said she's more of a glass half full kind of girl, right?"

"Pretty much. In truth, I can't believe how this thing is all shaping up."

"For instance?" he asked.

"Like the general contractor we selected? Turns out he's built amusement parks all over the world. The subs are a combination of guys he's used on other projects, people my father recommended, our manufacturers recommended people and members of the suppliers' own staff are installers."

"Sounds like you guys are all over it."

"Ted, I can't believe these people we're with, Hannah and Dru. I knew Hannah in college and she was a fierce golfer, but in addition to sports of all kinds, she was on the Dean's List, President of the sorority and who knows what all. She's the most positive person I've ever met, ya know."

"I do know, Dru's the same way. Even during the blowup at the BOA, he knew he'd prevail. It's like he willed the outcome he wanted, nothin,' stops him, it's amazing."

"You're pretty amazing yourself, darlin," she said.

"Hold that thought until tomorrow afternoon."

* * *

The next day, Ted ran into the house, grabbed Libby and made their way upstairs.

"It's the middle of the day," she said in mock shock. In the glow of the aftermath, they fell asleep.

"Mom, Dad, where are you?" shouted their sixteen-year-old daughter Emily as she searched the house.

"Ted, wake up! Emily's home!"

"Why the panic, Lib?"

"C'mon, get up, your daughter's home."

"She lives here, she belongs here, she's allowed to be here, Libby."

"You're naked," she chastised.

"I couldn't do what we just did as well if I had my clothes on, could I?"

"So not the point!"

As Libby tried to get out of bed, Ted reached out and wrapped his arms around her in a playful embrace that stopped her just as the bedroom door flew open.

"EEWW! What are you doing, why aren't you at work somewhere?" cried Emily as she stormed out of the room.

"Remember when your father caught us on the porch?" asked Ted.

"Of course, who could forget a thing like that? But Daddy wasn't so bad. How about the summit meeting with my mother the next day?"

"I wasn't a big fan of either occasion, frankly. Your dad scared me witless."

"Guess what, Dear Heart, this was worse," she said as she rose and got dressed.

Ted finally emerged from the bedroom to find his wife and daughter laughing gleefully in the kitchen.

"There's Mr. Wonderful now," said Emily. Ted looked stunned, grabbed a cup of coffee and repaired to the M/Tstudy. The girls continued their hilarity as he left.

Women, I'll never understand any of 'em, he thought.

The next day at Casa Reynolds, the boys filled the girls in on their meeting with Adair and Ralph Meyers and Bill Lattimore. In turn the girls filled the boys in on the status of their side of the project. The info swap thus completed, Hannah and I repaired to Keuka Lake feeling the effects of a long tiring day. We were dining on the dock by the lake, courtesy of the Barefoot Contessa's two bags of food and a loaf of Italian with a jug of Bully Hill's 'Grower's Red.' We were short on meal prep time and long on appetite. Our days were becoming more hectic and we loved every minute of it. We discussed our upcoming schedules for the umpteenth time.

"Libby's background meshes perfectly with the demands of a pit-bull straw boss. She provides terrific expertise honchoing around the contractor troops. They respect her knowledge and skill. Her father trained her well."

"You're not doin' too bad your own self, dearie. I'm impressed with your sourcing out all the carnival type stuff and scheduling it," I said, proud of Hannah's skill.

"It's not much different than preparing for a trade show, really. Lord knows I've had tons of experience with those, so it's goose to paté."

"I hope with a better outcome than for the goose."

"We'll see, won't we?" she snarked in response.

"Our lives are truly blessed to have so many opportunities to get involved with people and projects like we have," I said.

"Indeed. What's on tap for tonight?" she asked.

"You mean after I walk the Beast and have my way with you? I'm open."

"Sounds like a plan but what about Riley? He likes to jump on our bed."

"As I said before, let 'im find his own girl."

It was a plan we executed flawlessly with extreme pleasure.

I drove down to Ted's office in the morning where we enjoyed coffee, courtesy of Ted's Keurig and my bag of Starbucks Italian Roast.

"What have you heard of our friend Henry?" I asked.

"Funny you should ask. I was talkin' to Steve Greatsinger the other day about the very thing. Turns out nobody's seen him or Rance Butler for about a week."

"Really, what do ya think's goin' on?"

"No clue. Bob Crandall hasn't heard a peep either so who knows?"

"Whatever it is can't be good," I said. "I have an idea. Let's ask Hank what's up. Watcha ya think?"

Ted mused a bit then said, "Couldn't hurt... Maybe I should call. He now considers you public enemy number *uno*."

"Like you haven't beaten him like a drum his whole life."

"True but he doesn't hate me, not really. I'm sure he's jealous and wants to beat me, but he holds no malice toward me. You on the other hand made a fool outta him, on purpose and in public."

Ted ended up calling to invite Hank to lunch. Just Hank, no Butler, but the call went to voicemail. Ted left a 'call me' message and hung up. A scant five minutes later Hank surprisingly returned the call and accepted an invitation to Bus Horrigan's the next day.

Meanwhile, Libby was discussing the schedule with the general contractor's head man, Jack Thomas. A former linebacker in school, he still looked as if he could hold his own on the gridiron. Standing six foot four at 230 pounds, he had no discernible fat, but a nose broken more than once told a story of many a set-to on the field. They agreed the site prep was a piece of cake. Jack recommended using the dirt from carving out the baseball stadium's playing surface to augment what was needed for the riding and hiking trails to make necessary contours—thereby saving a bundle.

Libby, who was an astute penny pincher eloquently pointed out she and Ted would pay back every cent Dru fronted, agreed with Jack and gave approval for the excavation and moving dirt as needed, ca-ching, ca-ching.

Libby also took the ingenious step of bringing a couple of horses to ride the property with the designer to assist in laying out the trails. By doing this they were able to ensure a positive experience for the public who could choose to ride through the subtle hills and dales of the land. The designer suggested places to plant saplings that would transform the relatively barren land into a lush venue for the riders to enjoy one day.

Reviewing the latest activity at dinner the next night Ted, Hannah and I heard this story from Libby. We marveled at the take charge foresight of the, heretofore, quietest member of the team.

"Still waters, men... still waters," offered Hannah, which made Libby blush.

"What's going on with the Hank deal?" asked Hannah.

"Ted's having lunch with him tomorrow," I said.

"Wow! Didn't see that coming," said Libby.

When she said it I jerked my head around, and Hannah saw a familiar look she'd come to fear. Not about to force me to divulge the cause she filed it away to ask me later.

CHAPTER 27

I called Bill Lattimore in the morning to discuss the press release of their acceptance by MLB and Brooklyn.

"I have some news," said Bill. "The new Brooklyn team will be the Colonials."

"Adair Meyers got her way, I see."

"Yeah, just like every woman I ever knew despite their protestations to the contrary," said Bill.

"Okay, but when can we go public?"

"Here's where it gets tricky, Dru. MLB wants to pick a date for maximum exposure. For us that means the All-Star Game Week or the World Series. I prefer All-Star Week, so as not to detract from the Fall Classic. The hang-up is Adair's brother Ralph. She sides with me, but since Ralph let her have the name decision, he wants the release date to be his, and he wants the World Series."

"Are you kidding me? Are we really talking about sibling rivalry here or what?" I said.

"I know, nuts isn't it? Ralph makes a good point in that the World Series would make the biggest splash for Brooklyn, but at the cost of the spotlight dimming on the Series."

"How about a compromise?" I suggested.

"That being?" asked Bill.

"We announce it the day after the Series ends, the very next day."

"Interesting, let me work on it. I'll get back."

***

Ted couldn't wait to tell me what took place at his meeting with Hank at Horrigan's which has been a friendly neighborhood watering hole cum restaurant, in Elmira, for decades. The décor is comfortable as is the food served by a young staff of pretty college coeds. Hank, as is his wont, arrived fifteen minutes late. After their last episode it was certain the wait staff would remember Hank when he arrived. They did and gave him wide berth. It was as if a predicted tsunami arrived.

Ignoring the hostess, he barged through the dining room to Ted's table, plopped himself in a chair and without preamble said, "What're we doin' here, Ted?"

Hank in his usual belligerent manner hardly ever wasted time on pleasantries augmenting his already tarnished reputation.

Not to be sucked into a confrontation Ted smiled, shook his head and calmly said, "Hank, we've been involved in a lot of the same projects over the years."

"You've been involved. I've lost every chance I had to be involved."

"I know you think it's you against me but I don't. I never go into anything thinking about how to beat you. It's more of how can I make this happen and get what I want?"

"Ted, it's the getting what you want part which stops me from getting what I want. It's as simple as that," said Hank.

"I know it seems that way..."

"Seems horse shit, look there's no other way to put it, period."

"Hank, the reason I asked you to lunch is to see if you would entertain not competing against me but joining me on this project."

Hank was taken aback. He said nothing, had no expression, no visible reaction.

"Christ, Ted, I don't even know for sure what in hell you're doin, you and that ringer from Michigan, McCann or McCauley or whoever."

"You know damn well it's McKenna, Hank . . ." Just then Ted rose to take a call. "Excuse me, it's an SOS." Recognizing Hannah's cell, Ted walked out of the restaurant into the parking lot. "Has something happened to Dru?"

"Not Dru, Ted, it's Libby. Meet me at the Arnot Emergency now. Hurry!"

An ashen faced, withered man wearing Ted's clothes looking out of *Little Orphan Annie* eyes, wobbled back into the restaurant, approached the table and said, "Sorry, Hank, I have to leave."

"Isn't that just swell. Thanks for stopping by."

"My wife's been in an accident... she's in the hospital... emergency... serious."

Ted turned and continued his Weeble-like gait out to the parking lot. Within a few steps he felt someone grab his arm. It was Hank.

"C'mon, I'll drive. What hospital, St. Joe's?"

"No, Arnot."

"What happened?" asked Hank with uncharacteristic concern.

"No idea... none at all."

Arriving at the emergency room, Ted was met by Hannah and Dru who, looking over Ted's shoulder, was surprised to see Hank Lewis. *Odd,* she thought.

"This way, Ted," she said leading him down the hall.

They arrived at the Emergency Room and saw Libby on the gurney covered in blood.

"What happened? What's goin' on? What's *he* doin' here?" I said, as I spotted Hank Lewis in a chair on the other side of the room.

"Take it easy. Ted was in no condition to drive so Hank brought him here from Horrigan's, and he's been here ever since."

Shaking my head I said, "Unbelievable. Okay, what happened?"

"As near as we can figure Libby was on her way home when a school bus came down Mt. Zoar hill and ran the light. The bus T-boned Libby and drove into the candy store on the corner. So far, three kids are dead at the scene, the driver DOA here. Ten kids admitted with various broken bones and head traumas. Libby has a lot wrong. Two broken legs, a broken arm, six broken ribs, head wound, probably concussion and she's in shock. Ted's with her now and he's a mess."

"What can we do?" I asked.

"Just be here, and play it by ear. I'm going to phone Emily and Patrick and ask them who else I can call."

"I'll go pick 'em up," I said.

"Better wait 'til you speak with Ted," she advised.

Ted appeared moments later, a bit steadier. "Dru, Hanna, thanks for comin'. I gotta sit down."

"Ted, I'm going to pick up Emily and Patrick," I said.

"Yeah that would be great, thanks. I need time to steady-up for them. Doc says she's probably goin' to make it. Long, long rehab though."

"Better than *no* hab," I said somberly.

"Ain't it the truth. Thanks, bud."

I left on my mission and Ted and Hannah saw Hank venture over.

"Ted, did I hear you say Libby'll be okay?"

"Hank? Where did you come from? Oh, we were having lunch. How'd you get here?"

"Ted, Hank drove you here," said Hannah.

"You were in no shape to drive, Ted. It was the least I could do. Anything else I can do for ya?"

"Thanks, Hank, I can't think of a thing. Thanks again."

Hank left without another word, leaving Hannah and Ted slack-jawed. Ted said, "Can you beat that? Hank's got a heart. Who knew?"

Soon I returned with the kids in tow. Hannah and I left to retrieve Ted's car from Horrigan's.

On the way over she gave me the situation report.

"This puts things in a quandary for now, doesn't it?" asked Hannah.

"Don't worry, we'll handle it. But yeah, things will be up in the air for a while."

That night Hannah and I stayed at Ted and Libby's. We saw to the kids getting off to school amid much protestation. They wanted to be there for their mom. They wanted to be there for their dad. They wanted to be of some help, somehow.

Mostly they wanted a day off from school. It was not to be. As a consolation I drove them to school and on the way back I reflected on how tragedy had been narrowly averted by Libby. I harkened back to the feeling I had just prior to Jon Fallon's "accident." I had the same feeling just before Libby's accident.

I don't want to experience that feeling again.

***

For the next two days get well cards, flowers, candy, balloons and all sorts of e-mails piled up at home, office and hospital. The doctor's news was very good. Prognosis: complete recovery with much rehab effort.

MLB's Bill Lattimore called to express shock, dismay and grave concern, offering if there was anything they could do, they would. Adair Meyers did pretty much the same.

Bill Lattimore also said the compromise I suggested was accepted and everyone was elated with the news. This time next year the new teams would be known to the world the day after the last game of the Series.

Pinch-hitting for Libby, Hannah met with Jack Thomas, filled him in, and told him to keep her apprised of developments until Libby got back on her feet.

CHAPTER 28

While winter approached quickly, Libby, now out of harm's way, came home from the hospital. I arranged for the McKenna Associates' corporate jet to whisk them all, kids included, down to Orlando, Florida, for some R&R. They spent a full month down there together, most of it hangin' out by various hotel pools.

Libby, still working hard on her rehab program, used a wheel chair to dine out and visit some of the tamer non-participatory sites, beaches and pools mostly. They kept up with daily project activities, meager though they were, but did accomplish a solid plan for scheduling every aspect of the creation of the facilities. The kids, much to their dismay, kept up with classes through the internet and Skype.

Upon their return to New York the weather was still brutal. We decided to stay at the lake for the winter to be close to any project developments, and pick up the slack while Libby recovered.

Snow patterns in the area had changed dramatically in the last fifty years from steady high annual snow fall to intermittent high accumulations. This winter, however, was a throwback. For several days, storms were heavy enough to hold Hannah and me captive at the lake house. A scheduled trip to our Lake Placid home had to be rescheduled.

Preparing places in the yard for Riley to conduct his business was challenging, what with winds and drifts and all, covering freshly snow-blown areas in the yard.

Horsing around with the snow blower on the uneven terrain of the yard was truly man's work. Hannah was too smart to mess with it. Eventually we weathered it all. The New Year dawned and site work began in earnest whenever Mother Nature periodically relaxed her grip on the area.

In addition to working on the installation of the amusement rides, Hannah was still wearing her straw boss hat until Libby got back, which was looking to be soon. Jack Thomas pretended to let Hannah boss him and the crew around until he realized he wasn't pretending any more. She knew what she was doing too. Some pair of women were these two.

After two more weeks Libby started half-days in the office four times a week, and one half-day per week at the site. During this time, roads were put in but not yet paved. A few basic carnival type metal buildings for the midway were erected and equipped. The riding trails and picnic and hiking areas were laid out. The baseball stadium playing surface was dug out and the subsequent mound of dirt harvested and spread around the trails as planned.

At the end of every day we looked with pride at what had been accomplished. Through all of this activity nobody mentioned to outsiders what was going on. People in the area knew something was being built, but thus far only unsubstantiated speculation existed, no facts.

The primary reason for the mystery was due to advice from Hannah's house manager and former British Ranger who delved into security services periodically. He used the tactic we used on the National Motors test facilities and manufacturing plants: high vegetation barriers with razor-wire fencing encircling the whole thing. I made a note to call Ivor the next day.

"Ivor, I love these euonymus bushes you suggested. They grow better than weeds with no end in sight."

"You've got 'em in your yard in Manhattan and Lake Placid," Ivor said.

"Ivor, you've been to Lake Placid more than I have this year."

"You've been a mite busy this year, Dru. When are you going to go up there? Any time soon?"

"I'm not sure. It looks like the weather is finally going to cooperate so the building of this thing is going to kick into warp speed. But I'll be in New York next week to meet with our baseball friends. I'll see you then."

"Bring Riley too. I miss the boy," said Ivor as he hung up.

The weather did not cooperate. Construction was placed on hold. A spur of the moment trip to Lake Placid was not in the cards either, so Hannah, Riley and I left for The City the next day. This was an opportunity for Hannah to meet with her staff and flesh out the promotional plan for the baseball team and the amusement park.

"What are your thoughts on what to call the amusement park?" I asked.

"I need to contact the city's parks people and Indians to see if we can use Emily's idea."

"Out of the mouths of babes, huh?"

"Libby told me yesterday, and I like it. After all, the demographics we're targeting is the tweeners and young adults. She fits that profile to a tee."

"What is it?"

"Eldridge Park."

"Hence, the need to get permission from the city, right?" I asked.

"Okay, I'd be surprised if we catch any flack from 'em though. Wouldn't you?" I asked.

"Not the city, not after the BOA dust up. They're afraid you'll pull the plug and bolt," she said chuckling.

"What about the baseball promo?" I asked.

"Well, you know about the name-the-team campaign. We can also leave the choice of the team colors to the fans too, since MLB is trusting us to do it."

"Oh boy, I can see chartreuse and orange named the Geckos," I said.

"You forget who's counting the ballots and making the decision public, sahib."

"Ah yes, sounds like every drawing for a customer golf outing I've ever seen. You know the boss of the best client always gets the best prize," I said.

"So that's how it's done?"

"That's how."

When Ivor met us at the brownstone he was greeted by a familiar ersatz chomp and a wagging bat tail from Riley, a handshake from me, then Hannah hugged him.

Ivor lead Riley into the kitchen to provide a healthy snack for the boy and began building our lunch which I'm sure will be a feast.

I was hanging out on the office sofa listening to the "Jersey Boys Greatest Hits" on headphones while Hannah met with her creative staff in her conference room.

As the founder of her own very successful PR agency Hannah had taken it to the pinnacle of creative achievement. Her crown jewel was the launch for National Motors' H2 car two years ago. It was the most successful car introduction ever.

During the meeting several ideas emerged for the Eldridge Park 2.0 project. Among them, an opening day gala featuring a country-western and a rock band performing on bandstands at either end of the park. To move from one to the other patrons would have to walk through the park and be exposed to games, rides and a myriad of activities.

"Won't that detract from the entertainment's audience?" asked an assistant.

"Not really. They probably would file the information away for use later when their sole purpose will be taking part in the park's activities."

Free admission was discussed and rejected under the 'no free lunch' proviso.

They took the lead from Hannah who said, "I never have liked giving away the product from the git-go. It's kinda like getting what you pay for, isn't it? Runs the risk of devaluing the place, since they'll recall getting in for free. Anything above free will seems like a gyp. Besides, the concert portion is free. The admission fee is the same as it always will be."

"I'm getting hungry. Is it lunch time yet?"

"About an hour ago," said one staffer.

"Okay, let's wrap this up. We'll open on a Saturday. We've hired the fireworks people from Baltimore, the ones we used for the National car launch, remember?"

"The Zembelli's, right?"

"Exactomundo, what do you think?"

"We're also giving away a car as the Grand Door Prize," she said.

"Let me guess, a National H2 model?" said her assistant, Janet Mustico.

"You, my dear, are on a roll."

Going back into her office she found me sound asleep or so she thought. I was fakin' it with headphones still holding my ears captive while I eavesdropped on my wife's leadership skills.

She shook me and said, "How the hell do you fall asleep to that?" as Hannah freed my ears. She held up the phones and heard not the falsetto tones of *Sherri* offered by Frankie Valli, but nothing.

At this point she began filling me in on the meeting's results. "What do you think?"

"I thought it was great the moment I heard it."

"Yeah, as if you'd say anything other than 'it's terrific, dear.' You know why?"

"Okay, why?"

"Cause it's terrific, dear."

"Does Justin or Kimberley know about their donation yet?"

"Not unless they're witches or clairvoyant, but I'll ask them before I go ahead. What do you think so far?"

"If there's any witchcraft going on it'll be you who plies it, Mrs. Wizard. I defer to the expert in developing PR ideas. It's why your company is so successful, dearie."

"I know, and thank you, but just like we've talked about, ask and it's given. We've done it our whole lives."

"We have indeed. Any more thoughts about the baseball promotional program, besides the name and colors contests?"

"At the moment nothing original, we can do the same things everybody does but just the successful stuff."

"Like?"

"For instance, fan appreciation nights. I want to develop some new and appealing ways to honor the fans besides just giving away free stuff. Not that I want to abandon giving away stuff. We'll keep the tried and true designated nights for promotional giveaways like caps, shirts, sun glasses, beach towels and what not. But instead of flimsy crap I want to spend more of your money to give better quality stuff. More team logos instead of promotional crap people—especially kids—don't give a rat's ass about. We want all the people to be excited about coming out to the game and enjoying the experience."

"We need to work on expanding the list," I said.

"We will. I just started working on it, and I'll put the pit bulls in the conference room on it. We'll be ready with a full plan before you know it."

"Trust me, I'll know it."

***

Later, Ted called to touch base on his New York plans and to run an idea by me.

"You're gonna think I'm nuts, but I've been wondering how to turn Hank from being an enemy into something more agreeable."

I was reclined in bed, but sat bolt upright. "You mean like a friend?"

"Well, I'm not sure I'll ever be able to call him a friend but I'm looking to lose him as an enemy," said Ted.

"Yeah, good luck with that. Light a candle or seventy, say a novena, go to Lourdes. Just stay away from Vegas. I wouldn't count too heavily on it."

"I know this sounds crazy, after all we've seen from him, but when I needed immediate help he didn't hesitate to step up and drive me to the hospital. I know. Lots of people would've done the same thing, but he's not one I ever believed would've done it... but he did."

"You're right, he did. I was surprised, actually flabbergasted, to see him at Arnot. I guess there's a scintilla of grace in that withered soulless son-of-a-bitch."

"Dru, he's only six months older than me, and he's not withered."

"He acts like he should be, and his face do look like a walnut shell after all," I said, with more than a little snark.

Ted leaned back and tried to stifle a laugh, but it was replaced with a perfect snort—which made me laugh. Then we both gave into a laughing fit.

"What do you have in mind, Ted?"

"The same thing I was trying to do at Horrigan's. Make peace."

"I didn't mention this before but you do know about leopards and their spots, right?"

"That's just it, Dru, I'm not sure Hank's a leopard. His whole life—at least since I've known him—he's always on the outside looking at everybody and everything. It must've been hard."

"Probably, of his own doing," I said.

"Ted, I'm a hard ass when it comes to bullies. I don't care how they get to be like they are, I just abhor the fact they're bullies."

CHAPTER 29

Fearing the worst, Hank took Ted's call. He was stupefied and stopped pacing when he heard Ted ask him for lunch—this time not at a restaurant but to his home. Hank had never been there, and wasn't quite sure where they lived.

Finally finding power of speech he said, "Did I just hear you right, Ted? You're inviting me to lunch with Libby and you at your place."

Ted couldn't help but laugh at Hank's reaction.

"I know, it's kinda surprising to me too, and Libby doesn't know what to make of it either. Hank, I just thought I wanted the chance to finish what we started in Bus Horrigan's the day of the accident."

"Ted, I hope you don't feel like you owe me somethin' for what I did that day. Anybody woulda," he said.

"Yeah, but the fact is *you did*. I admit I was surprised," said Ted.

"Horseshit, Ted. You weren't even aware I did it, you were so far out of it."

"You're right, Hank, I was out of it. I just want to get off my chest what I was going to say then, okay?"

Hank rather reluctantly agreed to the invitation, got the directions and planned on it two days from now.

This is nuts. What the hell could he possibly be up to? Hank couldn't help wonder if Ted had something more than an olive branch up his sleeve.

When Hank told Rance Butler about it he was taken aback by his reaction.

"Hank, why the hell can't you see the man just wants to thank you? Why do you immediately suspect some sinister motive?"

"Cause that's what I'd be doing," said Hank.

Shaking his head Rance said, "Yeah, you probably would." Hank looked startled at this comment and began to fidget with his prized ring as Rance continued. "You have nothing to fear from Ted Reynolds. He's won every encounter you two have ever had. You're the one who wants to get even."

"I believe that's enough outta you, dip-shit."

***

Ted was more nervous than Libby had ever seen him. He kept checking the table outside, making sure the umbrella was positioned properly to block the sun for the third time.

"Ted, relax. It's just a guy you really don't like coming, not the pope."

"I know it's nuts, but I just want this to go well. If it doesn't I'll feel stupid."

When Hank arrived Ted showed him in and Libby joined them in the entryway. Everyone shook hands and they went into the living room. Hank noticed Libby not in the expected predatory way but he noticed she was favoring her left leg more so than the right. On the whole he was glad to see she didn't appear to be in any pain.

"I couldn't help but notice you're recovering remarkably well, Libby. Glad to see it," said Hank.

"Thank you, Hank, I've been lucky. Ted says I must be part cat for the way I'm on my feet. If that's true, I don't need to go through eight more of these things."

"Yeah," Hank said chuckling. "Nine lives, I get it."

"Hank, I want to thank you for what you did for Ted. It was very kind and helpful and we appreciate it."

"Libby, as I told Ted, it was a scary moment and I didn't think Ted should drive. I just did what everyone in that position would do."

"Would you like the dollar tour of the house?" she asked.

Hank weighed his options as he chewed his lip, not immediately responding. He glanced at everyone, figured she wanted to show it off, so he agreed to take the damn tour—as if he gave a rat's ass about their living conditions.

They ended the tour at what Libby said was the empty study—which to Hank's eye was vaguely familiar and full of furniture, office equipment and papers.

"What an interesting room," said a complimentary Hank.

"It should be," said Ted, "it's as close to his study as I could get it. Just a bit bigger here and there," said Ted.

"Whose?" asked Hank.

"Mark Twain," said Ted.

Hank started to laugh with more glee than Ted would have thought possible. Soon all three were laughing with only one knowing why.

"I thought you said E-M-P-T-Y study... not MT. I couldn't figure out with all the stuff in here why you'd call it 'empty.' Of course, it's familiar, but I've never been inside the actual study. Just seen it on the campus."

Ted and Libby laughed again, even harder for the knowing why.

"We're eating in here if that's all right," said Libby.

"Okay, sure."

While they were eating petite filets and macaroni salad with iced tea, Ted said, "Hank I want you to know that I never did anything under-handed in any of the business dealings in which we've been in competition. Never bribed, snuck looks at rival bids, played any games, or used tricks to gain an advantage."

"I never said you did. At least not to anyone else. There were a few deals I knew I had the best offer and still lost, though. Rance Butler says it's because people like you better'n me."

Hank averted his eyes from both of them. Libby felt he looked sad and lonely. At this moment she felt sorry for him... she got over it quickly though.

"Who knows how these things are really decided? I just wanted to tell you face to face that I never cheated you in any way."

"Okay, I believe you, Ted."

"Hank, I just want to show you I'm serious about this, want you to hear what I'm doing here, want you to know why I'm doing it. Then I want you to think about it, and consider joining me and Libby in the thing, okay?"

Hank was speechless. He sat fingering his diamond and onyx ring at a rapid pace, round and round his finger it twirled. He looked at Libby and Ted then shook his head. It seemed as if he lost his ability to speak.

Finally he uttered, barely audible, "Why are you doing this? You feelin' sorry for me, or what?"

The hard edge in Hank's tone raised the hair on Ted's neck, but he silently talked down the urge to punch the son-of-a-bitch in the face... hard.

I knew this wouldn't be easy. *Why do I want to offer this prick anything?* wondered Ted.

That's what he thought, what he said was, "Hank, I don't get it. I'm not trying to pull a fast one, and you don't need my help. I just thought it might be a good deal for both of us. I never believed I was the sharpest tool on the marquee so I thought with a project of this size... I... we... could use some extra knowledge. Don't make me regret this, please."

Hank was stunned and amazed. A man he believed to be his sworn enemy was offering him something. He didn't know exactly what, but nobody had ever offered him anything in his entire life. Not his parents, brother, sister, teachers, nobody, no how. He was always the one who made the offer, never the recipient. Why the hell were they doing this? Nobody is this altruistic, or are they just nut jobs?

"Ted, I've never been offered something for nothin' in my life."

"Whoa, hold on, Hank. I'm not offering something for nothing. I expect something... you and your expertise are what I need and want."

"Are you asking me to buy in?"

"Hank, I don't know how to make in any plainer. Do I need to speak slower or what?"

Hank was still flummoxed, he didn't appreciate 'the speak' slower comment, but oddly it didn't set him off on a temper tantrum like it normally would. *What the hell is going on here?*

Ted's patience was waning. It felt like he was dealing with a recalcitrant child. Part of him wanted to take Hank by the scruff of the neck and shake some sense into him.

Instead Ted reached deep into his soul and said, "Hank, I need your help. If you didn't exist I would still need help. You, however, do exist, and I would be a fool to bypass using your abilities because of some silly feud I never really was a part of except in your mind. Now will you or won't you join me in this deal or what?"

"How the hell do I know, Ted? You haven't told what the damn deal is."

"You're right I'm kinda asking you to buy a pig in a poke, so here's the deal. We looked at a property in Big Flats, as you know. Our plan was to build an amusement park similar to the old Eldrige Park."

"I was going to create a planned community on that land," said Hank with an edge to his voice.

"I know, I spoke to Steve Greatsinger and he told me my bid was accepted. But I'm not going to put the park there. What I'm proposing is we—you and I—go ahead with your small planned community idea, what do ya think of that?"

Hank, got up and started his ring fingering routine, and began to pace about the room.

"I admit it sounds interesting but I can't get over why me? I've been a pain in your ass forever. The only person who's been halfway decent with me is Rance Butler. The only reason for him is I took the blame for something he did in school when we were kids. I've never done squat for you."

"Goddamnit, Hank. Why does it have to be *quid pro quo* in everything you do? Can't people do each other a good turn occasionally?"

"Not been my experience. I don't do nice things for people, and people never do me any favors unless they want something."

"You just mentioned Butler. What's he want?"

"I don't know, he hasn't told me yet. But I'm expectin' it."

"You're hopeless. Do we get together on this, Hank?"

"Probably not." Hank sat down and looked a bit forlorn as if he'd lost his best friend or just realized he never had one to lose.

Ted looked at the man in front of him and felt bad for him. He realized this reclamation project was going to be harder to accomplish than anticipated, or not at all possible.

"What are you and your buddy McCraw doing around here?"

At first Ted didn't get it. "Who's McCraw?"

"C'mon, don't be cute. The guy I saw you in Morretti's with. The guy tryin' to buy the Holding Point land."

"You mean Dru McKenna?"

"Whatever," Hank dismissively answered.

"Hank, you are a bona fide beauty. Dru and I are working another project, and in case you didn't get the memo, the court ruled against you about your right-of-way gambit. That game is over. So what about the Big Flats deal? One last time, in or out? I'm outta patience."

"Lemme think about it, okay?"

Ted could not believe what he heard. It stopped him dead in his mental tracks. He couldn't fathom the pain Hank must have been afflicted with to cause him to work so hard at being an asshole.

"Sure, but let me know soon, okay?"

Hank got up and left without shaking hands.

"Poor thing, he must have been totally ignored his whole life," said Libby.

Ted thought about it the rest of the night.

* * *

Hank drove the back way to Harris Hill and parked near an old abandoned glider field. He reflected on what just happened, trying to figure out why Ted seemed to want to be friends, or friendly, or friend-ish. *Yeah, friend-ish,* he thought. *But why me?*

Hank realized nobody ever liked him. And his giant secret was, it killed him, every day.

CHAPTER 30

Ivor and Riley returned from the morning patrol around the 'hood. Upon seeing me and Hannah at the coffee station Riley bounded up and gave us each a morning chomp and an opportunity to rub his back.

"The boy does know how to get what he wants," said Hannah.

"He's my boy, after all," I said with a sly wink at Hannah. She just shook her head, poured coffee and headed to her office.

The day was to be devoted entirely to promotional plans for the new amusement/baseball openings. The weather for this early spring had been more pleasant than expected. Therefore, we were way ahead of construction schedule. Keeping the lid on this thing was going to be hard. We needed to restrict news reports until the All-Star game in July.

"Dru, come in here. I need you," Hannah yelled.

"Sounds like you just invented the telephone," he said.

"Huh?" she asked.

"It's the first thing Alexander Graham Bell, or Don Ameche, said to his assistant, Watson."

"Geez, the stuff you know. I just had an idea. We don't have to hide the Iroquois Amusement Park. We can announce it now or soon and not mention the baseball part of the deal. Whatcha think?"

"What the hell is Iroquois Park?" I asked with, what I'm sure, was a bewildered expression, which made Hannah snort. "The look on your face is priceless. 'Out of the mouths of babes' has struck again. Ted's daughter's class is learning about the Five Nations history in school, and she got all het up about Indian lore especially in the area. She asked her mom what she thought of Iroquois Park for the name instead of Eldridge 2.0."

Stunned I said, "I guess security is shot in the ass, huh? I mean if one kid knows a secret, I bet all her friends and their families know. Basically in two days the whole town knows, right?"

"Ye of so little faith. Libby swore her daughter to secrecy and she says it'll stick."

"Uh huh, we'll see."

"Even if it's out there, we're not gonna show it to anybody. Baseball's still secure," said Hannah.

"Okay, but it would be easier to keep a lid on the baseball part until the MLB announcement in October if that doesn't happen. I'll have to run it by Bill Lattimore. I guess if the town knows about the amusement side it could quell curiosity. It's only a couple of months until the World Series. I'll call Bill today."

And I did. As suspected we could go ahead with the amusement announcement. Bill agreed it was a good idea to hide something in plain sight. I thought of something else, and put in a call to Ivor.

"Ivor, put your security consultant hat on. How hard will it be to bring in very tall pines to shield the baseball stadium from sight? We're gonna open the amusement section a couple of months ahead of the World Series and want to hide it from incoming patrons.

"Not hard but expensive. If you want to foot the bill, it's a good idea," said Ivor.

"Okay, set it up ASAP. And thanks."

I called Ted and caught him up on Hannah's idea, Ivor's plan and MLB acceptance. In turn I was filled in on the Hank Lewis situation.

"Let me get this straight. You were gonna essentially give the rat bastard the Big Flats land for the planned community project?"

"Not exactly. We were to be partners but he turned his nose up at the whole deal and walked away. Now I think eventually I'll develop Columbia, Maryland 2.0 myself. Screw him. I was gonna be partners by letting him do the majority of the work in lieu of a buy in."

"What does he think you'll be doing instead of working with him?"

"I told him about the amusement park idea so he knows you and I will be working together on it."

"No mention about baseball?"

"None."

"You know when he finds out about the baseball aspect he's gonna flip out, right?"

"I don't think so. You shoulda seen how he acted when I introduced the whole thing to him. He kept asking why I was doing this, over and over."

"Leopards, my friend. He's going to think you tricked him again when he finds out your ploy to keep him away from somethin' so much bigger than a few houses, Ted."

"I'm thinking out loud now, but I'm backing down on my rant. I still think I can reach the guy," said Ted more hopeful than realistic.

"You are something, my friend, and I admire you for it. Me, I'd punch the SOB into the middle of next week."

"I know it's a long shot, and maybe initially he keeps up the jerk persona, but when I show him the economic sense of it I'll win him over, just wait."

"I hope you're right, I really do. I doubt it, but I do hope you win him over," I said.

The next few days were spent putting our heads together on the promotion of Iroquois Park. We made lists of entertainers to feature, celebrities to invite including Iroquois Nation reps and other festivities. Across-country race for local high schools, an area band competition as well as a singing competition, came to the fore. With all that, Hannah still felt something was missing. She knew there was an idea circling but not ready to land.

She assumed the position of a Law of Attraction advocate and with thumbs circling to touch her middle fingers she intoned, "Please give me the blockbuster idea I need."

I had been working in her office, heard her and asked, "Whadja say, hon?"

"Just practicing the art of ask and it is given."

"Good idea. Lemme know when you get it," I said.

In the afternoon we decided to return to Keuka. The next day, right after breakfast we hit the road in separate cars.

Morning dawned in a downpour. The rain-laden clouds, tired of carrying their burden, let loose. The stark panorama of the now sodden hills, populated by forlorn trees, droopy, and cold made the trip dreary instead of enjoyable.

I was thinking about the conversation Hannah and I had the previous night. I told Hannah about Ted's overture to Hank and my skepticism.

"Dru, I trust Ted's judgment. I don't know him well, but somehow, I trust him," she said.

"Oh, I trust Ted too, it's Henry Wallbanger whom I don't trust as far as I can throw my voice."

"I didn't know you were a ventriloquist."

"I'm not."

"Oh."

* * *

Hank was in his opulent office mulling over Ted's offer. "He's up to something, I just know it," he said to Rance Butler.

Butler was witness to many of Hank's rants over the years, and never understood what drove him to hang around the guy. Oh sure, Hank took the blame for him in a schoolhouse misunderstanding, but it wasn't like Hank saved his life or somethin'. Maybe it was the curiosity of the thing. Like looking inside of a precision Rolex to see what made it tick. Or maybe trying to understand what a man with every material thing available to him would be so consumed by envy to the point of being unable to count any of his blessings, let alone all of them.

"Why do you always look for the worst in people, Hank?"

"Simple. I always find it."

"What're you gonna do?"

"I think I'll accept the offer, keep my eyes open, and see what he's got up his sleeve."

"Good idea, but it's probably only his arm."

Libby and her crew of builders were making huge strides. One entire side of the midway amusement booths were erected and work was beginning on the other side of the meandering street. The bandstands were completed, and the mild weather allowed for foundation pouring for the roller coaster, carousel and bumper car attractions.

Hannah promised to drop by to see it herself and she did just that. "Wow, Libby, you're humming right along. I'm impressed," said Hannah.

"Me too, Jack and these guys are great. I really don't have to do any bossing. I show 'em the plans, and boom it comes alive. Their experience shows."

"Libby, what's your take on the Hank situation?"

"I'm not as sure as Ted seems to be, but if Ted can weather Hank's insecurities he may turn the man's life around. If he can't, he may kill 'im. Hank is a very exasperating individual."

"Dru doesn't think it'll work, but mainly because—among Dru's many attributes—patience is *not* numbered among them," said Hannah.

"We'll have to see. Dru's main concern is if Hank finds out about the baseball part, he's afraid of what he'll do to get even."

"Ted's worried about that too. I don't know what Hank could do, but he's a step away from being one of the most vindictive people on the planet. It could go very badly."

"Okay, it looks like you have control of your end, now I've got to finish the promotion stuff. I'm about halfway there," said Hannah.

Hannah decided to drive up to Keuka via the back way over the hill through Watkins. She recalled taking this scenic route with Justin and Kimberley.

The trees were all leaved up and flowers were blooming. The pastoral scenery was breathtaking. The early morning's precip encouraged the blooms to emerge. Today, like the rest of the early spring everywhere, the area was coming alive.

Serendipity is a wonderful event. It's responsible for so many great achievements, it's always welcomed. It was now. While thinking of Justin and Kimberley, and therefore National Motors, a serendipitous thought barged into her Hannah's imagination, which solved her big promotional challenge.

CHAPTER 31

When I arrived at the M/T office, I called Adair Meyers to reveal the total scope of the project. I hadn't mentioned the amusement park side of things before.

"I didn't tell you about it before because it wasn't a sure thing."

"And now it is?" she asked. She was silent for only a second then added, "This is a horse of a different color, isn't it?"

"It is, but what we're thinking is both attractions will enhance the other symbiotically. Attendees of the ballgame will file away the amusement attractions they see coming into the stadium, to be checked out in the future. The parking areas are deliberately routed past both the stadium and the park, so they are visible to both sets of patrons."

"Who thought that up?" asked Adair.

"My wife Hannah, actually. Whatcha think of the idea?" I asked.

"In a word, brilliant. Your wife must be congratulated, as you must be also for listening to her."

"Yes, ma'am, I think so too. It's not the first time." I didn't mention the threat I feared from Hank Lewis mainly because I hoped it wouldn't be necessary.

My next call was to Bill Lattimore, "Bill, I want to bring you up to date on our project. The stadium field has been dug out, the plans finalized for the start of construction, and weather looks promising."

"How's your amusement park plan going?" asked Bill.

"That's where it might get a little tricky."

"Why don't I like the sound of that?"

"Easy, Bill, I'm a bit of a mother hen when it comes to my projects. It seems Ted has a nemesis that is not likely to be pleased by any of this."

"Why not?"

"It goes back a long time but most recently it was this guy we beat out for the land," I said.

"What was his idea?"

"As near as we can figure he wanted to build a planned community, or so he says. Ted's beat him out of every project they've gone head to head on and the guy wants to get even. The latest episode of this saga started when Ted asked me in for the baseball end. He showed me two parcels of land. The one we're using and another in Big Flats, New York.

Bill Lattimore was standing now and began to pace about the office, he wasn't thrilled with what he was being told but did not interrupt.

"I advised Ted to put a bid in on the Big Flats project as a red herring to the nemesis."

"What's this guy's name?"

"Henry Lewis. We thought when Hank heard about this bid in Big Flats he would stick his nose in the tent and try to snatch it away, and that would keep him out of our hair. Hank had no idea of Ted's baseball plans. I advised Ted to think about letting Hank outbid him in Big Flats. If it didn't work, we'd invite him to join Ted in the planned community idea..."

Interrupting Bill asked, "Why would you do that?"

"Look at it this way, it's better to have an enemy inside pissing out of the tent than an enemy outside pissing in."

Bill chuckled, "I see what you mean. Where does everything stand now?"

"Hank's mulling over Ted's offer."

"Dru, I detect you're concerned about all this, am I correct?"

"A little. It bothers me to have Hank this close to finding out about the park and baseball. I'm afraid how he'll react. We believe

Hank is the thorn among all us roses. He might feel betrayed and seek revenge."

"Violence?"

"Not exactly sure, but when he found out about the Holding Point land he snapped up other worthless property to impede access. We filed an injunction which was ruled in our favor to put an end to it."

"Didn't he find out what was happening then?"

"No, we haven't told anybody what the plan is."

"So, this is just a heads up kind of call, huh?"

"Yeah, I have a number of strong contacts to help if it gets messy, but I thought maybe you'd have a few more."

"Okay, just let me know. By the way, or BTW as my grandson says, did you tell Adair Meyers about this?"

"Not about Lewis. I filled her in on the amusement park concept. Do you think we should discuss Lewis with her?"

"Only if the need arises."

With all bases covered in New York, we focused on the job site and awaited Hank's next move.

The site prep was mostly done, the stadium dirt moved to appropriate places. New dirt was brought in to complete the site work and the trails as construction continued. Thus far there's no word from Hank.

Hannah spoke with Justin Powell and asked how sales were going, and was thrilled to hear National Motors had not only set a record for new car first year sales, but also for company all-time one year sales. She was very pleased to receive such positive news which made the reason she called infinitely easier.

"Justin, has Kimberley told you what our friend Libby is up to in New York?" Hannah said.

"Something about baseball, right? You guys are using our cottage while you help, huh? "

"You got it. It turns out Dru worked his magic..."

Interrupting, Justin said, "So when's the first game?"

"I see you remember how effective Dru is. Right now we're building the new stadium and trying to recapture the flavor of the old amusement park in the area."

"Eldridge?" he asked.

"We're not using the Eldridge name since it still exists, although in a vastly diminished state."

"I knew it was still there. I thought perhaps you bought it."

"No, what we did buy was an enormous plot of land from the college, out by the Domes, so we had tons of room. Libby thought recreating the old feel of Eldrige in its heyday would be cool."

"Very cool, we all had great times there. What about Dunn Field, why aren't you using it?"

"Too costly to bring it up to MLB standards, and the location limits the attractiveness of game attendance to area visitors."

"Yeah, I remember the stadium was lacking. It was a big factor of why they lost the original Pioneers, or at least Baltimore's affiliation. What can we do to help?"

"This is a big favor, maybe I should get Kimberley to run interference for me."

"C'mon, Hannah, after what you and Dru did for this company, Kimberley and me. How many cars do you need?"

"Wow! What, are you clairvoyant or somethin'," she said only semi-amazed. Justin was semi-smart his own self.

"What else could it be? I haven't touched a baseball for a while, so I'm sure first pitch duty is out?"

"We were hoping for an Eagle and a Falconeer to give away in a promotional event."

"What are the team colors?"

"We don't know yet. One of the major promotions is to name the team and colors."

"Yikes, here comes the Chartreuse-Strawberry Posse," he said.

"No, fool, those are the cheerleaders."

After both had a good chuckle she continued, "You know how it goes. We'll pick out the one we like best, and there's your winner."

"What if ten submit the same name? We give ten cars?"

"Of course, what would be unfair about it?"

"You mean other than the shaky car company losing its shirt?"

"Yeah, you mean the record setting one you were bragging about a few minutes ago?"

"One in the same. Let me know when and you get four cars in the color of your choosing, make it five, okay?"

"Oh, Justin, thank you and thank Kimberley."

"Hold on, she's right here and wants to say hi."

I was talking to Ted about the attraction he had for bringing baseball back. "How did you decide to do something that has such a history of failure?"

"I grew up loving baseball. Dad started taking me to games when I was six or seven. We had a concrete wall in front of our house which served as a dike to keep the river from flooding into the neighborhood. Dad used to draw a chalk strike zone on the wall and I pitched to it every day."

"Didn't the ball ever go over the wall?" I asked.

"All the time. I wasn't supposed to go over the wall to get it but if I wanted to get the ball back I had to. Lost a good many balls that way. Couldn't find 'em in the weeds."

I smiled, "They say when you die all secrets are revealed."

Ted said, "What I want to know is who was behind Lincoln's and Kennedy's assassinations? Why do liberals believe socialism can work when it's failed everywhere it's ever been tried? Where do lost golf balls go? I get balls in the water and off-course property but I've lost 'em in the trees, the rough, even in the fairway. Where the hell are the rest of 'em? But most of all where the hell did those baseballs go?"

"So that's how the spark was kindled?"

"Yeah, I suppose I just loved the game, played it a long time."

"Did you want to turn pro?" I asked.

"Sure, I was pretty good until I tore muscles in my back. I was a pretty fair hitter but pitching's where I shined. Anyway, when I got financially secure I got this crazy idea to do something to help the area economically and give it an opportunity to have some fun. This place has been good to us and it's kinda my way of reaching back and saying thank you."

I was struck by how relaxed and composed Ted seemed. I often saw hyper activity in driven men, which caused them to lose focus on the goal and spin off onto the path of catastrophic failure ending in ruin. As I watched Ted sitting calm, cool and collected I was sure it wouldn't happen to him.

"I must say I'm surprised you never mentioned makin' money."

"Well sure, I want it to be successful and if we do it right the money will be there. But only if we do it right."

"Any word from Hank?"

"Dru, I get the sense everything I said went in one ear and ricocheted off his stone mind and bounced right back out. But not all of it, I think he kept the idea for himself to use later, somehow." Even though relaxed, Ted seemed to be waiting for the sword of Damocles to drop.

I pondered then said, "Call 'im again. Follow up, push him."

"I had the same thought this morning."

"Two great minds," I said.

"With but a single thought. Hope that doesn't mean we're operating with one brain between us," finished Ted.

"Make the call, Ted." He dialed from his cell and it went immediately to voicemail. I reached into my pocket and pulled out a phone,."Use this. It's what cops call a burner. Hank won't know who it is in case he's screening calls."

Ted accepted the phone and said, "Which he probably is." He dialed and put it on speaker.

"Who the hell is this?" answered an irascible voice.

"It's me, Hank. Ted.

"I didn't recognize the number," said Hank.

"Yeah my cell's dead, I borrowed this one. How you doin'? I was hopin' to hear back from you."

A long tense silence followed. Ted said, "Hank, can you hear me?"

"Yeah, Ted, I hear you. Why are you calling?"

I couldn't believe Hank's retractable attitude. He seemed genuinely touched when Ted invited him to join the project.

Listening to Ted's end I could tell he was mystified. Now, I wonder, *what in hell happened?*

"Hank, what's goin' on? The other day when we talked you acted like you were pleased about this deal. What's changed?"

"Ted, I can't buy your somethin' for nothing offer. Nobody's ever included me in anything. Not ever. Family, so-called friends, nobody ever. Then you come along, after burying me in every deal we've fought over, and offer to be partners. Let bygones and all that shit. Well, I'm not buying it. Nor am I stupid. You want me out of the way for some reason. Hold me closer. Yeah I read the Art of War too. But I'm not fallin' for it, ya got me?"

Ted rose and looked as if throwing the phone through the window was a good idea, but instead said, "Sorry I bothered you, Henry. Goodbye."

Ted stood up, looking like he wanted to hurl something, anything. So deep into his Hank induced funk he jerked when I stood up, looking ready to attack.

"Whoa, hold on, big guy. Didn't mean to scare ya," I said.

"Sorry, Dru. It's just Henry the Hump."

"I can see how he could get you revved up." We spent a few minutes discussing how our clever plan fizzled.

"Ya know, you have to give the devil his due. Hank really is astute. He nailed it. He may not be sure, but he's got the gist of us keeping him away from something. He doesn't know it's baseball, at least not yet."

"When he starts putting his spies on it he'll eventually come up with the answer," said Ted.

"Here's what he's gonna do. In the next couple of days he'll call and accept your offer," I said.

"The camel's nose will be in the tent."

"I'll bet it'll be a Wednesday."

"Why Wednesday, Dru?"

"Think about it."

I filled Ted in on Hannah's ideas, and we decided how to integrate the plans with the scheduled announcement at the World Series in October. At that point she'll turn her creative horses loose on the colors and name promotions.

"I just stopped by on my way to the golf course, to see if you wanted to play."

"Not today, Emily has a lacrosse game this afternoon, so I'll take a rain check. Besides I'm not much of a player, but you have a good round."

I went over to Binghamton to play En-Joie Golf Course. This public course had hosted a PGA tournament for a number of years. It was the smallest market tour stop on the PGA schedule and was very successful. Local Elmiran, Joey Sindelar—now on the Senior Tour—won it twice. Mike Hulbert, another Elmiran, also won it. One of Joey's wins featured a hole in one. A Senior Tour event was now the annual pro tournament in the immediate area.

Since it was open to the public, it was easy to get on and I enjoyed it immensely. I shot three over seventy-five and marveled at the way the senior tour guys torched the course, shooting in the low sixties.

Libby and her crews were plowing ahead of schedule and everything was flowing smoothly, so far. Hannah's plans were ahead of their JIT schedule—*just in time*. All the pieces of a very intricate puzzle were fitting together in perfect order. There were some unexpected delays due to manpower issues and equipment problems but they weren't impossible to overcome. An event planned for today was switched to some other day without much hassle. Stuff like this was all part of preparing for an event, any event, you name the event they never run smoothly.

One night a few weeks later, Hannah heard me get up at two a.m. I headed out to the deck and she followed a few minutes later.

"What's got you worried, hon?"

Turning around but not startled, I answered, "I wish I knew. Just one of my random concerns. I can't explain it, nor put it to rest."

We hung out on the deck, and talked about my worrisome night.

"You'll figure it out, you always do."

"What if this time I can't?" I asked.

"Thomas Corbett McKenna IV, buck up. No wallowing here, I won't have it." Eventually we went back to bed, got a couple more hours of sleep but the nagging concern was still hovering in my mind when *The Good, the Bad and the Ugly* ringtone harkened. My fears were about to be confirmed.

CHAPTER 32

"It's Bill Lattimore," said Hannah, handing me the phone.

Taking the offered phone I said, "Bill, what is it?"

"I've got some bad news and felt sitting on it would only make it worse," said Bill.

"Oh, boy! I knew something was wrong, I've felt it for a couple of days."

"How? It just happened late last night," said Lattimore.

"It's a long story and I'm not even sure I understand it, let alone be able to explain it. What's happened?"

"Adair Meyers' brother died last night, heart attack they think. Anyway, she just called and told me she can't go through with the deal for the Brooklyn ball club."

"Holy shit! That's awful," I blurted. "Not about the deal, but about Sonny," I backpedaled. "How's Adair doing, how's she feel?"

"As you can imagine she's crushed. They were extremely close," said Bill.

"Is there anything we can do?"

"Dru, I have no idea. You might want to call her and find out yourself. She might like to hear from you guys."

"Thanks, Bill, I'll do that very thing."

"I'm sure this is a shock to you as well. Let me fill you in on what Adair told me. It seems the baseball idea was mostly Sonny's and she just went along because he wanted it so."

"But I thought *she* was the spearhead of this," I said.

"She was looking forward to it because she loved her brother. Sonny was planning to remove himself from the real estate side of their empire, and Adair was going to assume a larger role there. She still wants to do that, but can't do both alone. So she's dropping the baseball plans."

"Wow, or holy shit, or whatever you're supposed to say. I'm speechless."

I sat down on the top step of the deck, visibly shaken. Hannah sat beside me and put her arm around my waist, waiting patiently to hear what was obviously wrong.

It brought back memories of two calls I received during the work on the National Motors project two years ago. Both calls involved unexpected deaths, and threw monkey wrenches into our plans. They also cost us dearly on a personal level.

"Hannah, one of these days I'm gonna learn not to answer this damn thing." I looked down at the phone as if it were a venomous snake, then threw it against the stone patio fireplace.

"Well, I guess we'll be shopping for a new phone, huh?" said Hannah.

"I don't think so. If I don't have one they can't get to me."

Hannah realized I was much more upset than she would've expected. She gently touched my face and sat close, not saying a word.

Finally, I stood up, looked down at the ruined phone and said, "Yeah, you're right, let's go get another one."

On the way to the mall I went over the things I had to do immediately. First, Ted had to be told. Second, we had to determine the feasibility of moving forward, with or without baseball, with the amusement park. And third, I had to figure out how to get out of the whole project, or at the least cost, if we decide to pull the plug. At this point I resolved to not let this whole deal fall apart.

"I don't know how, but we're gonna get this done," I mumbled with more resolve than feasible.

"Yes, dear," said Hannah.

"You didn't hear me. You couldn't have."

"As if I need you to tell me what you're thinking."

I shook my head and thought, *Witch!* But my thought was interrupted.

"Don't you dare call me a witch, Dru McKenna!"

I smiled and said, "Yes, dear."

With my new phone all reprogrammed and ready to go I called Ted to tell him we were on our way.

When we arrived, a note on the door sent us around to the pool area.

"Hey guys, welcome back to Casa Reynolds and our oasis," said Ted. As if on cue, Libby came out carrying iced tea and grilled chicken salads.

"Hi guys, dig in," said Libby.

Hannah looked at me with great intensity and mouthed the words, "Not now."

I took the hint, nodded and ate the food, chit chatting until we finished.

"Okay Dru, what's up?" asked Ted.

I bought some thinking time by looking down at my shoes, as if a simple painless way of dropping the bomb would be lying there to help me. It wasn't.

I looked at Ted and said, "I got a call from Bill Lattimore."

"Oh boy, judging by the expression on your face this can't be good. Lay it on me."

I reprised the story and watched Ted slowly rise from the table and walk to the edge of the pool.

He paused at the edge. Then he stepped in, clothes and all.

Startled, to say the least, we all jumped up and ran to the edge of the pool.

Before any of us could jump to his rescue, Ted surfaced.

"I always wanted to do that," he spit out some pool water and pushed the hair back from his eyes. "Seemed like the perfect time."

"Honey, are you okay?" asked Libby, grabbing a beach towel from the back of a nearby deck chair.

"Okay? I don't know. I'm numb, I know that. I'm facing ruin nostril to toe nail, it's that complete. I know that. But okay, I don't know that."

I reached out a hand and helped pull Ted out of the water.

"I'll change in the cabana, be just a minute," said Ted, taking the proffered towel from Libby.

Returning with trunks and a navy blue T-shirt that said BITE ME! in fluorescent orange, he said, "Alright, fill us in from the beginning," as if jumping fully clothed into the pool had been normal behavior.

Shaking my head, I told the entire scenario.

"Wow! Didn't see that coming. I'm dead meat if this craters now. Way beyond extended. I guess all Hank had to do to win was sit tight."

"Hold on, Ted. Dru and I have been in the soup before and collectively we'll think of somethin'," said Hannah. After all, we're clever and resourceful people," said Hannah, for about the bazillionth time.

We spent the rest of the day mulling various aspects of our fix but in the end we were still up a tree.

Sleep did not come easy for any of us that night. The new day didn't hold much promise either. For my part I sat down on the dock looking for Daisy's green light. I recalled a memory from early childhood of a movie about *The Great Gatsby*. I thought it was a biography. It was set in my grandfather's heyday, and knowing that, I asked him if he knew Gatsby.

In a real sense I now felt like Gatsby might have. You create a dream and have it almost in your grasp only to see it slip away.

I felt a tangible pain in my gut. Letting down Ted and Libby, not to mention Hannah was unthinkable. I vowed audibly not to fail them.

It was times like these where my strength of will shines its brightest, I thought.

Yes, I was confident, yes I'd done it before, many times to greater and lesser extents, but I wasn't always totally sure. What I was sure of was the fact quitting was not an option. Neither was failure. *A dosage of luck wouldn't hurt either.*

At breakfast on the dock I said to Hannah, "I think I'll call Lattimore and see if he has any ideas. Right now I don't have a clue."

The call to Bill brought both consternation and relief.

"Dru, glad you called, I've got more news. I'm leaving my position at MLB at the end of the year."

Boy, the hits they just keep on comin', I thought.

"Why would you do that?"

"Easy, big guy. I'm too young to retire but too old to keep up with the travel requirements of this job."

I stood up and began pacing about the deck, worry etching frown lines I'm sure Hannah could see.

"Well, isn't this day off and running?" I replied.

"I've got more news," said Bill.

"So far I'm not all that pleased with what you've reported, Mr. Cronkite. Is this gonna be good or bad?"

"That's up in the air, but I'm buying the team from Adair. I'd like you to join me."

I looked at Hannah with what I'm sure was a peculiar look, mainly because that's how I felt... peculiar.

I said, "Bill, let me call you right back," and hung up. I sat down and put my head in my hands.

Looking up I said to Hannah, "You're not going to believe this. Bill just asked me to join forces with him to buy the Brooklyn team from Adair."

"She's really selling?"

"Yeah, turns out the whole baseball thing was her brother's idea. She's going to oversee the real estate business. Bill is resigning from MLB to become an owner and asked me to join him."

"Holy cow, some turn of events, huh? What're you gonna do, are you interested in running a team?"

"Slow down, lady. One question at a time. I'm more flattered than interested. After all I just met Bill at the beginning of this project, and it's not even my project really," I said. The idea of becoming really involved in the running of a major league team, wow. I had never featured becoming an owner and play a role in running a team, after all, what the hell did I know about it?

The fact Bill was actually soliciting my participation was flattering, to say the least. To say the most it was unthinkable, or was it?

I had to think about it for a while. Time's up I saw, I thought, I saw, no way could I do this. I pictured what each day would entail and I blanched at the notion. Baking cookies for Mrs. Fields would be more diversely appealing or maybe on a par. In any event I came quickly to my senses and realized the actuality would drive me nuts.

"My, my, Mr. Humble. Dru, you cast a pretty wide shadow you know. Did you ever Google yourself? It's four pages, so far."

"No, I never Googled myself, would it hurt?"

"Droll, very droll, you didn't answer, aren't you the least bit curious?"

"Not really. I know all about myself and don't give a fig about what Google has to say about me."

"Again, what about running a baseball team? Think about it, wouldn't it be fun?"

"I like lending a hand... rebuilding... creating a solution for struggling companies. But I never thought about running anything," I said. I rubbed my chin as I contemplated briefly what running a baseball team would be like. What if this is an overture by Bill to elicit my financial participation in the club?

Rumination finished I said, "I better call Bill back."

Bill Lattimore answered, and I thanked him for the offer but explained I was helping Ted Reynolds, and I'd rather consult with companies in need of help than run one. Having said this I wondered if this turn of events would turn out to harm Ted.

"Bill, does this ownership change affect the deal with Elmira for a Double-A League team?"

"Not at all," replied Bill. "I assume you're still involved with it, so we'll be happy to continue on," said Bill.

"That sound you heard was a sigh of relief," I said. We chatted a bit, I wished Bill luck and he did the same.

Chapter 33

The day before the announcement in New York, Henry Lewis was pacing around his lair like a lion on the prowl for prey. Tired of it he went to his desk to think. Hank leaned back in his throne-like office chair and said to himself out loud, "What the hell is he up to?"

'Face value' was meant for stocks or money. Not people's word. He didn't take Ted's words at face value any more than he believed anybody else's. No, he was sure there was a game going on. He just didn't know what it was yet.

Picking up his cell he bellowed, "Butler, get your ass over here, right now!"

Butler couldn't respond yay or nay because Hank had already hung up.

An hour later, Rance Butler trudged into Hank's office.

"Took your time, I see," said Hank.

"Yeah, I was in Watkins, Henry."

"Didn't I tell you about calling me Henry? The name is Hank, I won't tell you again," said Hank for the bazillionth time.

Rance Butler got a cold look on his face, squinty eyes, and his pursed mouth looked as if it had been formed by a stiletto on a victim of a knife fight. Hank had not seen this expression from Butler before.

"Go pound sand up your ass, Hen-RY. I'm not your lackey, serf, gopher, your nothin', get it? If you want something from me, ask politely or else shove it. I'm leavin'."

"Jesus Christ, Rance, don't be so goddamned touchy. I'm in a bind and I need your help."

"You have a funny way of askin' for it, don't ya think?"

"C'mon, you know it's just my way. Lighten up." Hank was taken aback by the forcefulness of Butler's words.

"Look, this Reynolds deal has really got me bugged. He offered me a part of it for some reason. Now why would he ever do that?"

"Beats the hell outta me. Wait a minute, have you checked with the city and county records offices? You know, anything he's doing would have to have land in it, right?" said Rance.

"Goddamn it, why didn't I think of that? Of course. While I'm at it I'll check out McKenna, too. I know about the Holding Point purchase, but he'll have to have permits and such to develop it. Let's go, we're burnin' daylight."

"Is that a request, Hank?"

"Yeah, yeah, c'mon, let's get a move on."

Rance knew it was as much as he could expect from Hank but at least he'd stood up to 'im. In a curious way he felt sorry for Hank Lewis. He looked around the office and despite all the trappings of success with which he surrounded himself, Hank seemed to be a failed human being, and what's more, he knew it.

The trip was no waste of time. The two men learned the scope of the Holding Point project went beyond the known amusement park and riding area. What they didn't know of was the baseball park plans. They didn't have a clue as to the team, especially since nobody had contacted Butler about the Pioneer name for several months. *Come to think of it, it was probably McKenna,* thought Hank.

"I guess they're gonna bring in a team with a new name," said Butler.

"No shit, Sherlock. Who gives a rat's ass about the name? That devious mook Reynolds was just trying to distract me from the Holding Point property. I knew it, I just didn't know why."

"C'mon, Hank, you tried to stop it and couldn't. Maybe you should've accepted Reynolds' offer. Right now you got nothin."

"We'll see Rance, we'll see."

And so they did.

Hank called an acquaintance connected with the Mets, and found out MLB was about to expand and add a Brooklyn team to the National League. Not only was Brooklyn getting back into MLB but Bill Lattimore was to be the owner.

"Got any idea if Elmira has anything to do with it?"

"How the hell did you get a hold of that? Nobody's supposed to know. Yeah, they're gonna be the Double-A franchise. Some high roller is backin' some local who has the hots for baseball. They're gonna announce it tomorrow."

"So now we have it," Hank turned to Rance. "Reynolds has been up to his batting stance in this all along. What can I do to get in on it now?" He looked as if he was on the verge of tears.

Hank couldn't help but think, with all the penance he should have built up from his past actions, if I cry, it may flood the town.

"I just can't catch a break, Rance. Never could."

"Ya shoulda taken Ted up..."

"Shut up, ya hump. Of course I shoulda. Tell me somethin' I don't know."

"I may just have the idea you're lookin' for, Hank."

* * *

"Wow, this is like a roller coaster in our park—we'll call it Mr. McKenna's Wild Ride," cracked Hannah.

I called Ted to give him the good news. He answered anxiously. I ripped the bandage off and quickly brought him up to date. I sensed the anxiety in his voice. When given the situation-report, Ted audibly released the pent up fear he'd been storing. Sounded like a zeppelin with a slow leak.

"Guess that sound was either tension abatement, or you sprung a leak," I said.

"I know, I was really worried," Ted admitted.

I told him of Bill Lattimore's invitation to join in the post-World Series announcement of the MLB expansion and the minor league designated cities. We agreed to meet Bill in New York for the All-Star festivities to plan.

Hannah and Libby would go along and we'd make a long weekend of it. The night before the event, three days before the game, Hannah apparently heard me muttering in my sleep... "What next, what next?" repeatedly.

She shook me awake. "Dru, wake up, honey," she said while slowly caressing my back.

Awake but drowsy, I rolled toward her and slurred, "Whadja wan'?"

"You were dreaming, hon. And I don't think you liked it. What's worrying you now?"

Now fully awake I answered, "I just have the feeling we'll need to solve more stuff. Sorry, did I wake you?"

"Not really. I'm having trouble shutting down my brain. I'm nervous about tomorrow and the aftermath in Elmira." Hannah didn't specify but I knew she was thinking about Henry Lewis, because I was too.

The two peas in a pod thing again, I thought, not for the first time. We mulled over what was scheduled then found some impromptu things to do in bed.

Enjoyed 'em too.

The next night we met Bill at the Waldorf, and were awaiting the announcement that may have been the worst kept secret ever: MLB was expanding. What was a much better secret were the final choices. The contenders were known but not the MLB cities, nor their affiliated minor league cities.

The ballroom at the Waldorf was the venue and New York was putting its best foot out there for everyone to see. The place was packed with guests gussied up like a Hollywood premier.

Finally Bill Lattimore introduced the Commissioner, Phil Malozzi, and without delay he simply said MLB was expanding. Surprisingly a hush fell over the room. Everyone held their collective breaths in anticipation.

When Brooklyn's announcement came the place erupted in raucous celebration. To say the news was 'well received' would be a gross understatement. When Bill Lattimore was announced as the Brooklyn owner there was a standing ovation.

He took the podium and began relating his plans, including the location for the minor league teams. A wild cheer went up when Elmira was announced as the AA franchise's future home.

"That's surprising," Ted said to me. "Either really knowledgeable baseball historians are here, or a bus load of Elmirans came down for the occasion."

"Maybe both," I said.

I was still ill at ease but didn't know why. This foreboding that assails me from time to time is not pleasant. Not every project I've encountered presents this foreboding, but it had been there for the last two in spades. I suppose when two or more people are struggling over money it's to be expected... but never enjoyed.

I'd be glad to see where this leads. I didn't have long to wait.

Arriving back in Elmira, Ted was greeted by a full-fledged bombshell. Hank Lewis had not only dropped his interest in the Big Flats property, but had bought several parcels surrounding Holding Point. It appeared Hank was intent on limiting access to the future ballpark and amusement park. That land was precisely where Ted had planned to place the two entrances.

How could he know? thought Ted. He felt the blow as if he had introduced his solar plexus to a fist.

"Libby, we're in more trouble. I don't have a clue what to do. I'm sorry."

"Ted Reynolds, buck up! You're not going to sit there and wallow in self-pity. You're better than that. You've taken Henry Lewis to school on every occasion you two have competed. We aren't going to lose now and that's final," said Libby with as much passion as Ted had ever witnessed. She stood and confronted him and proclaimed,

"And don't forget, we're not alone in this deal. Let me call Hannah."

* * *

I answered the phone while Hannah was in the pool. "Hi Libby, what's up?"

"Dru, we got more problems with our friend Hank Lewis."

"I know, Libby, I just heard it from Bob Crandall. The college didn't own two strips of worthless land just outside the center of the property. They were used for rail access when trains serviced the area. I find it hard to believe those two strips of land seal off the area. What's up with that?"

Libby put Ted on the phone, who heard my last question.

"Dru, didn't you see those strips when you went out there?"

"I was only there once. Didn't realize those pieces were the drawbridge across the moat. Bob Crandall drove me around. I should have noticed but he never said anything either."

"I'm not sure he realized how strategic they were, Dru. You got any ideas off the top of your head? Because with as many real estate deals I've been involved, this is a first," said Ted.

I told Ted I had to think about it. Overwhelmed again, I decided what I most needed to do was play with Riley. I went down to the pool and filled Hannah in on the latest news and told her I was gonna take Riley for a walk to think. She was not surprised. She'd seen me do it often.

"I'll call Libby," she said.

Riley and I went to Keuka State Park located on the northeast side of the lake. We roamed around for a bit, went down to the water and out on the dock, and I sat while Riley jumped in the water for a swim. Watching him paddle around brought a smile and a feeling of how lucky I was to have that dog in my life. He's truly a member of the family. When Riley got out I still hadn't figured anything out, but I felt better. It was almost like watching my boy swim around—knowing he knew I'd be there for him—gave me a boost to resolve this issue like I had done so many times before.

On the drive back to the cottage we passed a boarded up old winery building. It apparently had been condemned as unsafe and was scheduled to be razed. Just like that an idea shot through my brain like a nova. *Aha!* I couldn't wait to tell Hannah. *Gotcha,* I thought.

We decided to go down to Ted and Libby's to share the idea in person. The closer we got to the house the more worked up I became. To have one piss ant of a human being be this disruptive to the best thing to hit the area in quite some time was infuriating.

"I think it's time we stop pissing around with this schmuck." I was angry and Ted saw it, which somehow made him feel better. It was as if he had faith in my ability to solve any problem and fix it, but how? Libby had told Ted of Hannah's concern that I was worried about some unforeseen cataclysm to come. After hearing of it Ted was really upset, for just a second.

"I see you're not too anxious, Ted."

"Forget that, whadda ya got?"

"Eminent Domain laws, you know 'em?"

A light dawned in Ted's eyes. "My real estate business has brought them to my attention from time to time. There have been more than a few disreputable local officials who are inclined to accept a contribution to rule favorably on a developer's plea. A building site without adequate ingress and egress is almost useless for nearly any kind of development."

"Yeah? Good. Who has the authority to enact it in the Holding Point area? Is it the Supervisor?" I asked.

"It varies. In the city, it's the mayor. In the county, the County Supervisor, and so on, all the way up to the Governor. In this case it's the County Supervisor, Linda Martin."

Could be trouble, I thought. I probably looked worried. I was, and wary too. I'm not a misogynist, but I've run into some Helen

Reddy, Hear Me Roar types, from time to time. Never mind the vulgar rant I'd had with her desk clerk!

"Do we know her? Is she a reasonable person to deal with, or a skivvy politician? Most important, any chance she could be a friend in court?"

"We used to date in high school, she's tops," said Ted.

Libby stared directly into his eyes, hands on hips ready to do battle.

"What happened with you guys?" I couldn't help but ask.

"She met a better man," Libby chimed in. "A good guy, funny as hell and smart, John Martin."

Turning to Ted, I had a huge grin and couldn't contain the chuckle, try as I might. "So she dumped ya, huh?"

"As if it hasn't happened to you, smart ass," he said.

In the morning we met Linda Martin, a short, pretty woman exuding confidence. Breakfast at Light's Bakery in Elmira was the chosen spot. Introductions made with sturdy handshakes to boot, Linda got down to cases, "What is it this time, Ted?"

"I've been fine, and you, Linda?"

"C'mon, Ted, I've got a full day. Haven't had my morning coffee and I'm cranky as hell, so out with it, okay?"

"Okay, it's my old friend Hank Lewis. He ..."

"Let me stop you right there. That's why I'm cranky. That pain in the ass jerk called me at five this morning. I didn't get to bed until three and he wanted me to support an injunction for preventing trespass across some sliver of land he just bought. Can you beat that?"

Hearing this I relaxed and smiled. We definitely had a friend in court.

"Well, yeah, that land is what we need to discuss," said Ted.

"Oh great, let's hear it," said Linda.

Ted filled her in on the plan for Iroquois Park, the whole deal including baseball and an uber-like Eldridge amusement park.

Upon hearing that Hank Lewis and his sliver of land threatened to halt the whole thing, future jobs, prosperity and entertainment for the area she postulated, "You want me to go for eminent domain, correct?"

"You got it," said Ted.

"So do you. Hank Lewis is the most odious individual I've ever encountered. It will be a joy to stick it in his ear. I'll call in every IOU I have if need be. I probably won't need to because I don't know anybody who doesn't loathe the man," she said with a look of indigestion.

Ted explained our eminent domain hopes and picked up the breakfast check when Linda left. We looked at each other as if a celebration were in order. We settled for a discreet fist bump under the table.

Back at Casa McKenna, née Powell, on the lake, the crew and I planned our chronological moves. In order were: conclude the land deal, get the baseball and amusement parks' engineers and contractors moving at optimum speed and contact MLB for the go ahead to release the news of the expansion dates and the details for the AA franchise. Not even the contractors, engineers or their crews knew all the details.

We decided I would fly to Detroit to inform the officers of McKenna Associates of my intention to sponsor a baseball team. Again details were withheld and tongues wagged in wild speculation. It amused my friends in Elmira to see and hear of it.

Morretti's, upon my return from Detroit, was the scene of Ted standing to make a toast. He appeared both joyful and nervous as he fidgeted with a napkin.

A commotion exploded in the hall leading into the dining room. Hank, in all his unruly self, bounded into the room, pushed Ted back against a nearby table, causing him to trip over a chair and crash into their waitress with a full tray of food. The Marx

Brothers couldn't have choreographed a more comedic scene. Ted, waitress, tray and food flew everywhere.

Ignoring all this, Hank Lewis announced to everyone within earshot in the crowded restaurant, "You son-of-bitch, McKenna," pointing directly at me, "you think this is over, not by a long shot, you slippery bastard."

The crowd gasped nearly in unison at the vehemence of Hank's words and of his facial expression which exuded malevolent evil.

"I'll be seeing you in court soon. All of you," promised Hank as he stomped out.

"Didn't see that coming," said Libby shaking her head.

"I did," said Ted, helping the waitress to her feet.

"Okay, boys, what now?" asked Libby.

"Not to worry. Dealing with bullies is my specialty. My grandfather taught me how when I was eleven years old," I said.

"Tell 'em the story, hon," urged Hannah.

"Yeah, I think we'd like to hear this," said Libby with an anticipatory grin.

"My grandfather raised me since dad died before I was born. He only had a few rules, and not being late for dinner was one of them. He thought it was the best time and place to find out what was going on in everybody's life and breed confidence in the younger members of clan McKenna to speak up and be counted. Anyway, I was accosted by a big kid in the neighborhood, Willie Holleran. He was about three years older than me. Willie pinned me to the ground and no matter how I struggled there's not much you can do when you're face down with a bully sitting on you. This adventure naturally made me late for dinner."

"I can see it comin'," said Ted with an ear to ear grin.

"I betcha can't," I said.

"C'mon, tell us," urged Libby.

"Okay, finally I was let go. I wasn't worried, I knew my granddad was a fair man and would understand I wasn't at fault.

Wrong! He didn't blame me, but rather gave me a command. 'Go to Willie's house and punch 'im in the nose.' "

"Are you serious?" asked Ted.

"Yep, I figured I was going to get killed. Willie outweighed me by a good twenty pounds and was two inches taller. His rep around school was that of a thug. Everybody was afraid of 'im. I walked over to the Holleran's, which was behind our house, with feet that felt like I was shod in iron boots. I finally approached the front door wishing I was either ten years older or not yet born. My wish didn't happen. I was on the Holleran doorstep, my last act on earth was about to commence."

Libby stood up as if she needed to defend me against whatever evil lurked on the other side of the door. It wasn't that at all. She just needed to get a glass of tea. Then she motioned to me to continue. I did.

"With the most fear I had experienced to that point in my life, I was paralyzed. Eventually I screwed up enough courage to ring the bell, hoping it didn't work. It did. His mother an overweight, frizzy haired woman, with a kid on her hip answered. She was clad in a drab house dress shrouded in a food splattered apron."

Ted inched forward on his cushion, in anticipation.

"Is Willie home?' I asked, wishing somehow he wasn't. Wish denied. 'They're all home,' she said, 'and you can take any of 'em widja if yer a mind to.' The beleaguered mother of six maniacs, Willie was her oldest at age fourteen. She turned and yelled, 'Willie, get your ass in here,' and then shuffled back to the kitchen. When he got to the door, Willie said, 'What the hell do you want, squirt?' "

I paused the tale to build tension and took a drink.

"So what'd ya do," asked Ted while Hannah was laughing.

"I hit him in the nose as hard as I could hit. You gotta understand when I was eleven, I was five foot seven and weighed 160 pounds, so I could hit."

"What did Willie do to ya?" asked Libby wearing a worried look.

"That's the odd thing. He grabbed his bleeding nose and ran into the kitchen cryin' for his mommy. I started to leave and Mr. Holleran, a balding, overweight, out of shape man said, 'I'll be seeing your father about this, kid.' "

"Grandfather, I corrected. I live with my grandfather. My dad's dead."

"Sorry, but that don't change nothin'. Tell 'im I'll see him tonight after supper."

"Did he?" asked Ted.

"Oh yeah, he came over. I could tell the size of my granddad surprised him. His eyes looked like dinner plates, and his eyebrows disappeared into his hairline. He gathered himself and started to tell my grandfather what I did. Before Mr. Holleran began the story TCM II held up his hand and stopped Holleran in his tracks. He told him he knew all about it. In fact he told him I was obeying his orders on how to deal with a bully such as his Willie boy."

Ted, Libby, and Hannah were all smiling now, and urged me to finish.

"TCM II asked Holleran if he wanted to make trouble 'cause if he did, he'd get the same thing. Holleran was speechless."

"Describe your grandfather, Dru," said Hannah.

"TCM II was six foot six and weighed in at 325 pounds, still hard as a boulder despite being in his seventies. Holleran quickly thought it over and left. I never had any trouble with the family again."

"How'd that make you feel, Dru?" asked Libby.

"Like I learned something... the value of self-respect."

"Is that what's in store for Hank?"

"Only if he chooses."

"Hold on, boys and girls, this is going to be some ride," said Ted.

That afternoon the four of us marched up to Hank's office and demanded to see him. He heard us and came out.

"Okay, McKenna, let me have it. How did you figure out what was goin' on?" said Hank.

"It wasn't really that tough, Henry, after the scene in Morretti's," I said.

"Yeah, right, I got that," said Hank.

"The reason was simple. Once I found out the guy who actually filed suit, it was obvious to us and the court, which ruled malice, so game over. We win, you lose, sound familiar?"

"What led you to that conclusion?"

"I'll make this easy for you, Hank. You know, for all his sycophant posturing, Butler hates you. And every time you've gone up against Ted the result is the same."

"How do you figure that about Butler?"

"Simple logic. *Everyone* hates you, Henry. I suspect you hate yourself. That's why I called you stupid. Oh, you're intelligent enough, clever enough, vindictive enough, but you don't believe other people matter. Not to you. You treat people like cattle or slaves only to be kept around to do your bidding. Henry, it doesn't take long for folks to grow weary of it and find their own desire for revenge."

"Call me Henry, one more time, Quadruple, and I'll punch your lights out," threatened Lewis.

"Henry, I've got ten years on you, and know how to fight. Don't be a fool. Much as I'd like to squash you like the bug you are, I don't want to hurt you."

"I'll show you what hurt is, punk. I got you by at least forty or fifty pounds."

"Yeah, mostly fat." The exchange told me that Henry, by resorting to a school boy threat when size was the most important factor, didn't know squat about fighting. I doubted he ever had a real one despite his abrasive nature.

I took a position an arm's length away from him and said, "I'd like to see you try that, Henry. I really would cause you are really askin' for it."

"Oh, you would, huh?" said Hank.

I was right, Lewis exhibited no skill or knowledge of how to fight. With his size he undoubtedly never had to. I blocked his telegraphed overhand right and nearly knocked Lewis back into the fireplace with a thunderous right cross to Henry's jaw.

Down went Lewis, tripping over the andiron and falling directly into the blazing fire. Hank tried in vain to extricate himself from the fiery pit.

Despite a powerful urge to leave him there, I stepped forward and pulled him from the hearth before he was immolated.

I rolled him over to quench his smoldering clothes. I suppose I saved his life. *Does that mean I'm responsible for him from here on out?*

"Only in China," I said out loud to myself, mainly because Hank and I were the only two in the room who heard my mumble... and he was out.

I was only semi-surprised I pulled him out. I truly wanted to let him lay there, at least for a while. After everything I've seen and heard, I felt toward him the same as I did toward Willie Holleran *and like every other bully I ever met*, recalling the Big Oil mook I hooked up with during the National Motors project a couple of years ago.

Finally Ted, Libby and Hannah came rushing over. They paused to take in the scene, then looked at each other and smiled.

Ted said, "Is he dead?"

"I don't think so, he has a head like a bowling ball. I think I broke my hand."

"Poor baby," consoled a mocking Libby.

"Nice touch, setting him on fire," complimented Ted.

Chapter 34

"So, it's over, huh?" said Hannah while wrapping two bags of frozen peas on my hand.

"With Henry, anyway. Now we gotta tie it all together," I said. "You know? Get the stadium finished, the park opened and watch the team begin the season next year."

"Yeah, then we'll figure out what to do next. I'm not letting you molt like last year," said Hannah.

"Yeah, after all, who needs R&R?"

"Before we start the search you can begin the saga of why your great-grandfather was called Red."

"Okay, you win. *After* we finish this project."

The activity of the next several months was exhausting and relentless. *Planning* is not nearly as complicated or physically demanding as *doing*. All of us were maxed out emotionally before the stadium was completed.

Thankfully Libby, with her dad's guidance, steered us through rough waters and finally completed the journey culminating in a beautiful state of the art stadium.

Watching the ten foot tall stainless steel name of Jon Fallon affixed to the stadium's façade was a source of immense satisfaction and joy. *A fitting tribute to my godfather*, I thought.

"Thanks, Jon," I said as we all watched the sign's completion.

"Amen," said Ted and Libby together, as Hannah hugged me and kissed my cheek.

The season opener was a year away but there was still much to accomplish.

* * *

Hannah continued work on the promotional program: the naming of the team, selecting the uniform designs, home and away, selling seats, working with MLB on rosters and a myriad of other details. Tied to the naming contests was the announcement of prizes for the successful entry. We deemed it fair that in the event of ties we would honor all the winning entries with season box seat tickets in perpetuity. We prayed there would be a manageable few. Working for us was the fact we hadn't officially named the park complex theme.

Hannah and Libby had been researching the area's history at the Strong Memorial Library and local Historical Societies. They came upon some interesting Indian connections dating back to the Revolutionary War. It occurred to Hannah that a tie to local Indians would prove to be a valuable promotional hook for the baseball and amusement parks, as well as the baseball team. We hadn't announced any preference for a theme or a specific Indian influence. We felt safe and secure the plan was still secret—that is, until a fifth grade class from St. Mary's Parochial school submitted an Indian name of Iroquois Park.

"Hey, Hannah," screeched Libby, eliciting as many glares as shhs from the library patrons and the hard-ass librarian. "Look what I found!"

Hannah stifled her laughter and read from the book Libby handed her, "This region is rich in Indian history. The Battle of Newtown in 1779 was fought at the behest of General Washington, to punish the Iroquois for atrocities committed in the village of Wyoming, among others, during the Revolutionary War. This battle pitted the newly formed Americans against the British and Iroquois comprised of six nations, the Senecas among them. On the advice of General Washington, an experienced Indian fighter, General John Sullivan did not fall into a nighttime ambush awaiting him. Instead he skirted the valleys and came at the opposing forces from the rear and won the day. Years later a prominent Seneca chief Sago-ye-watha, known as Red Jacket for his penchant for donning a British red coat given to him by his allies, was present at a peace treaty signing in 1791. This agreement formally ended the hostilities between the Indians and Americans and resolved all territorial disputes."

Hannah's beaming smile lit up the library's stacks. *Now we have a theme to run with throughout the project,* she mused.

Hannah shared the idea to build the project around local Indian heritages with Ted and me. To reinforce the decision, Ted told of his Boy Scout's troop hiking on Harris Hill and finding a slew of ancient arrowheads during these adventures, not to mention a goodly number of rattlesnakes. They picked up the arrowheads, not so the snakes. Also, with Major League teams already using names such as the Braves and Indians and minor league teams, like the Syracuse Chiefs it seemed like a good fit. She also thought of it as an opportunity to honor a heritage with dignity and the respect due it and avoid the controversies Cleveland and Washington fought to overcome every year.

The idea was well received by Ted, Libby and, of course, me. After all, I know where my best interests lie, not that I had a better suggestion to offer.

Now the theme could be expanded upon and the resulting promotions planned.

The team personnel became the focus, and for guidance we phoned Bill Lattimore. As expected, the parent team, the Brooklyn Colonials, would be responsible for staffing the front office and players for Elmira. Bill was curious about the team name and counseled us that he had final approval.

Ted saw surprise on my face and wondered why I didn't reveal the name.

Anticipating his question I said, "It's too soon. I want to have the plan further developed before I share it with you, Bill." I wanted to make it harder for him to '86 it. I knew after he could see Hannah's plan, he'd agree.

"Okay, we have our direction, now we have to select a name and get going with colors, uniform design and all that stuff," I said.

"Hold on, Roy Rogers, aren't you forgetting about the 'Name the Team' and colors contest and all that?" chastised Libby.

Ted and Libby sat back in their lounge chairs with a gotcha attitude stamped on their foreheads. We were sitting around the pool basking in a delightful summer day, ostensibly together for a planning session when it turned into a 'come to Jesus' meeting.

Ted and Libby looked at Hannah and me, trying to decide who was in charge. Hannah's faced flushed when she was het up about something while my stoic demeanor revealed not an inkling of my thoughts. Ted said to Libby, "I know Dru is gonna win this, in the end. I don't think Hannah will mind, though. Whadja think?"

"I'll take that bet. What's at stake?" Libby asked.

"What else? Your virtue."

"In that case you win," as she picked up Ted's hand and led him into the house.

Hannah looked perplexed and asked, "What's that about?"

I laughed and said, "I believe romance is in the air."

Hannah followed my drift and chuckled to herself.

After the two of us enjoyed a swim, Hannah decided the cabana would be a charming place for a rendezvous with destiny our ownselves. I agreed wholeheartedly as evidenced by my stupid grin and the drooling tongue hanging outta my face.

That evening all four of us glowed from our afternoon delight, as we discussed the agenda.

I explained that the team name and colors contest would go on as scheduled with only the outcomes already settled.

"We can't leave this up to chance. Ted, you and Libby own this team and you both should pick the name," I said.

"So the contest is a sham?" asked Libby.

"Not exactly the words I would've chosen, but yes. There will be a winner. A deserving one, no doubt. But we need to begin the planning process immediately," I said.

"So this is like the trade show raffle idea, huh?" said Hannah.

"What's that?" said Libby.

"Companies attend trade shows because it's an opportunity to attract new customers and give thanks to current ones by wining and dining them. On the show floor an individually numbered raffle ticket is given to everyone who stops by their booth. At the moment of truth the tickets which had been placed in a rotating drum are turned, a pretty girl is asked to pull THE winning ticket and announce the winning number. The number given to the best customer in attendance is put aside beforehand and given to the girl who pretends to pull it from the drum and the deed is done, maximum bang for the prize."

"That's not fair, is it?" said Libby, recalling this conversation when we first announced it.

"What? You'd rather see some mook from Chateauguay, who you'll never see again, walk off the winner?" said Ted.

"Let's vote on names, Libby. What say you?"

"Okay, I like the Iroquois Park name with the team named the Senecas."

"How about the colors?" I asked.

"Dark green and purple, like Wimbledon," she answered.

"Ted?"

"I'll go along with Brooklyn. Royal blue and white, except I'd add a touch of green to the color scheme."

"Wow, this is gonna be easier than I thought," said Hannah.

"Then it's settled. I agree," I said. "But not with you two, with Hannah."

"Wait, what the hell are you talking about? You two didn't agree with any of us," said Ted.

"I know, pity that, I was hoping you would agree... with Hannah."

"Are we back at the trade show again?" whined Libby.

"Yep," I said. "Look, this really is in Hannah's wheel house. It's how she earned the house we have. She's great at this stuff, trust her," I said.

"Okay, so what are the colors, Hannah?" asked Ted.

Hannah appeared to be a bit sheepish after being spotlighted by Ted.

"Since we're going with the Indian concept we should use appropriate colors to that theme: red, orange, black, gold and white."

Ted and Libby looked at each other, "Of course. Colors best suited to Indians."

"You know we're gonna have to be careful with the mascot selection and how he acts. We don't need tribal leaders comin' down on us with flaming arrows," said Ted.

"No sweat, guys, we already have it," I said.

In unison they said, "We do?"

"Sure, it's Red Jacket, the Seneca chief we read about. He'll preside over the line-up presentation to the umpires at the start of each game. Maybe he can sit in front of a Chief's tent over the fence in center field, standing to encourage cheering from the crowd. At the seventh inning stretch he can supervise the grooming of the field and bases, confer with the umpires, make a show of it, nothing that can be misconstrued as inappropriate for a chief. Whadja think?"

They looked at each other and agreed it sounded good.

"Beats a purple aardvark or something of a similar ilk," I said.

"It might be a good idea to get the imprimatur of a local chief to act as a paid consultant," said Ted.

"Yeah, that would be cool. Good idea, hon," said Libby.

"Ted, how about you and I go visit Bill Lattimore and fill him in and beg for some good players?" I said.

While Ted and I were preparing to head to New York, Libby and Hannah were supervising the amusement park construction and the attractions wrap up.

Thanks to Libby's expertise in straw bossing the contractors and subs, the entire park would be finished ahead of schedule which amazed everyone. Hannah noticed I didn't seem to be tortured by some Sword of Damocles or fear of doom.

I, of course, wondered if I was overlooking something. There was always something.

* * *

Arriving in New York, Ted and I hoped Bill Lattimore would fall head over tea cups with our ideas, but we weren't sure. We filled him in on the progress, both with the stadium and the team promotional plans, progress pictures included. Upon hearing the choices for the team name and the local historical connection, including Red Jacket, he was pleased to have this segment of the building of his Class AA league affiliate fall into his lap due to a childhood dream of Ted's. So far, so good. We let out sighs of relief.

When it came to begging for quality players we needn't have bothered. It was already in place. Each major league team had placed six names to be eligible for selection by the new franchises from the Major League teams. Each expansion team chose, in turn, players to be designated for assignment to Class AAA, AA, upper A, lower A, and rookie leagues. In addition the two new teams would have first four picks in each round of the amateur drafts of college and high school players. A coin toss would determine who went first.

Bill said he promised to look out for the Senecas. Given the people involved, namely me and Hannah, and the wherewithal we brought, he wanted us to be successful from the git go.

"Tell me more about that area's Indian lore," said Bill.

"Okay, here are two off the top of my head," said Ted. "As Boy Scouts we hiked around the ravines of Rorick's Glen and Harris Hill among the rattlesnakes, if you can believe it. The area is famed for being the glider capital of the world despite this slippery aspect. The Indian legend has it the ravines were formed by the tears from an Indian maiden who sat on a plain longing for her love who promised to return to her but never did. Another version says the cross erected on a hillside is to commemorate an Indian maiden who threw herself off the cliff because of an unfaithful lover." This caused a bit of a stir in the room as everyone contemplated a situation that would compel a person to fling herself off a cliff to be a personal horror.

"I'm afraid the truth is much tamer. A Frenchman, Eugene Berthod, who owned a tavern on the property, erected the cross in memory of his mother back in France. But I always chose to believe the Indian lore," said Ted.

Sitting with a stunned expression Bill focused on Ted and said, "Rattlesnakes, really?"

"I know, right. I don't even like driving past there now," said Ted.

"I hate snakes," Bill said.

I shivered at the thought of walking among them my own self.

"Bill, do we get to have any say in who gets to be on the team?" asked Ted.

"Sorry, Ted, but it's our business, yours and mine, to develop players to help the parent club. Our baseball people are charged with the responsibility to not only select the players for our affiliates but the MLB club as well. We'll put the players in the appropriate levels according to their skill. The first few years we expect there to be a lot of fluidity based on performance. I suspect one of the hardest choices to accept will be when we promote a player performing at a very high level from your team leaving a void and make it harder for you to win. Your fans will be upset, but that's the purpose of the minors... development."

"Yeah, I get that, Bill. I don't expect a roster of All-Stars, but I don't want to see over-rapid promotion at our expense either," said Ted.

"Ted, think of it as a company with branch offices. Each office is a profit center whose purpose is to add the most to the bottom line of all the branches. Those employees are vying for promotion with each other. When someone is promoted, an opportunity opens up to replace them. Hopefully, the Peter Principle isn't in play, and the company grows and prospers," Bill said.

"Okay, Bill, I'm just worried that after the glitz and novelty fades we don't end up holding an empty bag," said Ted.

"Ted, if we do this correctly, and with the staff I've hired, I believe we will... the bag won't be empty," said Bill.

CHAPTER 35

A few weeks later, all the construction was finished on the amusement park and Jon Fallon stadium. The announced contest for the team name and colors poured in. There were two cuts, then narrowed down to the final five. The names fell into several categories: Indians, animals, and quirky names like in colleges, i.e. Red Storm, the NBA, i.e. Thunder. Local ties were included in suggestion like the Twains and Gliders.

Team color suggestions resembled a color wheel found in all paint stores. After a few weeks, and close to announcement day, Hannah saw the wisdom in having picked our own choices.

Hannah and I left this to Ted and Libby. Thankfully no entry failed to match our choice. One of our first entrants, the 21 fifth-graders from St. Mary's on the Southside of Elmira, nailed the overall complex name of Iroquois and team named of Senecas, thanks in no small part to Emily Reynolds. To insure secrecy we invited all entrants who made the final cut to a prominent position at the game. There were five and they would enjoy box seats and authentic team hats at the ceremony held before the game.

We held back on revealing the winning names to build suspense, anticipation and excitement. All would be known at the pregame ceremonies. Of course the players knew—after all they had to dress for the game but were forbidden to tell anybody. We were serious about this to the extent we confiscated their cell phones until game time. Thankfully they bought into the hype and were eager to see the fans' reactions.

Hannah and Libby were floating around on Cloud # Nine. The amusement park had opened a month before baseball season to a capacity throng. The ticket price to get a feel for the gross from the games and rides, food concessions, the horses, the picnic areas, the whole shebang was proving to be wildly successful.

The five of us went to the picnic area five days after the opening, and of course, Riley was with us. We spent the day enjoying a lunch of baked chicken, potato salad, cole slaw, apple pie and Arnold Palmers. Riley had water. Then we rode the rides and played most of the games. Hannah scared me with her manic enjoyment of Whack-a-Mole. I made a mental note not to anger her. I vowed to keep her away from mallets when I was around.

The plan for unveiling what had been going on behind the fences and trees at north end of the former Elmira College property a few weeks after the park opened. Baseball was back in Elmira. Spring Training was upon us. All the surrounding towns were abuzz with anticipation. Tours of the stadium coincided with the tag-a-seat promotion for season ticket packages. The season would officially begin in early June.

Ted, Libby, Hannah and I had gone to spring training for a couple of days to look over the prospects. Fittingly, the Brooklyn Colonials bought, spruced up and set up training camp in Vero Beach at the site of the original Brooklyn team. They changed the complex's name from Dodgertown to The Colony, home of the Brooklyn Colonials. We thought the team looked pretty good and we hoped for a successful run. Their uniforms were generic gray with only Brooklyn stitched on the front. Bill said they really did want to hype the suspense, and reporters of all media pestered them continually. Not even the team was told the uniform designs. The red, white and blue Brooklyn uniforms were unveiled in April and enthusiastically received.

Opening day for our Senecas was upon us, the whole town was pulsating with palpable excitement. Anticipation of the team name, color and uniform design announcements along with the player introductions was running high. Two famous bands, one rock, one swing, began performing at ten a.m. til noon at each end of the park. They were scheduled to pick up again after the game and play until midnight.

The festivities included fireworks, before and after the game to entertain the crowd, win or lose.

The first thing on the agenda was the announcement of the name and the contest winner.

"I would like to introduce all twenty-one members of the fifth-grade class of St. Mary's school, who named our team, The Elmira Senecas," announced the public address man. A roar accompanied the announcement.

Before the player introductions, the presentation of the uniforms and colors by a squad of members of the VFW took place. The crowd gave an enthusiastic welcome to the vets clad in the new uniforms.

The team name Senecas was emblazoned across the chest of the white home uniforms in red, outlined in black and gold while the numbers on the front and back were turquoise trimmed in gold. Ted chose to go old school and leave off player names on the back. He was trying to replicate the glory days of baseball when the Pioneers were most popular. Also, as a matter of team policy, the players had to show the colorful stirrup stockings. These were black with alternating stripes of red, white and gold. Topping off the uniforms was two choices of hat colors. One cap was a black cap with a red bill with a gold script E. The other was an all red cap with the gold E monogram. Away uniforms displayed the traditional road gray with red Senecas also trimmed in black and gold with turquoise numbers, front and back, framed in gold. The away stirrup socks were turquoise with black, gold and white stripes. There was no clear winner of the color contest, so we picked a Marine vet who had lost an arm and foot and his family as the recipients of the award.

Another surprise for the fans was the team mascot who rode in from center field astride a pinto pony sans saddle but on a turquoise blanket. He was dressed as Chief Red Jacket, an actual

Seneca chief during Revolutionary times. Fittingly, he was wearing said jacket that was presented to him by the British during the Revolutionary War.

The uniforms, colors and mascot were greeted by a thunderous ovation. Finally the players were announced with stirring beating of several drums performed by a drum corps of US Marines. The players also entered the field through the same center field gate Chief Red Jacket did. They ran down a red carpet trimmed in white, gold and black. The home team dugout was on the first base side of the diamond and the visitors, The Binghamton Mets, on the third base side. Both teams lined up on the baselines between home plate and first and third bases to await the National Anthem.

Chief White Deer, a local Seneca, was designated to throw out the first pitch with a ball presented to him by Red Jacket. It was now time to play ball.

The two pitchers were twenty years old and threw very hard, topping the radar gun at over ninety-five mph. Andy Yeager, the Seneca pitcher, was displaying surprising insight as to the most effective way to approach the opponents. Mixing speeds and pitches he showed superb control striking out seven, giving up one hit and walking one through five innings.

Jake Martin, the Binghamton Mets' pitcher and son of Linda and John Martin, matched Yeager with no runs allowed and striking out six.

The sixth inning proved to be difficult for both pitchers. Andy Yeager gave up a single then a double, runners on second and third. He then walked one and struck out one when Scott Reid lined a bullet down the short left field line for two runs. After walking the next batter he induced a 6-4-3 double play grounder to get out of the inning.

In the bottom of the sixth Elmira returned the favor, off relief pitcher Joe Scaramajapak, with catcher Bobby Wynn's double to right. Following a hit, batter Austin Mack slammed a long home run to deep left center for a three-two lead. A tight game with several highlight reel defensive plays on both sides held the fans in their seats for the entire game.

The ninth inning was packed with as much drama as a Hitchcock movie. The Mets' leadoff hitter hit a screamer down third base. It apparently hit the edge of the turf taking a wicked hop hitting the third baseman in the throat. The ball dropped in front of him. He picked it up and rifled a throw to first nipping the runner by a half step. Two walks later, the Binghamton first baseman looped a pop fly behind third base. The shortstop racing toward the stands slid toward the seats and made a one-handed grab before smashing into the fence. Two outs. The next batter lined a hard hit ball into right field. Ron Gilland raced in from right field, scooped up the ball and fired a laser throw, like something out of Star Wars, and the runner was a dead duck at home, game over. The Senecas win 3-2! The crowd went nuts.

Opening day for the amusement park had drawn an unthinkable crowd, which continued up to the arrival of baseball, for an economically depressed area. Hope for fiscal recovery seemed to appear on the horizon, if we could sustain it.

The throng of fans attending the first ball game was also more than anyone expected. A capacity crowd, colorful pageantry, emotional tributes to fallen area soldiers, fireworks all combined to provide a showcase for a jewel the area residents could savor with pride and which summoned remembrances of past glory for those old enough to recall them. The area now had such a great place in their midst which was a long time coming but well worth the wait. The fact the home team Senecas won was icing on the cake.

For the name-the-park contest, a ten-year-old heart patient, Tommy Dulaney, was chosen to represent St. Mary's. No other class member would ever argue with the choice. Three months later Tommy succumbed to a delicate heart operation. A plaque honoring his memory inscribed *Inspiration* is permanently affixed to his Seneca color seat to be permanently unsold. It was the first retired seat in professional baseball. The team's colors contest included almost unimaginable combinations from the world of the absurd. A fair and honest selection was not possible so the four of us threw our choices into a hat and Libby picked the winner. Hannah's choice of red, blue, and turquoise, with gold accented letters and numbers, turned out to be the winner. Hannah could win no prize so we selected a Marine Corps vet, home after three tours in the Middle East—who had been awarded three Purple Hearts, a Silver, and Bronze Star—to receive a National Motors Eagle and four season tickets for all the Senecas' home games.

The team name winners were the kids from St. Mary's. Tickets for them and their families were presented and then they were honored and applauded. A replica plaque in honor of Ralph Meyers with his likeness embossed on it was presented to his sister, Adair. The actual plaque was to be permanently displayed on the home team dugout. Tributes were given to all three. A dry eye in the stadium that day could not be found.

The team, like most, had ups and downs, but on the whole, finishing second in an eight-team division was deemed a great success as the 410,000 plus attendance verified. In honor of the Senecas' owners, a commitment to fund cool uniforms, several youth diamonds around town and equipment was made to be continued as long as the team drew profitable attendance figures.

Some of the players would be moving up to AAA at times during the year and would be invited to spring training with the parent Colonials next year. Two were called up in September to fill out the parent club's forty-man roster toward the end of the MLB season as most teams did.

The concerts during the summer were big hits as well. Money rolled in and the created jobs were a financial boon to the whole region. Summer and fall had not been so exciting in the area in a long, long time.

Hank Lewis never became the acclaimed citizen he aspired to be. His personality continued to rub everyone the wrong way. He had modest financial success. His Big Flats planned community was realized but never achieved the status of Columbia, Maryland. He would never best Ted Reynolds in anything ever. Sadly, his charitable work for the Notre Dame Orphanage continued in secrecy.

Baseball and entertainment were the vehicles used to achieve the dream of one man and his wife. A man had a dream and another man and his wife made it happen.

Hannah, Riley and I left for our house in New York shortly after the season's end.

"Hannah, did I ever tell you how my Great-Grandfather came to be called Red?"

"You're kidding, right?" Hannah twisted in her seat and said, "Let me tell you, Buster, it better be finished by the time we get home."

"We'll see."

ACKNOWLEDGMENTS

To be a member of Year of the Book writing group has afforded me the opportunity to continue a recently developed passion... writing. Led by our guru, Demi Stevens, we share our efforts, give critiques, and kudos wherever possible.

Her organizational skills, spirit, and patience are greatly appreciated. The group's encouragement and support helps us all slog through a sometimes difficult path.

I am grateful to all the members including: Gloria Bostic, Patty Collamer, Mary Pat Hough-Greene, Maria Hillegas, Elva Winter, Marian Condon, Sondra Lambert, Jacqui Doyle and Joan King.

www.ingramcontent.com/pod-product-compliance
Lightning Source LLC
Chambersburg PA
CBHW071310200626
46813CB00015B/938